## CASTONBURY PARK
### A Regency Upstairs Downstairs

**Survival of the fittest is fine, so long as you're the one on top…but the family that has everything is about to lose it all…**

The Montagues have found themselves at the centre of the *ton*'s rumour mill, with lords and ladies alike claiming the family is not what it used to be.

The mysterious death of the heir to the Dukedom, and the arrival of an unknown woman claiming he fathered her son, is only the tip of the iceberg in a family where scandal upstairs *and* downstairs threatens the very foundations of their once powerful and revered dynasty...

D1421843

# Montague Family Tree

**KEY:**

|  |  |
| --- | --- |
| ↔ | Legal Marriage |
| — | Child |
| – – – | Suspected illegitimate child |
| ⋯⋯ | Sibling |
| ▬ | Half sibling |

Hannah Stratton
Housekeeper
b.1766

Adam
b.1784

Jamie
b.1786

Giles
b.1788

Henry
(Harry)
b.1791

Kate
b.1792

Edward
b.1796
d.1815

Duchess of Rothermere
b.1767
d.1800

Duke of Rothermere
b.1758

Charles
b.1761
d.1797

Claire
b.1787

Phaedra
b.1796

Ross
b.1787

Araminta
b.1795

*Dear Ross,*

*Nephew, I hesitate to ask, because I know you are busy
and your life is currently in India, but I would really
appreciate your calm head and guidance at this trying
time. As you know, we have been led to believe that my
dear son Jamie is dead, but to complicate matters I have
just this morning received a letter informing us that
Jamie was married, and that his new wife and young
son are in the grounds of Castonbury Park. The truth is
yet to be determined, for I thought I knew my son better.
But, Ross, I would be most grateful if you could return
to help your family and use your persuasive nature to
discover what this woman wants and what indeed did
happen. I believe she may be able to shed some light.*

*But please, however, be discreet. We cannot afford any
more scandal to be unearthed whilst you are here.*

*Yours,*

*Rothermere*

First published in Great Britain 2012
Mills & Boon, an imprint of Harlequin (UK) Limited,
Eton House, 18-24 Paradise Road, Richmond, Surrey TW9 1SR

© Helen Dickson 2012

ISBN: 978 0 263 90186 3

52-0912

Harlequin (UK) policy is to use papers that are natural, renewable and recyclable products and made from wood grown in sustainable forests. The logging and manufacturing processes conform to the legal environmental regulations of the country of origin.

Printed and bound
by CPI Group (UK) Ltd, Croydon, CR0 4YY

# The Housemaid's Scandalous Secret

HELEN DICKSON

For my husband, George, with love—
he has provided unconditional support and
encouragement throughout.

# Prologue

Cholera had killed Lisette's parents. Suddenly, at nineteen years old, she found herself homeless, penniless, with no family and no purpose in life. She was adrift but she would survive. She could survive anywhere, but she belonged nowhere.

Unable to remain in her beloved India, she was to travel to Bombay, where she hoped to work her passage on board a ship bound for England.

Lisette had enjoyed living in an Anglo-Indian society in Delhi. Her father had been an eccentric academic, a linguist and a botanist, working for the University of Oxford in India. It was through her father's friendship with the Rajah Jahana Sumana of the state of Rhuna that she had met and become a close friend of the Rajah's daughter, Princess Messalina.

Messalina was being escorted to her wedding in Bhopal and suggested Lisette travel part of the way with her as one of her attendants. Not wishing to draw attention to herself Lisette was dressed as a native girl, for to travel openly as an unescorted English girl was unthinkable.

Lisette had parted from her friend when the rains came. It was a light sprinkling at first that washed the dust from the air. Then, as the lightning pranced closer in a flashing, sizzling display of the storm's power, a torrential downpour marched across the land, turning the roads to mud and causing the rivers to overflow. The people Lisette was travelling with reached the banks of a wide, fast-flowing river at the only point of safe crossing for twenty miles upstream and down. Usually the banks here were lined with *dhobis* busy with piles of washing, *mahouts* bathing their elephants and children playing and splashing in the shallows.

The rain had stopped some time ago. The last rays of the sinking sun catching the river glittered on the rushing water in a haze of gold. The bridge creaked and swayed with the pull of the current. It was almost dark, but rather than wait until morning by which time the bridge could have been washed away or become impossible to cross, the travellers decided not to postpone their crossing.

There were so many people and conveyances and bullocks milling about the bridgehead that Lisette was in danger of being crushed to death. Panicking she tried to turn back but she was carried forward by the frenzied crowd. She saw the red uniforms of British soldiers trying to bring some kind of order to the chaos but to no avail. One of them, an exceedingly handsome and masculine British officer, was familiar to her, although they had never been introduced. He and his orderly had ridden part of the way with the rajah's procession—the presence of British soldiers had provided added protection against marauding bandits.

Trying to keep his horse from bolting from the melee ahead, Colonel Ross Montague watched the unruly multitude push onto the bridge. Light was fading fast but when he caught sight of a star-spangled bright pink sari he was transfixed. He recognised it as belonging to one of Princess Messalina's attendants. He could just make out her slender figure crushed against the rails and trying desperately to hang on. What she was doing there he did not stop to wonder at, for at that moment she was in serious danger of falling off the bridge that was dipping precariously under the weight of the crowd.

The next minute, to her horror, Lisette found herself flung into the raging torrent. With night drawing in it was difficult for the majority on the bridge to see what had happened, but looking down on the scene, Ross had a clear picture of it and immediately flung himself out of the saddle, quickly shedding his red jacket.

'Leave her, man,' his companion shouted above the

din. 'There'll be many more in the water before this evening's done.'

'Hold my horse, Blackstock. The life of a soldier calls for a far greater degree of proficiency in dealing with the unexpected than is required of the average man.'

'But to jump into a fast-flowing river is in excess of your official duties. It's insane—suicidal.'

With a grin, Ross tossed him the reins and his jacket. 'I'll be back.'

Pushing his way towards the bridge, he shouted to make himself heard above the tumult of yelling voices and the thunder of the water rushing below.

The current sucked Lisette deep into the river. Breaking the surface, choking in the thick, muddy water, she didn't see the figure that dove off the bridge after her. She tried to swim but hampered by the weight of her sari it was impossible. Desperately she tried to grasp at anything that would prevent her from being washed away, but the force of the water defeated her and swept her a hundred yards or more downstream until she crashed into a tree. The bank had been washed away but mercifully the tree's roots were still secured. Grabbing at a branch she groaned when it cracked and gave way. Somehow she managed to grab another, but the long green leaves slipped between her fingers. Her heart wrenched with despair. She couldn't drown, not when she had come so far.

Suddenly she felt something slide about her waist, then knock against her legs. For one horrified second she thought she was about to be eaten by a crocodile, but then hope flared when she felt a hard body pressed to her own.

'Cling on to me,' a voice yelled in Urdu above the roar of the water.

Spluttering and thrashing Lisette desperately tried to do as he asked. Again she reached out to take a fresh grip on the tree and this time she managed to grasp a branch and hold on. Dragging herself and her companion towards it she emerged through a canopy of leaves, her sopping wet veil wrapped around her, half covering her face. The man managed to half drag himself into the branches and hauled her up beside him. Exhausted from their exertions and panting for breath, they were still for a moment. Then, seeing she was in danger of slipping back into the water, the man's arms were about her once more.

Eventually he managed to edge along the tree towards the bank. Feeling sand beneath his feet, he pulled the woman he had rescued along with him and lay down with her on the sandbank, out of the water. The night was now pitch-black and he daren't move any further. His breathing was laboured and his arms and legs ached, his body battered and bruised.

The woman clung to him in a frenzy of terror. 'Are you all right?' he asked, his mouth close to her ear.

Though she made no sound he could feel the rise and fall of her breast against his own, while the feel of her warm, wet body and every slender curve and line of it spoke eloquently of a woman, not a child.

'Are you hurt?'

She did not reply, but she shook her head in a helpless gesture that might have been either agreement or dissent, and for some reason, that small despairing gesture cut him to the heart and he tightened his arms about her, whispering foolish words of comfort. For a moment her body shuddered and she lay her head against his shoulder. Wrapped together, the darkness of the night and the danger of falling back into the river forced them to remain where they were. The night wind arose and blew strongly off the water, and the girl in his arms began to shiver in the cold air.

After a while Lisette ceased to shiver. It was strangely comforting to lean her aching head against her rescuer's shoulder. With his arms tight about her, she was conscious only of an unfamiliar and inexplicable feeling of being safe—a feeling she had longed for since the day her parents had died and she had left the safe and familiar walls of her home. She did not know why the presence and the touch of this man should give her this warm feeling of safety, and she was too battered and bruised and physically exhausted to figure it out. It was enough to feel protected.

In fact, the closeness of him was dizzying, so much so that she hardly knew her own thoughts. She felt pleasurably wanton feelings rippling through her, and instead of trying hard to stifle the feelings, she allowed them to flood through her. They were overwhelming sensations, so new and strong that they frightened her. She moved slightly, as though to pull away from him, and his arms tightened in response.

It was a long time since Ross had held a woman in his arms, and though he could not see her face distinctly, the feel of her firm young body moulded against his made his blood throb through his veins. 'Hold still, my lovely. It's not safe for us to move until we have light. Until then we have no choice but to cling on to each other and keep ourselves warm.'

Had it not been for that softly rich voice, Lisette would not have relaxed into his secure embrace once more, little realising the devastating effect her thinly clad body was having on him. Her heart was racing now, part of his heart, his body... Her face was uplifted and she strained her eyes to see her rescuer. His lean features were starkly etched, his eyes translucent in the ghostly light. It was impossible to make out anything more, but she knew it was the soldier who had accompanied the rajah's procession.

Ross held her firm. He felt the softness of her silken hair, the stirring pressure of her small, round breasts against his chest, and even in this dire situation, he ached to sample this woman more thoroughly.

Lisette's mind reeled and the next moment she felt the warmth of his mouth on hers. She gave herself up to this, her first kiss, savouring it with a sensual awakening as the stranger's arms held her captive. It lasted no more than a moment, but it was enough to stir the strange feelings until she became acutely conscious of her innocence. The trembling weakness in her body attested to its potency. She found her lips entrapped with his once more, and though they were soft and gentle, they flamed with a fiery heat that warmed her whole body. Her eyes closed, and the strength of his embrace, the hard pressure of his loins and his hand cupping her breast made her all too aware that this was a strong, living, healthy man, and that he was treating her like a woman, indeed desiring her.

In that moment Lisette tried to still the violent tremor that had seized her, but his powerful, animal-like masculinity was an assault on her senses. She was unable to resist him and she felt her body offer itself to this man, this stranger, and in that instant they both acknowledged the forbidden flame that had ignited between them. Right there, with the river raging all around them, they exchanged a carnal promise as binding as any spoken vow.

When her leg slid sideways and she felt the cold lap of water against her flesh, reason flooded back to her. She had no doubt that this man would take her there and then if she did not halt things now. Having been properly brought up and having consorted with an Indian princess, no one should treat her like this. This man thought she was a native girl, so as a native girl she must behave.

Sliding her lips away from his, with her mouth against his ear she managed to say, 'Please don't do this. Would you take advantage of an innocent woman when she has nothing with which to defend herself? Am I fair sport to be ravished like this? Would you make me an outcast for the rest of my days?'

Hearing her words Ross shook his head and gathered her to him again. With an effort he restrained the urge to take her lips once more for he must not. 'You are right. I have no wish to take you—not here, not like this—delightful though the prospect might be. I go too fast. What you are doing away from the royal procession is not my concern—and you do seem to have a penchant for getting yourself into trouble—but now that I have found you I contemplate a much grander bedding for you and me. We will talk about it when we get out of this damned river.'

Hearing the male arrogance edging his voice, Lisette swallowed drily. 'Then tell me where you plan this bedding so that I can avoid it,' she exclaimed, knowing that what he was saying was wrong…and yet it was so wickedly exciting, like nothing she had ever experienced before.

Ross gave a small sensual laugh, sending shivering pulse beats through her body. 'Nay, my lovely girl. Do not think you can avoid your destiny. I am a soldier, but I have been in India long enough to know your culture is full of the mysteries of destiny and fate and other fantasies. When we kissed I felt the desire in you. Deny it if you can.'

Lisette was helpless in denying it. How could she, when she had felt it too?

'Rest easy,' Ross said, his arms gathering her against him, 'while we wait out the night.'

With nowhere to rest her arm Lisette placed it around his waist and closed her eyes.

As the water continued to rush around them, Ross did the same, knowing there was the danger of the water rising. If it did, they would not survive the night.

When dawn broke up the darkness of the sky, Ross opened his eyes to find his arms empty of his companion's soft warmth. Panic seized him and he cursed himself for allowing himself to fall asleep, but he had truly believed she would be safe in his arms. Standing up, his eyes did a frantic search of the water round about, but there was no sign of her.

Thankfully the river level had fallen during the night and the bridge hadn't been washed away. Without any difficulty he managed to make it to the bank. On reaching it and looking at the ground, he saw the small footprints of a woman coming out of the river. This in itself put paid to the theory that she had been washed away. But there the trail ended. She had vanished as if spirited into thin air.

He was astounded at the strength of his relief that she was alive, but then he felt a strange sensation come over him and he could hardly believe it himself when he realised it was pique and a helpless, futile sick anger against fate and himself and the foolish instinct of his kind that had driven him to leap unthinkingly to the rescue of a drowning native girl. And now the ungrateful girl had simply got up and left him; the sense of loss and disappointment would come later.

He was affronted because having endangered his life to rescue her, she had left without so much as a farewell, slipped from his hands as unexpectedly as she had been placed into them. He set off to look for his horse and young Blackstock, determined to banish the native girl from his mind. But all the way to Bombay he did not stop looking for the girl in the pink, star-spangled sari.

* * *

The events of that night were a hideous jumble in Lisette's mind, and reaction had her in its grip. On opening her eyes and seeing the river level had fallen, careful not to disturb her companion, she had gotten to her feet and looked down into his deeply tanned and undeniably good-looking face. His closed eyes were fringed with black lashes and he was tall, his chest broad and hard muscled. His luxuriant dark brown hair and clean-shaven face enhanced his masculine good looks.

Her heart stirred. How she would like to get to know him better, but there was something inside her telling her to flee, not to become entangled with this man whose only thought when they had been locked together had been to bed her. And so, shaking so violently she could barely walk, troubled by doubts and fears and a haunting sense of insecurity, she had left her handsome rescuer and made it to the riverbank.

Fortunately she spotted the people she was travelling with encamped on the other side of the river. Reclaiming her bundle she carried on with her journey to Bombay.

## Chapter One

Surviving tropical storms, pirates and a thousand other discomforts in the cramped quarters allotted to her on board ship, Lisette was relieved when she arrived in England, a country of bucks and beaux, Corinthians and macaronis. It was said that the old King George III had lapsed into incurable madness and his son 'Prinny' had been made regent. As the ship made its way up the river Thames, she went on deck. Against a marbled sky of grey and white, London was spread out before her—streets and houses, church spires and the dome of St Paul's.

Lisette felt no attachment to England. It was a long way from the India that she loved, with its tiger hunts and elephants, oriental princes and potentates glittering with fabulous jewels living in medieval state in fantastic marble palaces. India had been her world for so long that England on this grey morning was a pale comparison. A swift vision of that lovely, mysterious country with all its smells, its vibrancy and blistering heat sprang into her mind with a mixture of pleasure and pain and she choked a little, and then swallowed. It was no time to be self-pitying, when she was on the brink of a new life.

Stepping onto dry land her legs shook like those of a newborn colt. After the relative quiet of the small cabin, the noise and bustle of the East India dock was jarring and chaotic. The Company was rich and powerful and well organised, owning the largest ships that used the port of London. The dock was a scene of great variety. The smell of tar and coffee beans, timber and hemp, permeated the air, along with other aromas which titillated her nostrils. Another ship of the fleet, the *Diligence*, had already docked and its cargo of tea, silks and spices from India and porcelain from China was being unloaded.

Although Lisette had seen many a dark face in Bombay and heard all manner of languages spoken, she was dazzled by the spectacle of foreigners and shouting sailors, uniformed men and those in styles of dress she had never seen before. That was the moment that the enormity of her undertaking came over her. She was in a country that held nothing for her. Even the faces looked alien. Fear sank into her but it was too late to do anything about it.

Stevedores carrying crates and trunks swarmed up and down the gangplank. One of them struggled to carry a barrel. On reaching the bottom of the gangplank he lost the battle and it rolled away in the direction of a prancing horse. The horse sidestepped to avoid it, causing its young handler to leap back or risk being struck by a flying hoof. The horse rose up on its hind legs with a snort of alarm, dragging the short rein from the man's grip. Finding itself unexpectedly free, with stirrups dancing, it then began to rear and prance with its hooves flailing, scattering everyone in its path. Raising a noisy furore amongst the crowds it was heading straight for Lisette.

She watched as it came closer. The horse had its ears back and nostrils flared, but it seemed to her that its head was still well up, which was a sign that it was not completely out of control. The only thing she could think of was to try to slow the horse. Unafraid, stepping into its path she began to walk towards the charging beast, holding her arms wide. When it was close she uttered a gasp of admiration, for it was the most beautiful chestnut horse and it was galloping straight at her.

'Oh, my God! Get back, woman! Get back!' the horse's handler shouted.

Standing only a few feet from the danger, Lisette heard the warning but stood her ground, not out of bravado but from sheer fascination as the magnificent animal reared up. 'Oh, you beautiful creature!' she whispered. Then, as if she were urging a child to do her bidding, 'Stop, stop, you'll hurt yourself if you're not careful.'

Reaching into her pocket for a sugared sweet, she held out a flat palm to the horse, which ground to a halt, snorting wildly and rolling big hazel eyes. 'Come on, you adorable thing. I'm sure you're going to like it.' The horse decided he would. He accepted the sweet as Lisette calmly took hold of the short rein and proceeded to stroke his quivering, satiny neck. With huge hindquarters and a barrel chest, he was a splendid sight. 'You're so lovely.' She sighed as the horse nudged her pocket for another sweet. 'But where have you come from?'

Suddenly a swift, agile figure appeared from nowhere.

'It's all right, Blackstock,' the figure shouted to the man who had brought the horse off the ship. 'I'll handle him. Give me that horse,' he demanded of Lisette, holding out his hand for the rein. But as he made to grab it, the horse flattened his ears, stamped his foot and lunged at him, knocking the man sideways so that he collided with Lisette and she started to topple back. Acting so swiftly his movement was a blur, he gripped her upper arms and hauled her forward.

She landed against him, her breasts pressed to his

chest, her hips welded to his hard thighs which felt as resilient as tempered steel. The breath was knocked out of her, leaving her gasping. His hands held her upright, his long fingers gripping her arms. His lips thinned, the austere planes of his face hardened and his fingers tightened about her arms. To Lisette's stunned amazement, he lifted her easily and carefully set her down a couple of feet away from him. When he released her arms she turned to the restless horse.

'Stop that,' she scolded, reaching out and jerking the rein reprovingly. 'You mustn't stamp your feet. Here, have another sweet.' The man, a soldier, stared at her. The expression his eyes contained—intensely concentrated—sent a most peculiar thrill through her. She blinked and stared back, and then it was as if she was seeing a dream awake before her. She knew this man. Her body and all its senses remembered him. She knew him by the rich, hypnotically deep voice, and the icy, needle-like chills that were her own response to him.

'Stepping in front of an out of control horse is a dangerous and extremely foolish thing to do,' he reproached sternly. 'Do you make a habit of it?'

'No, and nor do I make a habit of talking to strangers—and never to gentlemen in uniform,' she replied, her light mockery laced with gentle humour.

He scowled down at her averted face. 'And that is your rule, is it?'

For the first time she turned her head and faced him fully. A salvo was fired. It struck home with a crushing weight. Lisette couldn't have realised that Ross Montague could not trust himself to speak. Her beauty was such that his breath caught in his chest. It brought home to him the starvation of his need to feel a woman's touch.

'Oh, absolutely,' she replied calmly.

With a will of iron, Ross clamped a grip upon himself. 'Rules are made to be broken—at least mine are. By me,' he said with an ease he little felt. 'You could have been maimed for life or worse. But it is clear that you seem to have a way with horses.'

'I was brought up with them in India where I have lived since I was a child. I love them and they seem to like me—and this is such a beautiful horse. If he's been confined on board ship for weeks on end no wonder he bolted like he did. I would say he could do with a good gallop.'

Beginning to relax as he looked at this enticing young woman in a dark grey, unadorned gown, his interest growing by the second, Ross gave her a slow smile. 'I agree, but he will have to be patient a while longer.' Having witnessed the entire incident and relieved no one had been hurt, this girl had amazed him. 'I've never seen anyone stand in front of a charging horse before. I am impressed. But you do realise that

the horse could have killed you, don't you?' She gave
him a look that was almost condescending, a look that
told him she had known precisely what she was doing
and that she was more than capable of dealing with a
runaway horse. He was indeed relieved that she was un-
harmed, though he was a little surprised at the strength
of his emotions.

Taking the rein, the horse jerked back and for a moment he wrestled with the animal, speaking to him in
a soothing voice until he calmed down. Fascinated,
Lisette watched him. She didn't know men could move
like that. His coordination was faultless. He was so
tall, large and lean but strongly muscled beneath the
splendid scarlet-and-gold regimentals that hugged his
broad shoulders and narrow waist without a wrinkle
or a crease. She felt she should leave him now, this
stranger—yet he wasn't a stranger, not to her. Was this
really the same man who had saved her life, the man
in whose arms she had spent an entire night, clinging
on to him for dear life lest she fall into a raging river?

Tall and arrogant looking, he was olive skinned, almost the colour of a native of India. His hair was dark
brown, thick and curling vigorously at the nape of his
neck. His eyebrows were inclined to dip in a frown
of perplexity over eyes that were watchful. It was his
eyes that held her. They were vivid and startling blue,
a shade of blue she had never seen on a man or woman

before. It was the deep blue of the Indian Ocean—or was it the colour of the peacocks' feathers that strutted cocksure in the grounds of the rajah's palace? His face was too strong, his jaw too stubborn and too arrogant to be called classically handsome. His features were clear cut, hard edged. Only his lips, with a hint of humour to relieve their austerity, his intelligence and the wickedness that lit his blue eyes, gave any hint of mortal personality.

'His name is Bengal,' Ross informed her, 'and he was given to me by a maharajah of that place. Sometimes I wonder if he's a horse at all and not Nimrod in disguise. The Hindus believe in the transmigration of souls and I'm not convinced that in some previous incarnation this horse wasn't a noble prince dedicated to hunting wild boar.'

'Then for the love of his sins it would appear he has now descended into the body of a horse with his love of the chase unaltered,' Lisette said laughingly as the horse nuzzled at her pocket.

Ross met her wide gaze and looked at her long and deliberately, studying the young and guarded face, noting the wariness and schooled immobility with interest. There was something about her, something vaguely familiar that attracted his attention. He had the impression that he had seen her before, but he could not imagine where. He saw a girl slightly above average height, graceful and as slender as a young willow. Beneath her bonnet her blue-black hair was drawn straight back and confined in a black net so that its shining, luxuriant weight tilted her little pointed chin up as though with pride.

When he looked into her eyes which were surrounded by a thick fringe of jet-black lashes, he felt an unexplainable pang of desire. They were intense, large eyes of an unusual honey-gold colour—or was it amber?—and they gave her whole face a magical look. In them were golden flecks of light, reminding him of the tigers of India. She had also acquired the lovely honey-gold skin that no longer looked quite English, yet could never be termed foreign. In fact, she seemed to radiate a feminine perfection, with all the qualities he most admired. Her soft pink lips were tantalising and gracefully curved, full and simply begged to be kissed—in fact, he'd come within a whisker of kissing them already today, but kissing a young woman before being properly introduced was simply not good form.

A flush of colour rose into Lisette's cheeks, embarrassed as this man studied her with such cool and speculative interest.

'So you have just returned from India.'

'Yes. My mistress has instructed me to look for a conveyance. Her husband, Mr Arbuthnot, has recently retired as a factor from the Company.'

'I see. And you are?'

'Lisette Napier. I am lady's maid to Mrs Arbuthnot.'

'And where is home, Lisette Napier?' Ross was intrigued and he wondered why, for he didn't often make conversation with maids.

'Wherever I happen to be—with my work, you understand.' Her voice was low and somewhat strained. 'Before that I lived with my parents in India since I was a small child. But after India—well…'

She felt his interest quicken. Ross bent his head to look into her face. 'Yes?'

'Well—it will be…different here in London.'

His teeth flashed in a sudden infectious grin. 'You will find it very different indeed from India's hot clime.'

'Yes,' she said, trying not to let herself sound too regretful.

'And your employer? Does she live in London?'

She nodded. 'Somewhere in Chelsea, I believe.'

He grinned. 'You will find it dull in comparison to India.' Ross knew he should take his horse and move on but he was curiously reluctant to do so. Goodness, what was wrong with him, standing here talking to a servant girl when he had things to do. Again his horse nudged the girl's pocket and with a laugh she produced another sweet, her hand stroking his neck to the horse's evident delight.

'You'll spoil the beast,' Ross found himself saying.

Lisette saw that in the place of idle amusement was a look of awakened concentration. As their eyes met she shivered with an involuntary surge of excitement. She felt that this was the moment when she should remind him of their previous encounter, and with a multitude of ways of doing so on the tip of her tongue, thought better of it and bit back the words. Explaining her reasons for travelling to Bombay dressed as an Indian girl might prove difficult and tedious, and since they were unlikely to meet again there was nothing to be gained by doing so.

'He deserves to be made a fuss of after enduring such a long journey. I knew someone who had a similar horse once. She…'

Her voice trailed away. Ross waited for her to speak, to tell him more, but she didn't. She merely stared into the distance as though she were alone, or he were no more important than his horse. Less so, for she evidently loved horses. He felt a strange sensation come over him and he could hardly believe it himself when he realised he was affronted because she was unconcerned whether he moved on or stayed.

He tried again. 'How long have you been a lady's maid?' he asked, doing his best to be patient, though it was not really in his nature. He had her attention again and she smiled.

'Oh—long enough,' she replied, studying him covertly, her gaze sliding over him.

Ross felt the touch of her gaze, felt the hunter within him rise in response to that artless glance. He almost groaned. 'And is it your intention to always be a lady's maid? Would you not like to return to India?'

A glow appeared in her eyes. 'Oh, yes—and perhaps I will, one day, but I have to make my own way in the world, sir...'

'Colonel. Colonel Ross Montague.'

Ross studied her for a moment, frowning. She was looking at him, silent and unblinking, in the same way the dark-eyed Indian women stared in that unfathomable way. Having lived there for some considerable time, he suspected it was something she had developed almost unconsciously over the years, through her association with some of those doe-eyed women.

Spending many years in India had shaped Ross's ideal of feminine beauty. He was no great admirer of European standards—the pink and white belles who had begun to invade India, accompanying parents attached in some form to the East India Company. With their insipid colouring, their simpering ways and carefully arranged ringlets, they set their caps at him, attracting him not one whit.

Ross sought his pleasures with the dusky, dark-eyed maidens, who offered a chance of escape from the stifling rounds of British social life, although there had been singularly few of late. This, it may be added, was not from lack of opportunity. Ross Montague was no celibate, but two things obsessed him—India, with its beauty and glamour and its cruel mystery, and the East India Company, with its precious collection of merchant traders from London who were conquering a subcontinent and maintained their own army administering justice and laws to the Indians.

In India fortune had done nothing but smile on Ross. Young men with ambition and ability could go far. He had served with distinction; working his way up through the ranks he had now been rewarded with a promotion to colonel. But on receiving a letter from home, he had felt the sands of his good fortune were running out.

One of his cousins had been killed in the bloody shambles of the battle at Waterloo and another of his cousins, the heir to the Montague dukedom, had been listed as missing somewhere in Spain. Bound by the ties of present and future relationships to the house of Montague, Ross had returned to England at a time when his presence was likely to be of great comfort to his relatives there.

But India held his heart and imagination and he had little time for anything else—and certainly not marriage. He hadn't wanted a wife before he'd joined the army. Nothing had changed.

'How old are you?' he inquired abruptly.

The unexpectedness of the question appeared to take Lisette by surprise, and she answered in unconscious obedience to the authority in his voice. 'Twenty,' she replied, having reached that age as the ship sailed round the Cape of Africa.

He raised an intrigued eyebrow, choosing to ignore her awkward response. 'And you have a place.'

Her mouth quivered, but then she looked away, rather awkwardly. She felt her heart tighten. 'Not beyond three weeks. Now my employer's husband has retired from the Company he is to move his family to Brighton where they have a full complement of staff already. I have been told I must seek another situation.'

As she stood there she looked vulnerable for the first time. Her air of impregnable self-sufficiency vanished and Ross saw her troubled and rather desperate. 'You have references?'

'Oh, yes—well, just the one. I can only hope it will secure me another position—even that of a scullery maid would be better than nothing at all.'

'Even though it would be a blow to your pride?'

'I'm truly not proud,' she said with a bewitching smile. 'I'm wilful, I suppose. Stubborn too. And head-strong. But not, I think, proud.'

At that moment appeared Lottie Arbuthnot, her employer's daughter, treading with care over obstacles and holding her skirts to her sides so as not to mark them on the many barrels and casks piled up on the dock. On reaching Lisette she pricked her with her needle-like eyes.

'Lisette! Here you are. Mama is becoming quite vexed. How long you have been in securing a carriage.'

Ross turned and looked at her with an apologetic gesture. 'The fault is all mine—or perhaps I should say it was my horse who waylaid her. Having been released from the confines of his quarters on board, he ran amok when he reached the dock. Had Miss Napier not been so adept at handling horses there is no telling what damage he might have done.'

Staring up at the handsome colonel, Lottie disregarded his comment about Lisette and with a simpering smile fluttered her eyelashes in what Lisette consider to be an appallingly fast manner. 'Then you are forgiven, sir. I am Miss Lottie Arbuthnot. Miss Napier is servant to my ma and me.'

'So I understand,' Ross replied with a wry smile, beginning to feel pity for Miss Napier.

Lottie's arrival rudely shook Lisette out of the trance that seemed to have taken over her. It wasn't until that moment that she realised she had lost all sense of propriety. Colonel Montague must think her forward and impertinent. Embarrassment swept over her, washing her face in colour. Lottie was a moody, spiteful girl who had made her life extremely difficult on board ship as she had tried to do her best for both her and Mrs Arbuthnot, to whom she owed much gratitude.

Mrs Arbuthnot had taught her the refinements of being a lady's maid. She wore a smart black or dark grey dress and starched muslin apron and cap and could dip a curtsey as gracefully as a debutante. But all through the voyage she had been at the mercy of Lottie's every whim. It must be Lisette who helped her dress, Lisette who brought her tea. Oh, that she would never have to see the girl again!

'Lisette.' Lottie spoke peevishly. 'See, your face is quite red. Are you unwell?'

'No, I—I think it must be the heat,' she stammered. 'Excuse me. I'll go in search of a conveyance.'

'Allow me,' Ross said, handing the horse to Blackstock, who appeared at that moment. In no time at all he had secured a conveyance to take Miss Napier and the Arbuthnot family to Chelsea.

As Lottie continued to prattle on, Lisette saw Colonel Montague was watching her steadily, and she sensed the unbidden, unspoken communication between them. *He knows what I'm thinking*, she thought. It may be all imagination but she knew he was as bored and irritated by Lottie as she was. She felt instantly ashamed, knowing that Lottie could not help being the person she was.

Feeling in her pocket for some sweets, she handed them to him.

He smiled at her. 'Are these for me or the horse?'

A gentle flush mantled her cheeks. 'For Bengal, of course. If he should prove difficult you might be glad of them.'

Lowering her head she bade Colonel Montague a polite goodbye and walked back to the ship, a step behind Miss Arbuthnot. Yet she continued to feel his presence behind her, large and intensely masculine. Her senses skittered—she clamped a firm hold on them and lifted her chin, but she felt a cool tingle slither down her spine and the touch of his blue gaze on the sensitive skin on her nape.

As she walked, Ross thought she did so with the grace and presence of a dancer. As she had told him of her circumstances, he had been taken aback when her look became one of nervous apprehension. How different she'd suddenly appeared from the girl who had stepped in front of his horse, when her proud, self-possession had raised his interest. At first, not knowing what was the matter, he had thought that perhaps she was ill, but then he'd realised that she was afraid. Though her assurance and confidence had aroused him, that glimpse of vulnerability had drawn forth emotions he had only felt once before—in India—with a girl and a raging river... A girl who had also moved like a dancer.

Emerging from the river and seeing her small footprints in the mud, assured that she had survived the night, he had determined to banish the native girl from his mind. But all the way to Bombay he had not stopped looking for the girl in the pink, star-spangled sari and thick, black oiled plait hanging to her waist. The memory of that night and the girl had stayed with him, the way the hot heat of a candle flame stared at for a few moments would burn behind closed eyelids.

Those same emotions made him want to protect this girl, to keep her from harm. His fancy took flight and he imagined himself as her champion, secretly carrying her colours beneath his armour next to his heart, watching that proud smile on her face turn inward to a sweet, imploring look of appeal. Before his imagination could propel him to even more exquisitely poignant pangs of desire, Blackstock told him he would make the necessary arrangements for his baggage to be sent on to Lady Mannering's house in Bloomsbury.

Ross immediately mounted his restive horse and nosed him away from the dock, the clip-clopping of the horse's shoes ringing sharp and clear in the bright morning air. But he had made a mental note of where

Miss Napier could be located, tucking the information into a corner of his mind to be resurrected when he so desired.

Light streaming through the long windows fell in bright shafts upon the black-and-white marble floor. Ross felt a warm glow. The house belonged to his widowed maternal aunt, Lady Grace Mannering. In his absence the house had lost neither its old appeal nor its very special associations with those happy years he had spent as a boy in London with his sister, Araminta.

Drawn by the bittersweet memories stirred by hearing lilting strains of a merry tune being played on the piano, he strode across the hall to the door of the music room and pushed it open to find Araminta seated at the instrument.

She stopped playing and turned towards the door and the man who stood there. Joyous disbelief held her immobilised for a split second, then she shouted, 'Ross!' and amid squeals of laughter and ecstatic shrieks, she bounced off the stool and burst into an unladylike run. Almost knocking him over she flung her arms around his neck in a fierce hug, laughing with joy and nearly choking him in her enthusiasm. Embracing her in return, a full moment passed before Araminta relaxed her stranglehold.

'Oh, Ross, dear brother, is it really you? You look

wonderful. I've missed you so much. I don't know what I would have done without your letters,' she gushed, hugging him again.

Pulling him down onto the sofa, his legs disappearing amid a flurry of skirts, all at once she launched into a torrent of questions ranging from where he had been, what he had been doing and how long was he going to stay, hardly giving him time to reply.

When he had the chance he studied her closely. Five years had gone by since he had last seen her and the girl he had known had been replaced by a lovely young woman. Her shining light brown hair was a tumble of rebellious curls and her eyes as deeply blue as his own.

'I'm happy to see you looking so well, Araminta,' he said, realising just how much he had missed his only sibling. 'I hardly recognised you. Why, you must have grown taller by half a head in the time I've been gone. You look so mature.'

'And you are very handsome, Ross,' Araminta declared breathlessly, 'and so distinguished in your military uniform. You are a colonel now?'

He nodded. 'I was promoted just before I left India.'

'Will you go back there?'

'Of course. I'm home on extended leave—for how long depends on what I find when I get to Castonbury Park.'

Learning of her nephew's arrival Lady Mannering entered. Her small, rotund figure was encased in deep rose silk and a widow's cap was atop her sprightly brown hair liberally streaked with grey. As she went to greet her nephew, her eyes were bright with intelligence, set in a soft, lined face.

After greeting his aunt affectionately, Ross sat across from her and looked at her homely face and the light blue eyes that had scolded and teased him and Araminta and loved them so well. His look became sombre.

'Cousin Giles wrote and told me about young Edward.'

Grace's eyes filled with sadness. 'Yes, it was quite dreadful when we heard he'd been killed. There was great relief when Giles came back. As you will remember Edward was so attached to his older brother, but now Giles has resigned his commission. What happened to Edward has affected him rather badly, I'm afraid. And if that weren't bad enough Jamie is still missing.'

Ross stared at her in stunned disbelief. His cousin Jamie Montague, heir to the magnificent Castonbury Park in Derbyshire, had been listed as missing in Spain a year before Waterloo. 'Good heavens! I was hoping he'd been found by now. Is there still no word?'

'I'm afraid not.'

'No body has been found?'

She shook her head. 'It's thought that he was washed away when crossing a swollen river before the push for Toulouse.'

'Then Giles stands next in line. Knowing of his love for the military life, he will be a reluctant heir.'

'He was in London recently. It would have been good for you to have seen him before he left for Castonbury. Still, I suppose you've been fighting your own battles in India.'

'I'll catch up with him there. Castonbury is still my home and I am eager to see my uncle. Giles must be feeling pretty wretched right now. With Edward dead and Jamie missing—and of course Harry busy with his work here in London, he's going to need someone close.'

'Family support is always a good thing at a time like this, Ross. All things considered, the Montagues aren't as invincible as they thought.'

Having been raised with the Montague children, Ross had come to look on the six siblings as his brothers and sisters, and his concern over the disappearance of one and the death of another affected him deeply. Added to this was the financial crisis that had hit the family following the Napoleonic wars. Although the Montagues courted danger, they were his family, to be defended to the death.

'On top of Jamie's disappearance, Edward's death will have affected my uncle very badly.'

'I'm afraid it has. Everyone is quite worried about him. The letters that Phaedra writes to Araminta tell of his declining health and that his mind is not what it was, that at times he seems to be a little…unhinged I believe was the term she used. Which reminds me. A letter has been delivered from Castonbury Park. It's from Giles. Would you like to read it now?'

'I'll do that when I go and change.' Ross frowned with concern. 'I shall not delay in leaving for Castonbury. But first I shall have to visit my tailor—which I shall do first thing tomorrow. After that I shall be free to go.'

'The Season is almost over. Araminta can go with you.'

'Are you to accompany us too, Aunt?'

'You know how I prefer to be in town. However, I will give you the loan of my travelling chaise to take you to Castonbury. It could do with an outing and it will give the grooms something to do. Do you require a valet, Ross?'

'I've brought my own man with me, Blackstock, a young subaltern in my regiment. I left him at the dock sorting out the baggage. He should be here shortly.'

In the privacy of his room, Ross opened the letter from his cousin Giles, and found he was greatly disturbed by its contents. It contained a hurried account of a mysterious woman claiming her son was Jamie's heir, and that the family was in dire financial straits. Indeed, the news was so dire it seemed as if the house of Montague was about to come crashing down. Giles asked Ross to go and see this woman, who was in lodgings in Cheapside, for himself, and afterwards to seek out his brother Harry while he was in London and explain the situation. Ross must also emphasise to Harry the importance of finding out what had happened to Jamie, and that it was imperative that Harry left for Spain as soon as he was able.

Folding the letter, Ross sat down to draft a note to his cousin Harry.

Before sitting down to dinner, Ross sought his aunt's company in order to see what other troubles might have befallen the Montagues in his absence. He was shocked to discover that his sister had broken her betrothal to Lord Antony Bennington, son and heir of the Earl of Cawood in Cambridgeshire. Ross was disappointed. From what he remembered of young Bennington the man was an agreeable sort. Was there any good news to be had? he wondered to himself.

'Araminta must have had good reason to cry off her betrothal to young Bennington,' Ross said with a troubled frown. Having played nursemaid, surrogate father and guardian to Araminta all her life, she was in part the reason why he had returned to England, to provide the final direction she needed to cross the threshold into matrimony. It would seem he was going to have his work cut out to have her settled before he could return to India. 'How has it affected her?'

'Araminta is a girl of too much resolution and energy of character to allow herself to dwell on useless and unseemly sorrow for the past,' Aunt Grace said. 'Naturally she was regretful for a while, but she has wisely turned her attention towards the future, which is vastly more important to her than pining for what is lost.'

'Do you know what happened to make her break off the betrothal? Did she not speak of it to you?'

'No, she did not. The only reason she would give was that they did not suit—but I heard from a reliable source that Araminta caught him in a dalliance with a young woman by the name of Elizabeth Walton.'

Ross looked at Araminta with concern when she walked in and sat beside her aunt on the sofa. Looking at her now he noted her eyes held a certain sadness, and Ross was not at all convinced that she had put her broken betrothal behind her.

'You haven't forgotten that we're going shopping tomorrow, have you, Araminta?' Grace said as they settled down to dinner. 'I thought we might start by visiting the Exchange. Of course, all the best shops are on Bond or Bruton Street. If we have the time we can go there after.'

'You may have to go alone. I swear I have the onset of a headache. I think I shall lie in, if you don't mind.'

'But I do mind. Fresh air will be more beneficial to you than lying in bed all day. I'll send Sarah in to pamper you if you like.'

'How very generous of you, Aunt Grace. You know I'm in need of a maid of my own, for while Sarah is diligent, she has so much to do. She is always in a hurry and knows nothing of dressing me properly. Little wonder I appear at dinner looking half dressed and my hair all mussed up,' Araminta complained.

Ross pricked up his ears and looked at his sister, an image of the delectable Miss Napier drifting into his mind. 'You require a maid?'

'I most certainly do,' Araminta replied adamantly. 'I've mentioned it to Aunt Grace before but she never seems to get round to it.'

'That's true,' Grace said. 'There always seems to be so much to think about. But I agree, Araminta, you really do need a maid of your own.'

'Then might I suggest someone?' Ross said, feeling a strange lift to his heart. 'I met a young woman yesterday. She's been in India and is employed as maid to a lady and her daughter who reside in Chelsea. Her position is to be terminated in three weeks and she is looking for another post.'

'Why?' Araminta asked suspiciously. 'What has she done?'

'Nothing. Her employers are moving to Brighton and she will no longer be required.'

Ross's suggestion cheered Araminta somewhat. She studied the almost fond smile upon her brother's face as he spoke of the girl and noted the gleam in his eyes. He seldom smiled, she knew, unless the smile was seductive or cynical, and when he was in the presence of his uncle, the Duke of Rothermere, he rarely laughed. It was almost as though he believed sentimentality silly and anything that was silly was abhorrent and made a man vulnerable. She was intrigued. Was it possible that he'd developed a special fondness for this maid?

'What is this extraordinary female's name and what does she look like?' Araminta asked, anxious to discover more about the girl who'd had such an unusual effect on her brother.

'Her name is Lisette Napier. She is quite tall, slender and dark haired. Her speech is as cultured as yours and mine. Her manners are impeccable and she is presentable.'

'And how old is she?'

'I believe she is twenty.'

'I see. Isn't that a little young to be a lady's maid?'

'And will she make a suitable maid?' Aunt Grace asked.

'I really have no idea about such things, but I'm sure Mrs Arbuthnot would not employ her if she wasn't any good at her job.'

'Well, heaven forbid if she's prettier than Araminta. It would never do for a maid to be more becoming than her mistress.'

'Oh, that doesn't matter,' Araminta remarked happily, having already decided to take Miss Napier on—for her brother's sake as well as her own need and curiosity. 'I should very much like for you to hire her, Ross.'

'I expect you could do worse than give her a chance— perhaps for a trial period of a month. See how she gets on.'

'Yes—yes, I will. Decent servants are neither easy to find, cheap to train, nor simple to keep. I would like to meet her first.'

Ross nodded and began to attack the roast lamb with renewed relish. 'I'll do my best. I have no doubt that Mr Arbuthnot's address can be located through East India House.'

The Arbuthnot family had been at home in Chelsea for a few days when Lottie dressed early and told Lisette to prepare for a trip to the Royal Exchange to do some shopping. There were some items she wished to purchase before she left for Brighton. Glad of the opportunity to escape the stilted confines of the house, where she found the work hard for both Mrs Arbuthnot and Lottie demanded their pound of flesh, and eager to

see more of London, Lisette put on her coat and bonnet
and prepared to enjoy herself for a couple of hours or so.

When the carriage turned in to Cornhill, both girls
were in good spirits. They stared with excitement at
the immense stone front of the facade of the Exchange
with its high arcades and column and the clock tower
reaching skyward.

Alighting from the carriage they went through the
archway where the arcade square of the Exchange
opened up before them. It was filled with merchants
and traders and hawkers of wares, mingling with people of all occupations and positions and gentlemen in
military uniforms. It was a fashionable place to shop
and used as a rendezvous, much frequented by beaux
waiting to meet a lady bent on flirtation.

'Oh, what a wonderful place,' Lisette murmured,
breathing in the different smells that reached her, from
roasting chestnuts to hot pies and horse dung. She was
captivated by the sight and would have stopped, but
Lottie was moving on through the yard. She hurried
after her.

Taking hold of Lisette's arm, Lottie was unable to
conceal her excitement, blushing delightedly when a
handsome young soldier touched his hat and winked
at her. 'I think I would like to have a look round the
little stalls in the yard first but the shops upstairs are
always the best.'

And so they passed a pleasant half-hour browsing among the stalls with Lottie dipping into her silk purse for coins to buy fripperies and handing them to Lisette to place in her basket. They mounted the staircase and strolled along the upper gallery. It was thronged with shoppers and Lisette found it difficult to keep Lottie within her sight at times. When she disappeared inside a shop to purchase some gloves, telling Lisette that she would probably be a while since she wished to browse, Lisette slipped in after her. She was distracted when some beautiful lace collars caught her eye. Pausing to take a look, she could only wish she had the money to buy one. It would certainly enhance the grey dress she wore day in and day out.

She had not been inside the shop very long when she had an odd feeling that she was being watched. The short hairs on the nape of her neck rose on end and her spine tingled. As she began to turn slowly to see if her suspicions were correct, she was half expecting to see Lottie behind her for she was sure now that she was only being fanciful.

Her eyes flicked round the shop and turning round she passed the stranger with hardly more than a glance, not even pausing for the sake of politeness as the man swept his hat from his dark head. Instead she lifted her skirts to descend a step.

Ross leaned back against the fixtures and smiled

his appreciation as his eyes caressed her trim back. Suddenly Lisette stopped, and sensing his eyes on her she whirled to gape at him, her amber eyes wide in disbelief on finding herself face to face with Colonel Montague—tall, lean and strikingly handsome, recklessly so, with magnificent dark brows that curved neatly, a straight nose and a firm but almost sensuous mouth. The lean line of his jaw showed strength and flexed with the movement of the muscles there.

'Colonel Montague?' the question burst from her.

'The same, Miss Napier.' Now having her full attention, he held his hat before his chest in a bow of exaggerated politeness, before taking her arm and drawing her aside.

He had appeared too suddenly for Lisette to prepare herself, so the heady surge of pleasure she experienced on seeing him again was clearly evident, stamped like an unbidden confession on her lovely face. For a long, joyous interval they held each other with their eyes, savouring the moment, enjoying afresh the powerful force that sprang between them. Then he smiled.

'Miss Napier! How odd to find you here.' Desire was already tightening his loins—and *that* with just the sight of her. He didn't understand why she had such a volatile effect on him, but he understood that he wanted her—he wanted her warm and willing in his arms, in his bed.

## *Chapter Two*

Lisette stared at Colonel Montague, her heart doing a somersault. 'It is?' His smile sent a flood of warmth through her body to settle in a hot flush upon her cheeks and other, less exposed places.

'Most certainly.'

Without relinquishing his hold on her arm, his touch igniting fires inside her, fires that flared to a startling intensity when he led her to a private place at the back of the shop. She found herself standing so close to him that she could almost hear the beating of his heart. He looked down at her so intently that he might have been trying to commit every detail of her features to memory.

As before, when he had met her on the dock, Ross felt a faint stirring of recognition, like the ghost of a memory long submerged, but it drifted away when he saw the warmth in her eyes.

He didn't waste time on unnecessary words of politeness. 'This is a trace of luck our meeting like this. Are you alone?'

She shook her head. 'No, I'm with Miss Arbuthnot. She wandered off. I suppose I must go and find her before I lose her altogether,' Lisette said, although she was most reluctant to do so on finding herself in the presence of Colonel Montague once more. She could not rightly say what it was about him that held her attention. She felt utterly fascinated, like a child beholding a favourite toy. He was quite unlike anything or anyone she had ever known.

Ross stared at her profile, tracing with his gaze the classically beautiful lines of her face, the unexpected brush of lustrous ebony eyelashes. He had never seen the like of her. She was quite extraordinarily lovely. She had an untamed quality running in dangerous undercurrents just below the surface, a wild freedom of spirit that found its counterpart in his own hot-blooded nature.

Something in his stare made Lisette's fingertips tingle. The tingle crept up her arms with sweet warmth, into her chest, and straight into her breast. She did her best to ignore the sensation.

'Tell me, Miss Napier, how are you finding London? Is it to your liking?'

'I have seen little of it. This is the first time I've been

away from the house, but I must confess that I am finding it all so strange—and exciting, of course, and so different from what I am used to.'

'I imagine you are missing India.'

Lisette was spared answering his question when a pretty, fashionable young woman dressed in a beautiful blue gown with a matching hat perched atop a riot of gleaming brown curls appeared at his side.

'Ah—so this is where you've got to, Ross. Little wonder I couldn't find you when you were lurking at the back of the shop.' Her eyes looked Lisette up and down, in an appraising way. A little smile formed on her lips. 'And I can see why. Will you do me the honour of introducing your companion?'

'Of course. Allow me to present to you Miss Lisette Napier. Miss Napier—my sister, Miss Araminta Montague. This is the young lady I spoke to you about, Araminta.'

Lisette bobbed a respectful curtsey, looking from one to the other. 'For what reason did you have to discuss me, Colonel?' she enquired, surprised and deeply touched to know he had spared her a passing thought.

'I recall you telling me you were looking for another position. When my sister mentioned that she was in desperate need of a maid, I thought of you.'

'And now we've met it will save us the trouble of writing to you,' Araminta said.

'Would the position be to your liking?' Ross asked,

cocking a quizzical, amused eyebrow. 'Although, when I recall you telling me that you are wilful, stubborn and headstrong, perhaps I should question your suitability!'

His wry tone made Lisette burst out laughing, and Ross found himself captivated by the infectious joy, the beauty, of it. He'd never heard the music of her laughter before, nor seen it glowing in her magnificent eyes.

'I also recall telling you that I am not proud, Colonel—although I would be honoured to be offered the post of your sister's maid,' Lisette said, fighting down a sudden absurd surge of happiness.

Standing against a backdrop of ribbons and lace, laughing up at him, Lisette Napier was unforgettable. Ross realised it as clearly as he realised that if he became her employer, there was every chance he was going to find her irresistible as well.

'My brother tells me your present position is shortly to be terminated. Is this correct, Miss Napier?'

'Yes. My employer will have no need of me when the family moves to Brighton.'

'Why don't you ask Miss Napier to come to the house, Araminta? It's highly irregular to carry out an interview in such a place as this and for you to be doing it. Shouldn't Aunt Grace—or is it the housekeeper who usually sees to the hiring of servants?'

Araminta gave him a cross look. 'Usually it is but since I am the one requiring a maid I shall have a say in who is employed to see to my needs. I am in London for the Season and will shortly be leaving for our home in Derbyshire,' she said, addressing Lisette. 'Would you mind?'

Lisette stared at her. Mind? Of course she wouldn't mind. From what she could recall of the English geography lessons her father had taught her, Derbyshire was miles away from London—somewhere in the north. That would suit her perfectly. Colonel Montague had thought of her when he knew his sister was requiring a maid of her own and put her name forward—like a friend would. She looked at him. Her heart was beating hard in her chest. She wanted beyond anything to accept the post since it represented decency, security, respectability and a release from the gnawing fear and uncertainty of the past months, and going to Derbyshire would certainly solve her current predicament.

'No,' she said. 'That would suit me very well.'

'Still,' Araminta said, suffering some discomfort when she was jostled from behind by an exuberant shopper, 'Ross is quite right. This is hardly the place, but I think you will do very well. Can you come to the house?'

Lisette shook her head. 'Unfortunately that's not possible. There is so much to be done before my employer leaves for Brighton. I shall be fully occupied.'

'Then come to the house when they have left. Ross

will give you directions. Present yourself to the house-keeper and we will take it from there. I shall tell her to expect you.' Tilting her head to one side she looked at Lisette with renewed interest. 'Did you travel from India on the same ship as my brother, Miss Napier?'

'No. I sailed on the *Portland*. Colonel Montague was on the *Diligence*—the first vessel of the fleet to dock in London.'

Araminta's eyes opened wider, more and more intrigued by the second. 'Then how did you meet?'

'My horse panicked when he was taken off the ship and Miss Napier calmed him,' Ross explained shortly, 'which was immensely brave of her and for which I was truly grateful.'

'Oh, I see. You are not afraid of horses, Miss Napier?'

'Far from it,' Ross quipped before Lisette could open her mouth. 'Bengal's a peppery beast at the best of times. She handled him admirably. But I cannot see that this has anything to do with Miss Napier being your maid, Araminta.'

Araminta looked at her brother and laughed. He really did look put out by her questioning. 'Forgive my curiosity. You know what I'm like. Now are you ready, Ross, or is there something further you wish to say to Miss Napier before we leave?'

Ross turned his back on his sister to speak to Lisette, giving her directions to his aunt's house in Bloomsbury.

Meeting her gaze he realised that when he had met her before and looked into her eyes, he had thought them strange. Now he could not understand how he had ever thought that. He now saw those astonishing eyes as the perfect expression of her unique self. Now she seemed absolutely perfect.

His voice was laced with concern when he said, 'Will you be all right? Would you like me to wait with you until Miss Arbuthnot appears?'

'That will not be necessary. I see Miss Arbuthnot is in the process of purchasing some ribbons. You have been most generous, Colonel, and to be sure I am grateful that you saw fit to speak of me to your sister. If she considers me suitable for the post, then I shall appreciate the shelter, protection and stability of the position and to be valued for the qualities I know I possess.'

For a moment Ross didn't move—he studied her with speculative blue eyes, pleasuring himself with the sight of her. 'Which I am certain you have in abundance. I'm happy to have been of help.' He reached out and took her right hand in his firm grip. 'I'm so glad to have met you again, Miss Napier,' he said, shaking her hand.

With her heart racing, Lisette sucked in a breath. For one definable instant she felt trapped. 'Yes,' she said, feeling utterly foolish. She was so aware of the touch of him, his skin against hers, the feel of her slim hand held in his broad grasp, and as she gazed into those penetrating blue eyes, she suddenly felt herself drawn to him as if by some overwhelming magnetic force.

She opened her mouth to tell him they had met before and to thank him for saving her life, then closed it again. As much as she wanted to she could not. A ribbon and lace shop was hardly the place for such an intimate revelation. And besides, to do so would bring about a change to their relationship. He would look upon her differently—he might regret the passion they had shared, feel ashamed, even, and decide against hiring her as his sister's maid. She desperately needed the security of this employment and would do nothing to jeopardise that. In any case, it seemed he did not recognise her as the girl he had rescued, and in the grey of London colourful, vibrant India seemed half a lifetime away.

'I shall look forward to seeing you if not in London, then in Derbyshire.'

Lisette could find no words to say, and merely bobbed a little curtsey and picked up her basket.

'Good day, Miss Napier.'

Leaving the shop, Ross's lips curved in a satisfied smile. He'd sensed the awareness that had flared at his touch, the quiver of consciousness she hadn't been able to hide. Known among his contemporaries to be single-minded in pursuit of what he wanted, he was supremely confident that in no time at all he would succeed in tempting the delectable Lisette Napier into his bed.

As Ross approached the modest lodging house in Cheapside, the only thing that occupied his mind was that even after the horrors of war were over, the Montague family was in trouble. Ross feared that the arrival of this woman, Alicia, and her child into their midst, a woman who apparently called herself the Marchioness of Hatherton, had the power to shake the foundations of Castonbury Park to the core.

On seeing her, his first impression was that she did not remotely resemble the conventional image of a noblewoman, not even a lady of fashion. Her hair was fair and neatly arranged, her gown simple and unadorned, and over her arm she carried the freshly laundered clothes of an infant. But not even her plain clothing or the fact that she had probably laundered the clothes herself could make this woman look common. Petite and slender, she held herself with a dignity, a calm intelligence and a self-assurance he had not expected. Her hair framed a face of striking beauty; her skin was creamy and glowing with health. Her eyes were light blue, with long curling lashes.

'I owe you an apology for turning up like this,' Ross said, having thought that by not giving notice of his visit he would put her at a disadvantage. She seemed surprised and a little agitated by his sudden arrival and her eyes darkened with anxiety, but her generous mouth curved in a smile of welcome.

'Not at all, Colonel Montague. You are most welcome. I thank you for coming to see me. I wrote to the duke informing him of the situation, explaining to him fully, in great detail, everything that happened before Jamie was killed.'

'My uncle had already been notified of my cousin's disappearance by the British authorities.'

'So I understand. I wrote telling the duke of Crispin, our son, who is the duke's heir now Jamie is dead. I made no claim to anything for myself in my letter, only that Jamie's son is taken care of.'

Which showed great delicacy on her part, Ross thought with cynicism. But could the family reconcile themselves to the fact that the Jamie they knew, admired and loved would marry without their blessing?

'I—I expected someone to contact me,' Alicia went on hesitantly, 'but…I did not know when or who it would be. Would you like some refreshment—tea, perhaps, or coffee?'

'No, thank you. I do not wish to put you to any trouble.'

Moving towards the fire she sat rather nervously on the edge of a chair and motioned Ross to the chair opposite. He did so, trying to read her.

'Is there anything more I can tell you?' she asked, trying to ease the tension in her voice.

'What was your reason for being in Spain?'

'I was employed as companion to a lady whose husband was out there. Sadly he was killed in action and she returned to England. Having already met Jamie by that time I remained behind and we were married. If—if you're wondering about my suitability, I was born into a respectable family. I was an only child—my mother died when I was quite young. My father was a clergyman in the village of Shafton in Wiltshire. Unfortunately when he died I was quite impoverished and had no choice other than to seek employment, which was how I came to be a lady's companion.'

For the next few minutes, with tactful consideration, Ross tried to test her on little things he recalled about Jamie—his appearance, things about his past he might have told her. His questioning seemed to unsettle her and he noticed how she clasped her hands in her lap to keep them from trembling.

'You—you must forgive me, Colonel Montague, if I appear a trifle vague,' she said. 'You must understand that Jamie and I were not together very long. I confess that most of his background is still unknown to me. I know he has three brothers—Giles, Harry and Edward—and that they are all military men.'

'Forgive me. My questions were impertinent.'

She seemed to relax. 'It all happened so quickly. Jamie had no time to write to his family to inform them of our marriage. Sadly he never saw his son.' She lifted her head and looked at her visitor, her gaze long and searching. This time there were tears in her eyes, and it seemed to Ross he read in them a profound sadness, tinged with reserve and pride.

She rose then and crossed over to a bureau, extracting some papers from a drawer. 'Forgive me. I am not entirely myself these days. Emotion lies too near the surface. I expect you would like to see these.' She handed the papers to Ross. 'You will see that one is a letter from an army chaplain confirming our marriage.'

'And the chaplain? Where is he now?'

'He was killed during the battle at Toulouse.'

So, Ross thought as he scanned the document, thinking it looked authentic enough, the marriage could not be confirmed or denied in person. How plausible it all sounded. But was she telling him the truth?

The other document was a birth certificate.

'Your son has been baptised, I see.'

'Yes, here in London.'

The birth certificate only reflected what the chaplain had been told.

'I…also have Jamie's ring.'

Ross took it from her. It was old, gold and engraved

with the crest of the Marquis of Hatherton, one of Jamie's titles, proof that it was his.

'May I ask how you come to have it in your possession?' he enquired, handing it back to her. 'Jamie's body has not been found and I find it difficult to imagine he would have removed it from his finger. It holds great significance and meant a good deal to him. He would not have left it lying around.'

'You are quite right to question me about it—and to be suspicious about how I come to have it,' she said, seemingly not in the least offended by what his words implied, but the worried look Ross had seen in her eyes earlier was still there and he suspected she would be relieved when his visit was over. 'But when Jamie and I married he was unable to obtain a wedding band so he gave me this until the time when he could give me a proper ring.' Looking down at it a wistful smile touched her lips. 'It was far too big for my finger,' she said softly, 'but he insisted that I should take it.'

'You will understand,' Ross said, 'that your letter informing my uncle of your marriage to Jamie came as a shock to him—as it did to the whole family.'

'I can understand that,' she replied, her voice quite calm, without surprise, as if she read his thoughts correctly. 'If they think I wrote the letter to stake my claim, they are mistaken. Jamie's death was a great shock to me also. Before I wrote to the duke I had already come to the conclusion that you would all be perfectly right to dislike me, and to consider me either a usurper or an imposter.' Taking the documents from him she placed them back in the bureau. 'I assure you I am neither of those things, Colonel Montague.' Her eyes held her visitor's for an instant before looking away.

Ross wished he could say making pre-conclusions were stupid, but found that he could not. Yet there was no shadow in her eye, no tone in her voice, that gave him reason to believe she was anything other than what she claimed to be. Jamie's wife.

'Jamie did tell me something of his home and his family. I am looking forward to meeting them.'

'Yes, the Montagues are a fine family.'

She bent her head, and Ross had a shrewd suspicion it was to hide a smile. 'I am sure they are, Colonel. Do you think I could pay them a courtesy visit? Would that be appropriate?'

For the first time since entering the house, Ross smiled. 'I am sure that could be arranged.' He got up to take his leave. 'I shall inform my cousins of our meeting. I am sure Giles will be contacting you.'

Ross had much to think about when he left the house. His mind was split in two conflicting directions. One direction made him wonder how much it had cost her to write to his uncle, the Duke of Rothermere—to make the swing from pride to humility.

For the first time since his cousin had gone missing, he found himself blaming Jamie for Alicia's situation. If she was indeed his wife, then considering the kind of work he was doing, surely he could have taken some thought for the future. In war sudden death could come at any time to anyone. He must have known that by making no provision, he left his wife to his family's mercy, to their charity. A letter home to his father would have spared all this.

The other direction reminded Ross that as a born sceptic, he wasn't entirely convinced about the validity of Alicia's claim. There were too many questions left to be answered for his comfort. It had been obvious from her manner and speech that her background was respectable, but was she clever enough and ambitious enough to raise herself from a lady's companion to a marchioness and ultimately a duchess? Or was she as she seemed to be—not ambitious, and innocent of any deviousness?

Another thought cast doubt. The Jamie he knew would have written to his family informing them of his intentions—could he really have been so blinded by his love for Alicia it had robbed him of all rational thought?

As soon as the Arbuthnots had left for Brighton, dressing simply and neatly in her most suitable gown and bonnet, Lisette presented herself at Mannering House in Bloomsbury. She was greeted at the door by a stiff-faced footman in dark green livery. On requesting to see the housekeeper he showed her into a glittering entry hall and told her to wait.

Feeling terribly nervous her gaze scanned the impressive hall. Never had she seen the like. This house surpassed her wildest imaginings. In magnificent splendour a marble staircase rose gracefully to the upper floors. A vase of sweet-smelling blooms beautifully matched and arranged had been placed on a side table beneath a huge gilt mirror. Folding her gloved hands at her waist, her body stiffened when, on looking up, she saw Colonel Montague.

She studied him as he slowly descended to the hall—his broad, muscular shoulders, deep chest and narrow waist—before lifting her eyes to his darkly handsome face. In a linen shirt, tight-fitting riding breeches and polished tan boots, every inch of Ross Montague's tall frame positively radiated raw power, tough, implacable authority and leashed sensuality.

For what seemed an eternity, she stood perfectly still, existing in a state of jarring tension, struggling to appear completely calm, clinging to her composure as if it were a blanket she could use to insulate herself against this man who disturbed her like no other. His gaze was steadily fixed on her and on reaching the bottom of the stairs he paused and they stared at each other for a second, with several yards of marble hallway still between them.

She watched him in fascination as he approached her at a leisurely pace. Her heart skipped a beat. He was certainly the stuff of which young ladies' dreams were made.

Looking down at her, Ross noted how tense she looked. Her beauty caught him like an unexpected blow to the chest. 'Miss Lisette Napier. How very nice to see you again. You had no difficulty finding the house?'

Her eyes were alight with pleasure and she glanced around her. 'Not at all. It is a wondrous house,' she said softly. 'You might have warned me.'

'If you think this is grand, then wait until you see Castonbury Park. So you are here to take up your position as my sister's maid?'

The deep, velvet tones of his cultured voice made her stomach flutter. 'If I am considered suitable,' she replied, giving a slight curtsey.

He smiled slowly. His guarded stare travelled over her, noting the gentle flush mantling her cheeks. He didn't think he would have much persuading to do to make her succumb to his desire. The young beauty was not the expert that he was at hiding her feelings.

'Since I am to be the man who pays your wages, Miss Napier, your interview with Mrs Whitelaw is a mere formality. It is my considered opinion that you will be perfect for the post.' He lifted one eyebrow slightly after his words, as though challenging her to question them.

Lisette's knees knocked beneath her skirts, threatening to give out as she faced Ross Montague in all his male magnetism. 'I want to thank you again for thinking of me for the position,' she murmured. 'It was… generous of you.'

'Generous?' he echoed, both raven eyebrows arching high.

'Yes.' She nodded fervently. Something in his stare made her fingertips tingle. The tingle crept up her arms with sweet warmth into her chest. She ignored the odd sensation with a will, lowering her gaze. 'I am extremely grateful. When Mrs Arbuthnot told me I would have to look for work elsewhere—and at such short notice—unaccustomed as I am to this huge metropolis, I confess I found the prospect of going from door to door seeking another situation extremely daunting.' Colonel Montague shocked her when he touched her gently under her chin. She caught her breath sharply as he tilted her face upward again and looked into his eyes.

Her gratitude appeared to entertain him—his chiselled face softened considerably as he held her gaze. 'I am happy to be of service, Miss Napier.'

Her heart pounded at the light but sure pressure of his warm fingertips against her skin.

He smiled and lowered his hand to his side. 'The Arbuthnots have left for Brighton?'

'Yes, this very day.'

'And you have brought your luggage with you?'

'Yes, sir, although I do not possess much, as you see,' she answered, indicating her one bag by the door.

'One of the footmen will see it is carried to your room.'

Lisette showed her surprise. 'But I have not yet met your housekeeper. I have my reference…'

'Which I have no doubt will give you an excellent character, but I prefer to judge for myself.' A woman seemed to appear from nowhere. 'Ah, here is Mrs Whitelaw. I'll leave you in her capable hands.'

Ross entered the hallowed rooms of White's, the gentleman's club in St James's, where he had arranged to meet his cousin, Lord Harry Montague. The rooms were cloaked in the quiet, restrained ambience, redolent of the masculine smells of sandalwood, leather and cigars.

He scanned the room, his gaze coming to rest on a tall, dramatically dark gentleman clothed in black. He stood watching the play at the hazard table. With no wish to join in, raising a brandy to his lips, the impression Harry gave off was of bored indifference. Lifting his head, the instant he saw his cousin, his handsome countenance lightened. The two strode towards each other and they met in the doorway to the card room, where they clasped arms, laughing.

'Good to have you home, Ross,' Harry said. 'Back for good, are you?'

'No—extended leave.' Ross took Harry's arm and led him to a table that offered privacy.

A worried shadow darkened Harry's eyes as he seated himself across from Ross and thought about the strangely vague note asking him to meet his cousin here. After politely enquiring about the health of Araminta and their maternal aunt, Lady Grace Mannering, he sat back and waited for Ross to enlighten him as to the purpose of this meeting.

'Glad to learn you made it back from Waterloo, Harry, but it was bad news about Edward,' Ross said, ordering a couple of brandies.

The emotions Harry suffered over the death of his younger brother at Waterloo and carefully concealed from others were evident now in the tautness of his clenched jaw as he glanced at his cousin. 'It is a tragedy felt by the whole family. It was one hell of a battle, but we finally got those bastards.' Drinking deep of his brandy he looked at Ross. 'Anything in particular you wanted to see me about? I got the feeling there was a sense of urgency about your note.'

Meeting Harry's arrested stare, Ross hesitated and then he said gravely, 'I've received a letter from Giles. He asked me to speak to you about Jamie.'

'Jamie's still listed as missing.'

'I believe he disappeared when the army made the push for Toulouse. He wasn't with the rest of them when they crossed the river. I understand he was swept away.'

'Jamie is…was a strong swimmer.'

'I imagine the current was too strong, Harry.'

'It looks like it. You know how I always looked up to Jamie.'

'I know. There is something else—a couple of things, in fact, that make it imperative that you go to Spain, to search for Jamie's body, or at least learn what happened to him as quickly as possible.' Harry gave him a questioning look when he hesitated, but waited patiently for him to go on. 'The first concerns the Montague finances. Shortly before Waterloo your father gambled on Napoleon winning the war. He sold his government bonds and lost a substantial amount of money. He took out a loan which has to be repaid.'

Harry stared at him with something like incredulity and amazement. 'Good Lord, I had no idea.'

'You've been in Spain. How could you?'

This was true, but Harry remembered the terrible

rumours that had ignited London when word reached the city that Wellington had lost the battle at Waterloo, causing panic in the financial markets and the stock exchange to crash. In their desperation, London stockholders had wanted out of their investments immediately, believing they would need the money to survive. The market panic was halted when news of Wellington's victory at Waterloo arrived, but too late for the countless innocent people who had lost their life savings, and hundreds of reputable merchants and noble families had been ruined.

'There are many outstanding debts,' Ross went on. 'The creditors are being held off for now, but the deadline for repayment draws ever closer. As you know Castonbury costs a ransom to run. As things stand, its income doesn't match its expenses by a long way. The danger is that along with the contents of the house it will have to be mortgaged to pay off some of these debts.'

Harry's skin whitened. He was clearly shaken by this. 'Good Lord! As bad as that?'

'According to Giles, it is. Your father's grief at the loss of Edward and the situation with Jamie sent him into a decline, and the guilt he feels over his haste to sell off his shares is almost too painful for him to bear. As you know, when your mother died, as the firstborn and according to her marriage settlement, her immense fortune went to Jamie. Your father is banking on the money helping the family financially if proof can be found of Jamie's death.'

'Well, it will all go to Giles now. You said there were two things, Ross. You have told me the first. What is the second?'

'A short time ago a letter was delivered to your father from an unknown woman. It was sent from Spain. The woman is called Alicia Montague. She claims to be Jamie's widow.'

Ross waited through a long moment of awful suspense, knowing exactly where Harry's thoughts would turn next. Finally, when he spoke, his voice was rough with emotion, as if the words were being gouged out of him.

'What is known about her?'

'On Giles's request I have been to see her.'

'What did you make out?'

'She is an intelligent woman—she is also likeable and quite charming. She has a child she claims is Jamie's heir, and she also has a letter from the chaplain who performed the marriage ceremony—and Jamie's ring.'

'But...that is preposterous. As the heir, on a matter of such importance, it would be so unlike Jamie to commit himself to marriage without consulting with or at least informing his family first.'

'I agree. However, having met her she could very well be the type of woman Jamie would have fallen for.'

Harry felt a prickling along his nape. His instincts urged him to use extreme caution in making any judgement. 'What do you think, Ross? Could this woman be an imposter?'

Ross sighed and shook his head slowly. 'I don't know that. In fact, in all honesty I don't know what to think, which is why the truth concerning the marriage must be determined—along with the facts concerning Jamie's demise—before disaster strikes.'

'And if it is proven that Jamie is dead and the child is indeed his son, then as heir the estate will pass to him on father's death. And Mother's money too.'

'It looks like it. And should no body be found, then it will be seven years before an act of Parliament is passed officially declaring Jamie dead. In the meantime his finances will have to remain untouched. You've been to Spain, Harry. You have knowledge of the country, and being attached to the diplomatic service in London means you are ideally placed to go to there and search out the truth. We need hard evidence that Jamie is dead.'

Leaning his head against the back of his chair, Harry closed his eyes and drew a long, deep breath. Spain! He didn't want to go back. Reminders of that time evoked painful, personal memories he preferred not to recall. And now Ross was asking him to go back.

'You are right, Ross. I must return. If this woman's claim cannot be disproved, then her son is heir. It could be devastating to the whole Montague dynasty. Dear Lord, Ross, how has it come to this? As youths we lived like princes, champagne was drunk as though it were water and guests invited to Castonbury Park to partake of the Montague's hospitality were open-mouthed at the liberality and display. We hunted with the best of the county, the stables filled with expensive hunters, the kennels full of hounds—the hunt servants, the display of wealth. How is it possible that it's in danger of disappearing? It cannot happen. We cannot let it happen. We have to stop it.'

Ross knew that Harry would do everything within his power to seek out the truth. The Montagues' attitude to family was possessive and protective. They were a warrior clan defending what was theirs at all costs, their instinct being to hold on to what they had won. 'What are your chances, Harry?'

Harry's eyes narrowed into a slight frown and his features took on a pensive expression. 'The answer is that I don't know.' His tone implied the chances were not extremely good, but then he had contacts in Spain who might be able to help him so it was not entirely hopeless. 'But to find out what really happened to my

brother is a mission I am duty-bound to undertake—
and to find out what I can about this woman and if her
claim is genuine. Leave it with me. I'll make arrangements to leave for Spain. Unfortunately I have com-
mitments to fulfil regarding my work here in London
so I am unable to leave right away. I'll write to Giles
at Castonbury informing him when I can depart and
again as soon as I have anything to report.'

Although Lisette had learned to contend with the
varying moods and whims of Lottie Arbuthnot, this,
she feared, was a different environment and a different mistress entirely. She had complete care of Miss
Araminta's wardrobe and it was her duty to clean and
repair any garment that needed it. She attended her toilet and arranged her hair—a task Lisette was taught by
the maid who had attended Araminta before Lisette
took up her position.

Her young mistress was a leading belle of the *ton*,
and to Lisette's despair she was unpredictable and prob-
lematical. But she was also warm and open and there
was something about her that Lisette liked.

She had completed her first week and was arranging
Miss Araminta's hair when there was a knock on the
door. Meeting Lisette's eyes in the mirror, Araminta
gave her a knowing smile.

'That will be Ross—impatient as ever.' She bade him enter.

Contrary to Araminta's comment, Ross sauntered in and made himself comfortable in a chair facing his sister. He'd made it a practice to visit her in her room each day, and although he kept his visits brief, he found himself nevertheless looking forward to them because it gave him the opportunity to see Miss Napier. Out of uniform, Colonel Montague was the very epitome of an elegant gentleman. With his dark hair brushed back and shining, he was the image of relaxed elegance in his black and white evening clothes and one well-shod foot propped casually atop the opposite knee.

'I thought I'd come and see what's keeping you, Araminta. We're expected at the Bosworths' in half an hour.'

'I know, and I'm sorry, Ross. As soon as Lisette has finished arranging my hair I'll be ready.'

'I'm sure they'll understand if we're a bit late,' he said, content to sit and observe the delectable Miss Napier put the finishing touches to his sister's toilet. Even his expression was casual.

Looking at Lisette through the mirror Araminta eyed her in watchful curiosity, noticing her wandering attention and the soft flush that had risen to her cheeks when Ross had entered. She wondered what lay behind her maid's lovely face, for she really was exceptionally beautiful and in the right clothes she would be stunning.

'Tell me, Lisette, do you speak any other languages besides English?'

'I speak Urdu and Hindustani,' she answered, aware of Colonel Montague's eyes observing her every move and willing herself not to think of it. 'My parents taught me well and were quite insistent that I learn the language in order to understand the people and the culture of India.'

'That must have been difficult.'

'Not really. I was young so it came naturally.' Suddenly she felt like disappearing into the floor, for her announcement might have sounded like boasting and probably branded her a bluestocking in her mistress's eyes. But it had done no such thing. It had only increased her mistress's growing respect for this unusual maid of hers.

'Do you play the pianoforte and sing too?' Ross asked with a teasing smile.

Lisette returned his smile through the mirror and said, 'Oh, no. I can't do either. I gave up the piano in frustration, and when I opened my mouth to sing, to my immense relief my mother covered her ears and gave up on me.'

'And do you like working here, Lisette?' Araminta asked.

'Of course. I consider myself extremely fortunate to be working for such a fine family.'

'I am glad my brother brought you to my attention.'

'Our meeting on the docks was brief. I'm surprised he remembered me at all.'

'I'm not. You're very pretty, Lisette. Exceptionally so, and never have I seen hair so dark as to be almost black—in fact, I do believe it is. It's a beautiful shade—exotic, even, the perfect frame for your features and creamy skin. Do you not agree, Ross?'

Caught completely off guard, Ross said cautiously, 'Forgive me, Araminta, I'm not sure what you mean?'

'Either you're extremely unobservant or else your eyesight is afflicted. I was talking about Lisette's hair. It's quite extraordinary, don't you agree?'

'I am sure Colonel Montague has many things to think about other than my hair, Miss Araminta,' Lisette remarked. 'It is black and quite ordinary, which I do not find in the least exciting and is a common shade in India.'

'You don't like it,' Ross summarized.

'Not really,' she answered, touching Araminta's light brown tresses with something like envy in her eyes, 'but one must be satisfied with what one is born with. I would imagine that living in India and seeing nothing but dusky skins and black-haired natives day in and day out you would find monotonous, Colonel Montague.'

'Not at all—quite the opposite, in fact,' he replied, his gaze shifting to that exotic hair twisted and coiled neatly about Miss Napier's well-shaped head, with not a hair out of place. His fingers ached to release it from the pins and to let the heavy mass tumble in waves over her shoulders and down her back, to run his fingers through the tresses and to smell its fragrance.

It began to register on Lisette that the expression on his face wasn't dislike at all. In fact, he really did look almost admiring—and she saw something primitive flare in his eyes, which stirred her alarm and which she chose to ignore. Meeting his gaze she favoured him with an irrepressible sidewise smile. 'You mean you really do like it?'

Ross liked it. He liked every damn thing about her. In fact, he wanted nothing more than to thrust his sister out of the room and snatch Miss Napier into his arms, to kiss the smiling mischief from her lips until she was clinging to him, melting with desire. She'd indicated a feminine concern about her hair, then calmly accepted it. This gave him the distinct impression that pretence and pretension were completely foreign to her, and that she was refreshingly unique in those ways and probably many other delightful ways as well.

He leaned back in his chair and steepled his fingers beneath his chin, continuing to watch her from beneath hooded lids. 'That is what I said.'

'And my brother's opinion matters,' Araminta said smoothly, regarding Ross with fascinated disbelief. It was time for them to leave for their appointment, but there was something about the undercurrents flowing between her brother and her maid, something so very strange about everything, that she was reluctant to break the mood.

'I am glad you think so, Araminta, since it is my opinion that Miss Napier is in need of some new dresses as befits her position—although it would be more pleasing to the eye to see her decked out in satin and lace.' He studied Miss Napier surreptitiously. Beauty was moulded into every flawlessly sculpted feature of her face, but her allure went much deeper than that. It was in her voice and her graceful movements. There was something inside her that made her sparkle and glow, and she only needed the proper background and situation and elegant clothes to complement her alluring figure and exquisite features.

'Really, Ross,' Araminta chided lightly, 'it's very ungentlemanly of you to remark on that.'

A lazy smile transformed his harsh features. 'Surely I haven't done anything to give you the impression that I'm a gentleman!'

It was the exaggerated dismay in his voice that brought a smile to Araminta's lips. 'Nothing at all, and if you must know a trip to the modistes to purchase

Lisette some new clothes is imminent—but ball gowns are quite out of the question.'

'Of course they are,' Lisette said quietly. 'It's quite ridiculous to contemplate such a thing—although Colonel Montague has my gratitude.'

He gave her a puzzled look. 'For what?'

Those candid eyes lifted to his in the mirror, searching, delving, and Ross had the fleeting impression that with time she might see straight into his devious soul. She obviously hadn't gotten his true measure, however, because a warm smile touched those soft lips of hers.

'Why, for providing me with this opportunity.'

Her gratitude only made him feel guilty about everything, more of a disgusting fraud, for letting her think of him as some gallant white knight, instead of the black-hearted villain who had every intention of luring her into his bed.

Having watched the byplay between Ross and her maid and quite enthralled by this teasingly flirtatious side of her brother, Araminta's eyes twinkled mischievously. 'Ross never forgets a pretty face, Lisette. I'm quite certain that if I hadn't mentioned that I was in need of a maid, he would have concocted some other means of renewing your acquaintance.'

Lisette flushed with embarrassment. 'Oh, I—I never meant…' She saw Miss Araminta's pitying look and knew she was being seen as completely besotted.

'No, of course you didn't. But be wary,' she said, meeting her brother's eyes with something akin to cynicism. 'Don't let my brother's charm sway you. Many a villain has been god-like in appearance, and such an attribute can be to the dire cost of the poor victims.'

And there speaks the voice of experience, Lisette thought, beginning to realise that her young mistress might not have come out of her broken betrothal as unscathed as some might think, after all.

She was proved right a moment later when Araminta pulled herself up straight and smiled, her eyes meeting Lisette's in the mirror. 'As clever as you are, Lisette, and looking as you do, you no doubt will want to find a husband eventually.'

Lisette stiffened at those words and tried to ignore the fact that Colonel Montague was listening most intently. She could not detect any hint of ridicule in Miss Araminta's voice, but she must be laughing at the very idea that someone might want to marry her.

'As a matter of fact there is nothing further from my mind, but if I were, I see nothing wrong with that.'

'Well, if marriage is your goal, pray let me dissuade you from it. You may think me something of a radical, but I have come to think that womankind is rendered helpless by her dependency upon men. At their mercy we are no better than rabbits in a trap. It is far better in life to remain unencumbered, if possible.'

'Thank you for your cynical view on the subject, Miss Araminta, but it is not a view I share. I would like to think that marriage is a partnership based on mutual love and respect, and companionship, not an encumbrance.'

'You are quite right, Miss Napier,' Ross remarked. 'I can see that when I single out the object of my matrimonial intentions, I would be wise to seek your advice.'

Over her shoulder, Araminta threw him a glare of mock offence. 'Ladies are not objects, Ross. Little wonder you have failed to secure yourself a wife. And if you did I can only assume that you would toss her over your shoulder, carry her off and beat her into submission.'

'You mean,' Ross said straight-faced, 'that *isn't* the way to handle the matter?' His gaze shifted to Lisette's in the mirror. 'What say you, Miss Napier?' He awaited her reply with more interest than Lisette realised.

Lisette saw the humour lurking in his eyes; she burst out laughing, and to Ross it seemed as if the room were filled with music. 'Ladies—that is *all* ladies, be they well-born or otherwise,' she clarified a moment later with a look that clearly implied his past experience had probably been with females of quite another sort, 'have very definite ideas of the way they wish to be treated by the man who wins their heart.'

'Please enlarge on that,' Ross said as she stuck another pin through a curl on Araminta's head. 'Just how do ladies like to be treated?'

'With respect, loyalty and devotion—and she wants to think that he has eyes for no one but her, that he's blind to everything but her beauty.'

'In which case, he's in imminent danger of tripping over his own feet,' Ross pointed out, grinning broadly.

Araminta shot him an admonishing look. *'And,'* she said emphatically, 'she likes to think he's a romantic, which you obviously are not, dear brother.'

'Not if I have to grope my way about like a blind idiot,' he teased. 'What else do ladies like, Miss Napier? I am all ears.'

Having said more than she had intended and spoken more sharply to Miss Araminta than was seemly in a maid, under her mistress's penetrating gaze some of Lisette's confidence slid away. Apart from Messalina she had never known how to converse with people her own age, and for the first time since leaving India, she felt gauche and ill at ease.

'I will leave you to work that out for yourself, Colonel. I am sorry, Miss Araminta. I was impertinent. I should not have been so outspoken when you voiced your opinion on marriage.'

'Why on earth not? I like people who speak their mind and you were quite right. I was very rude and there was no call for it.'

Standing up and smoothing her satin skirts, Araminta felt a new respect for her maid. Lisette knew her role but to be sure she was no dullard. Her impish smile and darting golden eyes betrayed the quick wit of an urchin. No doubt she had already knitted together the strands of Araminta's own tragic story from below stairs gossip. Still, she was aware of Lisette's capabilities and had already come to value her honesty and discretion. In just one week she had assumed far more than her intended measure of responsibilities and in doing so had made herself indispensable.

## Chapter Three

Seated beside the window to catch the light for her sewing, Lisette was surprised when, following a brief knock on the door, it suddenly opened and Colonel Montague strolled in. Her heart missed a beat. His grey coat of Bath superfine hugged his broad shoulders, its excellent cut emphasising his broad chest and much narrower hips. His dark hair glowed softly in the sunlight slanting through the windows. With rigid calm she placed her work on the table in front of her and, rising, she bobbed a small curtsey.

He stopped just in front of her, and stood gazing into her eyes with a thoughtful expression. He seemed to peer down into her very soul.

'Miss Napier,' he greeted her, his blue eyes aglow, a beguiling little smile on his lips, 'how pleasant to see you and how well you look. Please, do sit down. I have no wish to interrupt your work. I'm here to see Araminta.'

Lisette did as he bade and sat back down, taking up her sewing. 'Miss Araminta is taking a bath. She shouldn't be too long—although sometimes she does like to wallow among the suds. Perhaps you would prefer to come back later.'

'I'm on my way out and would like to see her before I go. I'll wait,' he said, unable to think of anything better than spending a few minutes with this exotic young woman. It was the first time since she had taken up her position that he had found the opportunity to speak to her alone.

Lisette was aware of his aroused interest. From beneath dark brows he observed her with close attention, and then seated himself in a chair facing her, and with quiet patience he waited, like a cat before a mouse hole. He was watching her steadily, and she sensed the unbidden, unspoken communication between them.

Ross was thinking low lovely she was. Her hair drawn back from her face and coiled in her nape was very neat and tidy, and her cheeks were smooth and slightly golden. She wore a grey woollen dress and a starched and frilled white apron tied at the back of her small waist in a large and perfect bow, hugging her slender contours and emphasising their softness, leaving him with an urgent longing to fill his arms with their warmth.

'I have to confess that in the beginning I wasn't convinced you'd turn up here,' he said softly.

In disregard of the doubt she had felt during the time she had seen him at the Exchange, she said, 'I had no choice. When the Arbuthnots left for Brighton, I had nowhere else to go. Besides, I am not all that enamoured of London and the thought of Derbyshire appealed to me.' She could feel his gaze on her bent face. With a stirring of irritation and something else she could not put a name to, resolutely she lifted her head and met his eyes. 'Have you had an edifying look at me yet, Colonel?'

Quite unexpectedly he smiled, a white, buccaneer smile, and his eyes danced with devilish humour. 'You don't have to look so irate to find yourself the object of my attention. As a matter of fact I was admiring you.'

Unaccustomed as she was to any kind of compliment, the warmth in his tone brought heat creeping into her cheeks. 'You must excuse me if I seem a little embarrassed, Colonel. I'm not used to flattery.'

'I was merely thinking how lovely you are, Miss Napier.'

She shot him an amused look. 'And how many women have you said that to?' she asked, a smile trembling on her lips.

'Several. And it's always the truth.'

'I dare say you'll be eager to see Castonbury Park again.' Lisette looked down and did another stitch, eager to divert the conversation away from herself and relieved that she had something to occupy her hands.

His fascinating lips lifted fractionally. 'Eager enough, Miss Napier. I am concerned with family matters just now and my uncle's health is not what it was.'

Lisette wished his voice was not so very deep; it made her nerves vibrate.

A moment passed before he said, 'I wanted to have a word with you, Miss Napier.' She raised her head and waited for him to continue. 'You don't need me to remind you how unusual it is for a girl of your age to be working as a lady's maid. I know my sister has great confidence in you—indeed you will find as time goes on that she will confide in you in a way that is perhaps not entirely fitting, but because we have given you so much, because we chose you over a more experienced lady's maid, I know you will always be discreet. I know you will soon pick up your duties, but the habit of loyalty cannot be bought. Do you understand me?'

Lisette nodded. 'Yes. Be assured, Colonel, that whatever Miss Araminta confides in me, will go no further.'

Holding her gaze he nodded and smiled. 'Thank you. I know I can trust you. Have you no family, Miss Napier?'

She shook her head. 'No. My parents died of the cholera in India. As far as I am aware there is no one else.' As she said this she thought of the letter she had dispatched just yesterday to her father's lawyer in Oxford informing him of her parents' demise, and then her thoughts turned to Princess Messalina. Though not related, she was the closest she had to family.

'You must miss your parents.'

'Yes, I do. Very much.'

'What was your father doing out in India?'

She smiled. 'My father was something of an eccentric as well as being an academic. Not only was he a linguist he was also a botanist. He was working out there for the University of Oxford.'

'And your mother? Did she like India?'

'Yes, although she would have gone anywhere my father asked her to go. They were very close. They met in Italy—she was half Italian on her mother's side.'

'Then that explains your hair colouring. The only other women I've seen with hair as black as yours are Indian women. It must have been a difficult time for you when you lost your parents.'

She nodded. Remembering that time, she thanked God that was over and she was here. 'Yes, it was. Ever since, I've felt like a pawn on a chessboard, with no choice but to move forward, one step at a time.'

When she resumed her work he began to speak of his

life in India, recalling his travels and battles and life with his regiment. Soothed by the deep warmth of his voice, Lisette was fascinated by his recollections, and glad of them too, for it brought India closer.

'My parents are dead too,' he said. 'My mother died when Araminta was born and my father was killed in France. He was the Duke of Rothermere's younger brother. My aunt and uncle took pity on us and installed us at Castonbury. We've lived there nearly all our lives.'

'Does the duke have a large family?'

'Six offspring. There is Jamie—the eldest, but he's currently listed as missing presumed dead. It's been very hard for the whole family. Then there is Kate. I haven't seen her in five years but I believe she devotes her life to worthy causes. You are sure to come into contact with her at Castonbury. She has her own ideas on equality between the sexes and is of the opinion that women should try and rise above their servitude.'

'It's easy for someone with means to be so forceful and outspoken in their opinions, but if she were to suddenly find herself without means, then she would come down to earth with a bump.'

He gave her a wry smile. 'Maybe so, but being the kind of person she is, she'd have a damned good try anyway.'

'I understand what you mean,' Lisette said, lowering

her head over her work. 'But one could also look upon so privileged a life as a great comfort.'

'I do not take my position for granted, I assure you. I fully understand and appreciate how fortune of birth has given me all the opportunities and physical comforts of life—and I think I can speak for my cousin Kate too.'

'It is far more than that,' Lisette replied, sudden passion in her voice. 'You have a place in the world. You know what it is and where you belong. That is a very comforting thing.'

Her sudden intensity startled Ross. She was clearly a person of deep feeling, and there was a great deal of passion there. It all lay beneath the surface.

'You can have no comprehension how it feels not to belong anywhere,' she went on with an odd little catch in her voice. 'To have no roots that tie you to a place and give you purpose. I envy you that.'

'You no longer have a home of your own so it is understandable that you feel rootless. But you shall find your place one day. Everyone does, eventually.'

She smiled. 'I do hope so, Colonel. Now, you were telling me about your cousins at Castonbury Park. Who else is there?'

'Giles, Harry and Phaedra. She is horse mad. She would have come to London with Araminta for the

Season, but she was still in mourning for her brother Edward. He was killed in the battle at Waterloo.'

'I'm so sorry. And you? Do you have many siblings?'

'There is just Araminta and me.'

'Where did you live before you went to Castonbury Park?'

'Here in London. My father, of course, grew up at Castonbury Park—the ducal seat. When he married my mother, who hated the country, they decided to make their home in London.'

'Did you like living in London all of the time?'

Looking through the window at the busy square, Ross shook his head. 'Not really. I like the country better. Fortunately my father had settled a sizable sum on both Araminta and me. My inheritance was quite substantial.'

'You didn't think to buy a house of your own?'

'Not then. I had my mind set on a military career and I always knew Araminta would be taken care of and marry eventually. Perhaps one day, when I am no longer a soldier, I will give the matter some thought.'

'When you take a wife, you mean—as most men do when they realise they need an heir.'

Ross's disinterested shrug and brief smile dismissed all the usual reasons for marriage as trivial. 'I have no intention of adhering to custom, now or in the future, by shackling myself to a wife for the sole purpose of begetting an heir. For a man such as I,' he said with mild amusement that failed to disguise his genuine disregard for wedded bliss, 'there does not seem to be a single compelling reason to commit to matrimony.'

Lisette studied him intently, her eyes alight with curiosity and caution, and the dawning of understanding. 'In other words you are married to the army.'

He grinned. 'You might say that. Since going to India I've been expanding my own assets there.'

Observing the glint in his eyes, she dared to enquire, 'And what is your enterprise of choice?'

'I invest in anything from tea to marble.'

Lisette stared at him. 'But you are a soldier.'

One dark brow rose. 'Among other things.' Finding conversing with her extremely pleasant, he shifted in his chair, making himself more comfortable. 'What would you like to do with the rest of your life, Miss Napier?'

'What can a woman do with her life? Men can do whatever they want, but if women are not wives, if they are without means, then what are their hopes? Domestic service is the only thing open to them.'

'You're quite wrong there, Miss Napier. A clever woman can do almost anything she likes if she would go about it as a woman should. Women as well as men can be as free as they choose to be.'

'In your world, perhaps, Colonel. Not in mine—as I have already pointed out.'

'In an ideal world they could be.'

'That is possible, but this is not an ideal world.'

'Just now you likened yourself to a pawn on a chess-board. If you are familiar with the game you will know that eight paces brings the pawn to the other side and she becomes a queen.'

'So if I just keep on going, I can be a queen,' she said. 'Even if there's already a queen—or more, on the board.'

He nodded. 'There can be as many queens as there are pawns—as long as the pawns are ambitious enough or lucky enough to go the full distance.'

She slanted him a curious look, understanding perfectly what he was saying—that if she was ambitious enough she could become anything she wanted to be in life. 'Are you by any chance a radical, Colonel?'

He grinned, his mouth wide over his excellent teeth. 'I would not go as far as to say that.' He became thoughtful. 'But I do have notions which do not always agree with those of my associates—especially here in England. Perhaps I have lived too long in India.'

'Or not long enough,' Lisette said on a wistful note. She was quite fascinated by this extraordinary conversation and by the strangeness of having it and her eyes glowed with their interest in his startling opinions.

'When I was in India I used to help my father collect his plants and sort out his specimens and send them back to the university. I hoped to carry on helping him with his work—it all seemed so probable then.'

'So, Miss Napier, will you continue being a lady's maid?'

She laughed lightly. 'Someone has to be. Someone has to look after the aristocrats and the gentry.'

'Quite right,' he replied with mock pomposity. 'I never do a thing myself if I can get the servants to do it for me.'

'But everyone should be capable of being self-sufficient. What would you do if you suddenly found yourself without anyone? Why,' she said, noticing his boots, 'look at your boots. Who cleans them?'

'Blackstock—my valet. I suppose you're going to tell me I should clean them myself.'

'No. You'd probably make a mess of them.'

He laughed at her pointed remark. 'As a matter of fact you're wrong. When I was a very small boy my father would make me clean my own boots religiously—riding boots, walking boots, everyday boots. I had to rub them until I could see my face in them. But you didn't answer my question. Do you intend being a lady's maid forever?'

Lisette put her work down in her lap and contemplated his question. 'Oh, I don't know. I haven't had much time to think about it since coming to England. But no, I don't think so.'

'Araminta speaks highly of you, says you're a real asset. She'd be sorry to lose you.'

'She won't. Not yet anyway.' She sighed. 'I would like to go back to India one day. I shall always hope something will turn up, but in my case—well, I'm not so sure. Maybe I could go as a companion to a rich old lady and travel the world.' She laughed. 'But listen to me. I sound like a dreamer. I'm sure it will pass.'

Ross did not laugh. 'What's wrong with having dreams and longings? We'd be nowhere without them.'

'But in the end I have to be realistic. I can't see my situation changing dramatically in the foreseeable future. This is the real world. No one's going to wave some magic wand.'

'If one believes in magic, it could come true.'

He fell silent and beneath his gaze Lisette could feel his eyes on her as she sorted out a tangle of vividly coloured ribbons, painstakingly unravelling them and rolling each bright satin strand into a neat coil. His manner was all consideration and regard as he made a study of her person with a strange sort of intensity she could not define. She looked as she always did, so she had no illusions that he had cause to deem her worth staring at.

It was with some amusement that she raised her

head and looked across at him. 'Colonel Montague, you study me most intently—as if I were an artefact. Or maybe I have a smut on my nose? Is that it?'

Ross leaned back in his chair. His eyelids lowered as his gaze raked over her with the leisure of a well-fed wolf. 'Your nose is perfect,' he replied, his voice husky. If ever he had discounted the possibilities that a woman's features could be flawless, then he was swiftly coming to the conclusion that Lisette Napier would set the standard by which all other women would have to be judged, at least in his mind. If her face wasn't at the very least perfect, it came as close to being so as he was able to bear. Several feathery curls had escaped their confines at her temples and in front of her ears, lending a charming softness to the hairstyle. In contrast to her dark tresses, her golden skin seemed more fetching by far than other ladies. A faint rosy hue adorned her cheeks and her soft, winsomely curved lips. As for her large, silkily lashed warm amber eyes, their appeal was so strong that he had to mentally shake himself free of their spell.

'I'm trying to read your expression,' he remarked, giving no indication of where his thoughts had wandered. 'And as for studying you as if you were an artefact, do not be offended. Artefacts are rare and mysterious things, intriguing and often difficult to interpret. It is not unusual that incorrect conclusions are made about them.'

Lisette's hands tightened on the ribbons in her lap. What was he saying? she thought wildly. That he did not see her as a servant? 'Are you saying that I am a mystery, Colonel? Because if so I assure you I have never thought of myself as either secretive or mysterious. I am no great mystery at all.'

Ross leaned forward in his chair, and looked at her as if she were of the utmost importance. 'I know very well what you are—but I also know you are a good person. I've never thought otherwise, not for one single moment.' He paused. 'I hope my sister is not driving you too hard. Accustomed to socialising with only the best in society, she tends to treat other humans as subjects. She is only happy if she is the centre of attention, being unreasonably demanding and imperious, and she takes violently against anyone who criticises or disagrees with her.'

Lisette smiled. 'You judge her too harshly. I have no complaints.'

He grinned. 'And you wouldn't tell me if you had. Your loyalty does you credit. However, I am hoping your calming influence will help keep her in line.'

'It's not my place to do that.'

'Nevertheless I live in hope.'

Suddenly remembering her mistress when she heard

her call from the bathing chamber, putting her work down Lisette stood up and smoothed her apron. 'Excuse me. I must get on. I'll tell Miss Araminta you are waiting.'

Lady Mannering's two well-sprung travelling chaises travelled north to the splendid Castonbury Park that was the principal Montague residence. The first was occupied by Araminta and Lisette, the second filled to capacity with Ross's baggage and all of the trunks of clothes and accessories Araminta had deemed absolutely essential for any extended visit.

Lisette enjoyed the journey through the English countryside. Watching Colonel Montague riding on ahead with Will Blackstock, she longed to be able to join him on horseback. There were times when he tethered his horse to the back of the coach and joined them inside, his long legs stretched out in the luxurious conveyance. She was conscious and more than a little uncomfortable beneath his watchful gaze.

The weather had turned pleasantly warm and he often discarded his coat. His pristine white shirt and neck cloth contrasted sharply with his black hair and dark countenance. His body, a perfect harmony of form and strength, was like a work of Grecian art and most unsettling to Lisette's virgin heart. Each time their eyes met her heart tripped in her chest. Araminta's artless chatter filled any silence that could have been constrained.

It was the second day of their journey. Strolling away from the inn where, after consuming her dinner, Araminta was making use of the facilities in the ladies' room, observing Lisette stroll towards a stream that bubbled over its rocky bed to the rear of the inn, Ross smiled slowly and with a wicked glint in his eyes sauntered after her.

Ross was beginning to discover the whole tenor of his life was changing with Miss Lisette Napier in it. Constant awareness of her presence kept him in a perpetual state of delighted confusion. The stream ran through a sunlit glade. Having removed her shoes and stockings, Lisette was dangling her feet in the cool stream. Gazing at her, he was struck afresh by her loveliness. It was easy to forget she was his sister's maid. What was difficult was controlling his physical reaction to her nearness. An exercise in fortitude, he thought grimly. His body was achingly aware of her, even though she occasionally favoured him with a distant glance from those cool amber eyes of hers.

His throat went dry as he stared at the exposed skin along the back of her neck. Her hair was fashioned into intricate twists at the nape of her neck. Tiny combs somehow held it in place, and it gleamed in the sunlight like jet. He wanted to go to her and take it down, slide his fingers through the heavy mass of it.

Becoming aware of his presence, Lisette turned and looked up at him. 'Oh—Colonel Montague! How long have you been standing there?'

A slow, appraising smile touched his lips. 'Long enough.'

'Long enough for what?'

His smouldering gaze passed over her. 'Long enough to come to the conclusion that you are worthy of a higher position than that of a servant, Miss Napier.'

Lisette's mouth parted slightly, and she stared up at him in surprise, unconscious of the lovely vision she presented. 'Colonel Montague, it would be most improper for you to think of me as anything else.'

'Oh, yes, I can—and I do,' he asserted. 'Am I intruding?'

'Why, no. Did you follow me?' Lisette enquired, unsettled yet strangely thrilled by his words.

'Do you mind?'

'Who am I to mind? As my employer you are at liberty to seek me out whenever you please.'

He cocked a sleek questioning brow. 'For whatever reason?'

'No,' she stated firmly, her beautiful eyes sparkling with mischief, '*within* reason.'

His mouth curved in a devilish grin and the slight

breeze teased a strand of his dark hair. 'Methinks you bait me, Miss Napier. If that is your game, then lead on. I will welcome your attention and the challenge.'

Lisette considered his words. She really did desire this man, that she could not deny, but having listened to the gossip of the other maids and being made aware of the serious repercussions should any one of them overstep the mark by forming any kind of relationship with gentlemen outside their sphere, she was afraid of the repercussions should she be found out.

'And where do you think it would get me if I were to give you my attention? It would create difficulties I can well do without.'

He grinned roguishly. 'It could be fun while it lasts.'

'Fun? Your arrogance really is quite amazing, Colonel Montague.'

In what was meant to be a display of mock disdain, her eyes skimmed his powerful frame. In the warmth of the day he'd removed his jacket. His white shirt was open at the throat. But her gaze faltered as the realisation flashed through her mind that there was nothing she could see she could poke fun at. He was hard and all lean, firm muscles.

It was clear he did not recall their meeting in India, that he had dismissed it entirely. She couldn't. When he looked at her as he was looking at her now, it made her recall aspects of that time in vivid detail—his warm, hard mouth and the feel of his hands and his body pressed against hers. It was wholly unnerving the way memories of lying alongside this magnificent man haunted her. Discomfited, she chastised herself for allowing her thoughts to suggest what her body wanted to experience again.

Unable to bear the weight of his heated regard, she withdrew her feet from the water and dabbed them dry with the hem of her skirt. Much fascinated, Ross sat on the ground, his broad shoulders propped against a tree trunk, his knee drawn up, where he rested his arms to enjoy more leisurely what had become his favourite pastime since leaving London: watching Miss Napier. She surely could not guess the depth of torture she put him through, for beneath his cool facade he burned with a consuming desire for her.

He was ever conscious of her, and whenever he saw her seated in the carriage with Araminta, she appeared trim and fragile, like a budding rose. But when he was close to her, Ross was painfully aware that though indeed she was neither very tall nor heavily rounded, she was very much a woman, and he wanted her.

Standing up, Lisette slipped her feet into her shoes, shoving her stockings into the pocket of her dress, denying him the pleasure of the sight of her slender legs by pulling them on. She watched him get to his feet.

Her mouth curved into a tantalising smile as she came towards him with almost sensuous grace.

When he took her hand her heart accelerated inside her chest. What charged it more, her horror of being seen alone in his presence, or the sensation of his strong fingers holding her hand, she could not say. He drew her to him, and she let him put his arms around her. It was nice.

She felt him shudder. Anxiously she said, 'What is it?'

He looked at her. 'Do you realise how lovely you are, Miss Napier?'

'Oh, no. I am quite ordinary. I have never pretended otherwise.'

'You hide behind your modesty—although modesty is an adoring quality and you wear it well.'

He was looking at her with such intensity she became still. Her cheeks were hot. She should have looked away, but she didn't. She went on staring back, with the wondering start of a smile, knowing she was lost, but not caring. He raised a dark brow and considered her flushed cheeks and the soft, trembling mouth. His gaze moved even lower and surveyed her bosom, until Lisette wondered wildly if he could see right through her dress. Beneath his steady regard, her breasts burned. This was not what she had expected. Everything seemed to spin—the light from the sun intensified, the trees seemed to close in. She waited for what was to happen next, and then she found herself held close in his embrace.

Her heart was racing now. The next moment he bent his head and she felt the warmth of his mouth. He pulled away a little, then kissed her again. The touch of his lips on hers was soft. Feeling a tumult of feelings well up inside her, she relaxed her lips in a faint echo of his kiss.

Unbidden, into Ross's mind came a memory, a memory that he had once kissed a girl like this before, and that her lips had been just as sweet—but he did not dwell on the thought and it drifted away.

Encouraged, he moved his lips against hers. Lisette could feel his breath warm on her face. He opened his mouth a little. She pulled away.

He looked puzzled. 'Don't you like it?'

In truth, his kiss evoked so many memories of the time when he had kissed her before, and all the times she had wanted it to happen again, that she tilted her head and allowed him to kiss her once more. There was nothing threatening, nothing violently uncontrollable, no force or dominance—just the reverse. This kiss was a shared pleasure and she gave herself up to the magic of it.

His lips parted and she felt the tip of his tongue. He

teased her lips apart. She relaxed. He sucked gently at her lower lip. She felt dizzy.

'Open your mouth,' he urged softly.

She did as he asked and felt his tongue again, touching her lips, passing between her parted teeth, and probing into her mouth. She was filled with the need to hold him, to touch his skin and his hair, to feel his muscles and his bones. Her tongue met his and she was thrilled by the intimacy of it. He held her for what seemed an eternity. There were no minutes, no measures, only sensations and heartbeats. Although her head was spinning with a sickening mix of forbidden love, desire, guilt and unworthiness, she knew she must steady her thoughts. He was the first to break the kiss. His breathing was uneven, his eyes burning with intensity.

Touching her face he looked down at her. 'You see how much power you have when you choose to wield it, Miss Napier.'

She did see. It awed her and excited her that she, who had travelled halfway across the world, who had convinced herself she had no influence over anything in her life, who had placed herself in the position of desiring a man who didn't remember who she was, had the power over the very man she so desired. Suddenly, ordinary Lisette Napier felt as captivating and alluring as any woman, and a joy she had never felt blossomed inside her.

'Was that your first kiss?' he asked.

'No,' she whispered, saddened because he didn't remember. 'My second.'

'And how do I compare?'

'It is not a competition, Colonel, but I will say that you compare equally as well.'

He looked at her in mock dismay. 'That is high praise indeed—but not high enough. Is that all my kiss was worth? I am insulted. I believe my kiss should be valued more highly than that. I am a lord and a military colonel, after all.'

'So was he.'

'Really? I must remember to ask you about him one day,' he murmured. 'Then we are equal in more than just kissing. However, I know you enjoyed the kiss as much as I, Miss Napier.'

He saw a hint of blush come into her cheeks, and he thought her the most enticing thing he had ever seen. Kissing her could be the prelude to all the delicious imaginings in his mind, imaginings that would compromise his honour and her innocence. He was a soldier and a gentleman, he reminded himself, something that had never been hard to remember. Over a lifetime of fulfilling the obligations and duties of his military position, of obeying the strictures of an upbringing of discipline, no matter what his rank and title, a true gentleman did not corrupt an innocent young woman, especially one in his employ, and he should step back. But by God he knew he wanted her.

He raised the stakes higher.

'There is nothing wrong in sharing a kiss,' he stated, now in a more assured tone. 'A mere kiss,' he said, his voice sounding low and husky, 'can be far more tempting than you realise. In fact, I think we might get to know each other better, Miss Napier. So long as we resolve to be discreet,' he said, having no wish to create a scandal by forming a relationship with his sister's maid. 'I don't think either of us would enjoy all the attention we would receive at Castonbury Park.'

Lisette stared at him in disbelief at what he was suggesting. Though her stomach clenched with fear she slowly smiled, for she could not deny to herself that she liked the way he touched her. But to become closer would be a dangerous game to play, one that she would not willingly choose to become involved in, not because it would be distasteful—for she found Ross Montague desirable in every way—but because she could never be anything to him other than his mistress, and she had too much self-respect for that.

'I think that what you are suggesting is an illicit attachment, sir—in which I shall be judged to be a scheming hoyden. I would despise myself—and you. I have done nothing to invite your attentions or encourage the feelings that have taken root.' She stepped away and turned from him. 'Excuse me. I must go back.'

Ross's burst of laughter halted the flow of words abruptly and Lisette spun round, her eyes flashing with indignant sparks.

'How quickly you rebuke me, as if you're sorely in the wrong. And there you are, all soft and tempting. And then you chasten me for looking at you and kissing you. Fickle woman,' he teased.

'You deserve to be rebuked,' she was quick to add.

'You think so?' Ross took her in his arms once more. He knew he was playing with fire, but it was the risk that made a game exciting. He did not want to give up the tormenting delight of being alone with her. It was like an addiction, an addiction to the game of testing his desire for her against his resolve.

And so he kissed her again—her hair, her cheek, caressing her lips with his own. He pressed her back against a tree, and his mouth travelled downward to where her neck disappeared into the collar of her dress. Lisette held her breath, and the fires of passion and wild, wanton sensations again began to flare within. A touch, a kiss, a look, and he could rouse her. What madness.

'Your heart beats much too quickly for you to claim disinterest, Miss Lisette Napier.'

Her lips trembled as he claimed them fiercely with

his own. For a long moment his hungering mouth searched the sweetness of hers. Then she pulled back. 'Please let me go,' she said, her soft lips still throbbing from the demand of his. 'I have been away long enough. I must go back. Miss Araminta might have need of me,' she announced abruptly, embarrassed by her own musings.

Gleaming whiteness flashed as Ross grinned down at her. He took her hand in his and looked deep into her eyes. His skin was warm to the touch and somehow reassuring. But he seemed too much of a man, too knowing and strong, too able to bend her to his will. She was dizzy with conflicting emotions and the turmoil made her momentarily speechless. She wanted to tell him to go away, and at the same time wanted him to lean closer and kiss her again.

Ross smiled and for a moment looked wickedly mischievous. 'I believe there is a danger of you stealing my heart, Miss Napier. If you do I pray you will be gentle with it.' He kissed both her hands and then released them.

Something in their exchange pulled Lisette back from the brink of dangerous recklessness, and she remembered the deference due to the man before her. No matter how much he desired her, she was his servant. She depended on him for almost everything, and he had indeed been generous to her.

'Colonel Montague, I—I beg you not to do this. You have been good to me. I…am in your debt. But I am maid to your sister. I can never be more to you than that.'

Her speech was halting. His eyes held hers as he said, 'We shall see. I find what is called fate often has the workings of most worldly hands. Sometimes a whim or a fancy, a base desire, can deny the best-laid plans.'

Ross did not try to detain her further. When she turned away he followed along in her wake, appreciatively watching her hips as they swayed with a natural graceful provocativeness. She turned languidly and looked back, smiling to herself when she saw how he strode after her with that slowly deliberate saunter that reminded her so much of a hunting animal.

It wasn't until she got back to the inn and went to the ladies' room to put on her stockings that she realised she had lost herself and all sense of propriety. She was quite horrified by her behaviour. Colonel Montague would think her forward and impertinent. Shame swept over her like a fever, washing her face in colour. He was her employer and she must see that nothing like that happened again.

After that, whenever she saw him ride by or join them in the coach she could hardly bring herself to look at him, knowing that if she did she would begin to tremble. He had a particular gift. He possessed a unique ability to compel and captivate with his words, and this, combined with his handsome features, meant there was no woman he could not persuade.

Over the following days that episode would stay with her. She did what was expected of her and tried to smother those feelings to which her heart had succumbed. But her pulse would leap at the sight of him or the mention of his name, and she could not quench the forbidden spark that smouldered in her heart.

Accompanied by Blackstock, Ross felt an odd sensation of unreality as he rode through the wrought iron gates of Castonbury Park.

The drive wound through the neatly tended deer park to the upper lake. Here a beautiful cascade spanned by a three-arched bridge separated the upper and middle lakes, the bridge providing a splendid view of the grand and impressive sprawling mansion with its Palladian central facade embellished with Georgian lavishness, the immense stone steps rising on either side to the marble hall behind the portico. Linked by curved corridors, at each end of this splendid building were the family apartments on the left, and to the right the usual range of domestic buildings—kitchen, stables and workshops, and at the back, almost hugging the house, stood the old chapel.

Being home again made Ross feel uncharacteristically nostalgic. It was five years since he had been to Castonbury but of his welcome he had not a doubt. His uncle, Crispin Montague, the Duke of Rothermere, was well-bred and well set up, and he presided over the gargantuan Castonbury Park.

Drawing Bengal to a halt in front of the house, before he'd had time to dismount at the basement door, which was the everyday entrance to the central block, it was already being opened by Lumsden, clad in his usual black. Lumsden had been the butler at Castonbury Park from time immemorial and had always possessed uncanny timing. Leaving Blackstock to attend to the horses, Ross looked at this old retainer and smiled. It was Lumsden who'd found him sampling a bottle of his uncle's French brandy when he'd been nine years old. It was also Lumsden—who was not averse to sampling a drop of His Lordship's liquor himself—who took the blame for the missing bottle, explaining that he'd accidentally dropped it.

At the moment Lumsden's eyes were passing fondly over Ross's face. 'Good afternoon, my lord,' he intoned formally. 'And may I say how good it is to have you home at Castonbury.'

'Good afternoon, Lumsden. It's good to be back. It's been a long time and sadly much has changed in my absence.'

'Indeed it has, my lord,' Lumsden replied gravely.

'Everyone is deeply saddened by the deaths of Lord Jamie and Lord Edward.'

'Yes, I am sure they are. My sister will be here shortly. I rode on ahead in order to get a clear view of the place.'

'You will see the fabric of Castonbury is as it was before you left—although in this present financial climate, you will observe unavoidable signs of wear and tear here and there.'

'I think we have the wars to blame for that, Lumsden.' Ross entered the large hall. It was an impressive room with sixteen columns supporting the weight of those in the magnificent marble hall immediately above. A small army of footmen and housemaids seemed to be lurking about, ostensibly going about their work. As Ross looked around him they stole long, lingering looks at him, then turned to exchange swift, gratified smiles. With his mind on getting cleaned up before his meeting with his uncle, Ross was oblivious to the searching scrutiny he was receiving, but he was dimly aware as he walked through the hall that a few servants were hastily dabbing at their eyes and noses with handkerchiefs.

Seeing a tall man with dark hair coming towards him he quickened his stride. It was his cousin Giles. They were the same age and of a similar height. Smiling, he held out his hand and the two hugged each other warmly. So much had happened to them both and the family as a whole since their parting five years earlier.

'Giles! It's good to see you.'

'You too, Ross. Damn good, in fact.'

Ross stood back, anxiously studying the deeply etched lines of strain at his cousin's eyes and mouth, but he looked better than he'd expected. 'You look like hell.'

'Thank you, Cousin,' Giles said drily. 'I'm delighted to see you too.'

Ross laughed and slapped his back good-humouredly. 'And I you. You have no idea how much—but I would like to see you looking better.'

'You can put it down to hard work. It's backbreaking work running an estate the size of Castonbury—and don't think that now you're back you're going to be allowed to escape,' Giles threatened light-heartedly. 'I'll have you hard at it first thing.'

'I'll be glad to be of help in any way I can.' Ross laughed. Dismissing the subject with a casual wave of his hand, he drew him towards the stairs off to the right. 'Let's go up to the library. You can pour me a drink before I go and change. Five years is a long time and we have a lot of catching up to do.'

Entering the library on the first floor of the house, that was the moment when Ross really did feel that he had come home. He had spent many industrious yet happy hours in this room poring over books. His gaze was drawn to the painted plaster busts of Greek and Roman worthies and he smiled when he recalled his uncle Crispin telling him they were intended to encourage studiousness.

The cousins sat in companionable silence on opposite sides of a log fire, its light shining on the steel fender. They each held a glass of brandy from which they sipped appreciatively. There was a slight similarity of features between the two, and like Ross, Giles was not very good at showing his emotions.

'How is my uncle?' Ross enquired. 'I understand he isn't well.'

Giles grimaced. 'No, he is far from it. He has good days and bad days and there is an inconsistency in his behaviour. His mind wanders and he sits staring at nothing for long periods. It came as a blow to him when Jamie was listed as missing during the push for Toulouse, and when young Edward was killed he seemed to retreat inside himself.'

'Is there still no news about Jamie?'

Giles shook his head, a shadow passing over his grey eyes. 'Nothing. You know I resigned my commission after Waterloo.'

'I was sorry to hear it. Did you have to do that? I know how much your career meant to you.'

'Duty demanded it. When Edward was killed and

with Jamie missing, Father summoned me back home. I was in London at the time. He pointed out most forcibly that now, as his heir, my place is at Castonbury. I never envied Jamie being the heir—the responsibilities. When I got back here, knowing that in all probability it would one day be mine, they became like jewels too heavy to carry, too valuable to neglect and too enormous to ignore. I believed it had all come down to me— or so I thought until we got Alicia's letter. If it turns out that she *is* Jamie's wife and her child his son, then if Harry can discover irrefutably that Jamie is dead, the child, Crispin, is the heir. It's all such a mess. You saw her in London?'

'Yes, I did.'

'What did you make of her? Is she genuine do you think? Is she telling the truth?'

'I honestly don't know the answer to that, Giles. She was convincing—though nervous, I thought. She has all the necessary papers.'

'Then we'll just have to see what turns up.' He took a long drink of his brandy. 'Coming home kept me sane enough to deal with the broken man who is my father, to deal with those who came to pay their respects and to hold together the frayed strings of the household. Although Aunt Wilhelmina does a sterling job of keeping things shipshape and the household in order. She is out at present visiting Lady Hesketh in Hatherton. She is expected back before dinner.'

'And cousin Kate?'

'My sister is off on one of her travels—the Lake District, I believe, but Phaedra is here. She will be glad Araminta is back from London. She spends most of her time with her precious horses but I think she's missing Kate. I cannot guarantee what kind of reception you'll get from father. As I said, you'll find him much changed.' He grinned suddenly. 'And you'll have to get past Smithins first.'

'Smithins!' Ross exclaimed, recalling that rigidly superior gentleman's gentleman, who rarely deigned to speak to anyone but his uncle, the duke. 'Good Lord, is he still here? I'd forgotten about him.'

'Come now, no one forgets Smithins. A legion of soldiers couldn't do a better job of guarding my father than he does. Even I have to get past Smithins to see him.' He laughed, beginning to sound more like his old self. 'Goodness, I'm glad you're home, Ross. There's a definite sense of the military about you. God, how I miss it. Your presence will bring back some normality to the house. And how is the adorable Araminta?'

'Still adorable and very well, considering her broken engagement. She'll be here any time. I rode on ahead. She is in transports over coming back to Castonbury. When the time is appropriate, she has planned parties and goodness knows what so I doubt you'll have a moment's peace and quiet.'

'I shall welcome it,' Giles said, getting up and walking over to the side table and pouring himself another liberal glass of brandy. 'It's just what this house needs to shake it out of the doldrums. Although be warned. Whatever activities she is planning, she will have to gain Aunt Wilhelmina's approval first. She hasn't changed.'

For the next half-hour they sat in congenial companionship as Giles gave him a detailed account of what needed to be done on the estate, which through lack of money had been neglected. He went on to tell him of myriad business ventures and family holdings the Montagues had managed to hold on to, but it was clear Giles was concerned about the state of the finances.

'I would like to help,' Ross offered. 'Not only have I come home to offer my support but also to offer financial help to tide you over until the family debts can be settled.'

'Thank you, Ross. That's extremely generous of you. I appreciate your offer but I cannot accept it—not yet anyway. I have money of my own and I'm managing to keep things afloat just now. We're banking on Harry coming up with firm evidence of Jamie's death. Although if it is proved that Alicia's son is indeed the heir, then Jamie's wealth will pass to him.'

'Think about it. I owe your family a great deal—especially your parents, who gave me and my sister a home when we needed one, and extended as much affection to us as they did to their own children. The offer remains if you should change your mind.'

## Chapter Four

Nothing could have prepared Lisette for the exquisite splendour that was Castonbury Park in the heart of the Derbyshire countryside. She saw it from a distance sitting like a grand old lady surrounded by beautiful parkland, timeless, gracious and brooding, its elegant beauty expressing power and pride.

When the carriage drew to a halt in front of the house, scarlet and gold-liveried footmen appeared and descended to strip them of the mountain of baggage. Lisette stepped into the bustling, alien environment that was to be her world from now on, acutely aware of the rich trappings of the interior.

The house was awe inspiring, the atmosphere of comfort and luxury, of elegance and a style of living she could never have imagined. The butler, Lumsden, stood aside as they entered, keeping a keen eye on the footmen to remind them of their duties as their eyes kept straying with frank approval to the young maid who stood beside Miss Araminta.

Unaware of their admiring looks, with her eyes opened wide with wonder and awe, Lisette followed her mistress along an assortment of corridors to the west block, where Araminta and other family members had their rooms. Lisette attended her mistress's toilet and helped her change into fresh clothes in which to meet the family, before seeking her own chamber. She was pleasantly surprised to find she had been allotted an adequately furnished room overlooking the park at the south-facing front of the house.

Having washed her face and tidied herself, Lisette found her way to the domestic quarters to introduce herself to Mrs Stratton, the housekeeper.

'Wait here,' a young housemaid by the name of Daisy said when she asked if she might see Mrs Stratton. 'She's in her parlour with Mr Everett, the steward. I'll tell her you're here.'

Lisette did as she was told, standing just inside the kitchen door and glad of it, for it gave her a chance to look at this splendid room which was a hive of activity. Every surface was so highly polished it reflected the light. There were two enormous tables bearing bowls filled with all manner of ingredients and chopping boards. There was much stirring and chopping and whisking at this table, a tumultuous frenzy, as dinner was prepared for the family. Covering a whole wall was a huge dresser that reached from floor to ceiling with what seemed to be hundreds of pieces of crockery of every sort, along with copper utensils, silver-covered dishes and much more. A massive range took over the whole of another wall, with an iron contraption with hooks on which to hang kettles and such like for roasting meat.

A young male cook in a pristine white apron and white hat was leaning over the range, the wooden spoon with which he had just stirred a sauce at his lips. He tasted the mixture speculatively, his darkly handsome face set in lines of deep concentration, then he turned to a kitchen maid and, with an air of one who makes a momentous decision upon which the lives of hundreds might depend, he said with a strong foreign accent, 'A half-teaspoon more of pepper, if you please, Nancy, and not a spec more.'

Lisette turned when a neatly dressed woman with a rustle of stiff black silk and a jangle of the keys secured to her waist appeared.

'I'm Mrs Stratton and you must be Miss Napier, Miss Araminta's maid.'

'Yes. I'm pleased to meet you, Mrs Stratton.'

'How is Miss Araminta? Well, I hope?'

'Yes, she is very well and meeting her family just now. The footmen are sorting out the baggage at present so I thought I'd come and familiarise myself with the routine in the domestic quarters.'

Mrs Stratton looked her over and what she saw evidently satisfied her. A woman with greying blond hair, she was of a gentle and quiet nature and treated the maids fairly and with kindness. Over the coming days as Lisette got to know her better, she would find that she was one of those rare women blessed with a temperament that was constant and reliable, and that her loyalty to the Montagues exceeded that which was normally expected of a servant for her employers.

On seeing Miss Napier's interest in the male cook, she smiled.

'That is Monsieur André. He has the entire superintendence of the kitchen, while several maids are employed in roasting, boiling and all the ordinary manual operations of the kitchen. I'll get Faith Henshaw to show you the ropes—she's Lady Phaedra's maid and extremely competent. I'm sure you'll be glad of her help.'

Lisette was immensely grateful. Faith—or Henny as she was addressed—was a few years older than she was. Very slim and with dark brown hair and always on the go, she was an experienced lady's maid, kind and thoughtful. She was to marry Sandy, one of the footmen. It was from Faith that Lisette learned of the household duties and the routine of the household.

\* \* \*

The day of Ross's return was one of high spirits at Castonbury. The housemaids gathered in corners and whispered between themselves. Mrs Stratton instructed Monsieur André to make up his favourite chocolate sponge cake, and the following morning Giles took him on a tour of the estate lest he had forgotten where he lived.

It was late afternoon when Ross made his way to his uncle's suite of rooms. Smithins, small, with thick white hair and his habitual poker face and keen eyes, met him in the anteroom to the duke's bedchamber.

'Welcome home, my lord,' he said haughtily.

'Thank you, Smithins. I've come to see my uncle.' When the valet made no reply, he looked at him enquiringly, raising his eyebrows. 'Is he awake?'

Smithins considered the colonel, inclining his head and pursing his lips in an effeminate manner. 'On the doctor's orders I gave him a draught earlier. It has relaxed him. In fact, I was about to get him into bed. I am reluctant to allow any new stress foisted on him.'

'I am not here to cause him stress,' Ross stated, struggling to hold on to his temper, somewhat put out at being kept waiting as though he were a casual caller.

'I'm sure you're not, Colonel, but—'

'I would like to see my uncle,' Ross interrupted in

a glacial voice, feeling impatience grow in him as the valet bristled waspishly. 'I will stay just a moment.'

Smithins sniffed and with his nose in the air turned towards the door. 'Very well, if you insist.'

Ross was admitted into the bedchamber. It was dominated by a huge bed decorated with palms and ostrich feathers and hung with blue silk damask. It was a comfortable, spacious room, but there was an air of tension about it which manifested itself in the old man seated in a chair by the window, and the slow metronome ticking of the clock which seemed to herald the coming of something the duke might not care for. The room was warm, for Smithins was of the opinion that warm air helped fragile lungs to breath more easily.

Ross went to his uncle. 'Uncle?'

The duke lifted his head then and saw him. Ross was taken aback at the sight. Even Giles's words had not prepared him for his appearance. All his life he had been a tall, well-built man, his face full, firm and strong looking. Now it was much altered, the life gone from it, drained and empty, the flesh already sunken into the shape of his skull. His eyes were a dead, flat grey. They had lost all their bright intelligence that he had always associated with his uncle. He coughed, gasping to take his next breath. Ross waited while Smithins gave him some water. Gradually some colour came to his face and his breathing became easier. His eyes lost their blankness and filled with an expression of recognition as they settled on Ross. But Ross could see that his uncle was half the man he once was, shrunken, bent, slower and bereft without Edward and Jamie.

When he spoke he was coherent, his voice low and thread-like. 'Ross, my boy, Giles told me you were back. You look well. India must agree with you. You are on leave? How long have you got?'

'A few weeks—longer if I am needed here.'

He nodded, his gaze drawn to the window which offered an extensive view of the park, staring with an air of fixed absorption of some secret worry. 'That's good. Giles will be glad to have you around. You know about Edward—and Jamie...'

'Yes.'

'Sometimes I forget...I think they are still here—and then I remember. I can't take it. Why don't they come home?' He could not go on for a moment and his hand fell away to his lap where it clutched desperately at the wool of the rug which covered his legs. His gaze remained on the window and the yellow gold wash of the sun on the curtains. After a moment, speaking slowly, almost to himself, he said, 'I cannot believe they are both gone from here—that all that life and vigour, that passionate conviction, that vital, hot-headed emotion that sent them to war is...'

With those words trailing off into silence, Ross

looked down into the face of the man who stared somewhere into the far-off distance into a nightmare world in which no one existed but himself. He knew everyone who came to see him, to stand beside his chair and express hope and belief that some miracle would bring his sons back to Castonbury.

Drawing himself up, Ross laid a gentle hand on his uncle's shoulder and nodded to Smithins to show him out.

It was chance that brought Lisette into contact with Ross following his meeting with his uncle. Upon climbing the stairs on her route to Miss Araminta's room, she found him at the top of the landing. They were not entirely alone, as two footmen were lighting the candles along the corridor where they met. She stopped awkwardly and looked directly at him. He seemed perfectly self-possessed. The shadows were resting softly along his cheek and chin. He brought his gaze down upon hers heavily and with a slight smile, reaching out his hand, he gently touched her cheek with the tip of his finger.

Lisette looked away, not on account of shame, but because his gaze was loaded with desire. He stepped back, dipped his head to her graciously before proceeding down the stairs.

After a moment she turned. Mrs Stratton was watching her from the shadows, and in that instant Lisette felt as if all her vices had been unmasked. She shrank back, ashamed of her conduct, and resolved once more to dispel all her absurd longings, however impossible this task seemed. After all, what right had she to entertain even for a moment, a desire for anything more than what she had now?

But— Oh, dear sweet Lord! To be embraced by him, kissed by him! She had never known such a feeling. It was as if every particle of her might come apart in his arms. Until that moment she had never known the true force of her emotions. It was like nothing else on earth. It contained in it all the fierceness, all the violence, of a hurricane. It was the very essence of the sublime.

Whenever they met, she did her best to avoid meeting his gaze, but he did not endeavour to avoid hers; in fact, he occupied himself with nothing else.

Despite Ross's homecoming, which should have been cause for celebration, dinner that night was a subdued affair in the grand dining room. The long table shone with silver and crystal ware. Up above the ceiling was richly decorated with a series of paintings of the four seasons and continents. Gilt-framed paintings of hunting scenes adorned the stone-coloured walls, and the white marble mantelpiece was supported by Roman figures.

Looking particularly regal yet wraithlike in a gown of saffron silk shot with green, her grey hair immaculately coiffed beneath an elaborate arrangement of feathers, the Honourable Mrs Wilhelmina Landes-Fraser presided over all of it. Diamonds and emeralds sparkled at her neck, earlobes and wrists. Seated at the opposite end of the table to Giles, she regarded the family with a stern eye and an attentive expression in her eyes as they settled on Phaedra and Araminta before nodding to the servants to begin serving.

As sister-in-law to the Duke of Rothermere she cared a great deal for the fads and fashions of the day, although she, unlike the majority of her contemporaries, refused to allow her tall, slender figure to run to fat. A stickler for protocol and doing the right thing, she had the aloof, unshakable confidence and poise that came from living a thoroughly privileged life. In this world of hidden meanings and unspoken rules, there was no mistaking her value.

Ross inwardly gritted his teeth. Aunt Wilhelmina was effectively the matriarch of the family. Acknowledging the power she wielded was something the Montague men had to do.

The meal progressed with Phaedra complimenting Ross on his magnificent horse, who had lost no time in making himself at home in the stables, and Giles sang the praises of his betrothed, the lovely Lily Seagrove.

'You'll be meeting her shortly, Ross—and her father, the Reverend Seagrove. He often calls to spend some time with Father and frequently joins us for dinner.'

'I remember Miss Seagrove, Giles. Not having seen her since she was a girl, I'm sure I shall find her much changed. This is excellent soup, by the way,' Ross commented, spooning the rather unusual but mouthwatering soup up. 'I compliment the cook on her culinary art.'

'We have a chef in the Castonbury kitchen—a Frenchman, Monsieur André,' Giles informed him. 'French chefs are in demand in London—in the hotels in particular. When Father was ailing, we lured Monsieur André to Castonbury with promise of future advancement if he could tempt Father to eat in order to maintain his health.'

'I'm impressed,' Ross said, having finished the soup and looking forward to the next course, which he had no doubt would be a culinary delight.

'Giles tells me you have been to see this woman who claims to have married Jamie?' Wilhelmina said, settling her sharp eyes on Ross. 'What did you think of her? Is she genuine?'

'I can't say. I found her likeable and quite convincing, but...'

Wilhelmina lifted her aristocratic brows. 'But *you* were not convinced.'

'Not entirely.'

'Did you see the child?'

'No, I did not.'

'I see. I would appreciate it if we kept this within the family,' she said, lowering her tone a notch with Lumsden and his minions close within earshot. 'Hopefully we shall hear from Harry very soon and it will put an end to this nonsense.'

'It may not be nonsense,' Ross remarked. 'I greatly fear that, like it or not, there is every chance that Jamie married the woman in Spain and that the child is his.'

'I believe the woman to be an impostor—an opportunist, out for all she can get,' Wilhelmina remarked sternly.

'Not necessarily, Aunt,' Giles dared to argue, draining his glass and nodding to Lumsden.

Lumsden went to an alcove where a huge trough of Sicilian jasper was filled with iced water and bottles of wine. Taking out a bottle of white wine he replenished the glasses.

'I read the letter,' Giles went on, 'and I have to say she came over as pretty genuine to me.'

'I think if you had troubled to read it properly—between the lines as I did—you would have realised that she is not what she seems,' Wilhelmina retorted. 'But if her claim is proven, then how could Jamie have let this happen—and for a child to have been born of their union is just too dreadful to contemplate and will set in motion all manner of inheritance issues. It is bound to cause bad feeling within the family.'

'It doesn't have to be like that,' Giles said.

'But it will happen,' she exclaimed sternly, having been brought up to understand that good breeding mattered more than wealth. 'For generations the bloodlines of this family have been unsullied. The Montagues are descendants of the nobility. Yet Jamie may have married an utter nobody, a person without bloodlines or breeding or ancestry to produce the next heir. We know absolutely nothing about this woman. Little wonder your father's mind is unhinged with all this going on.' In supreme frustration, she turned her ire on her nephew. 'You must see my point, Giles.'

Giles leaned back in his chair, his expression wry. 'Very well,' he said amiably. 'It is certainly desirable and fortunate to be well descended, but until it is proven otherwise we must give her the benefit of the doubt.'

Wilhelmina cast him a killing glance, but she said nothing more on the subject and the rest of the meal passed in silence.

Three weeks after coming to Castonbury, while her mistress was dancing her feet off at the Assembly Rooms in the nearby town of Hatherton and entrancing more beaux, Lisette sat in Mrs Stratton's comfortable parlour sharing a cup of tea and mending some fine Brussels lace on one of Araminta's petticoats.

When Mrs Stratton was called away to attend to a crisis in the kitchen, feeling strangely restless and in need of some fresh air, Lisette put down her work and, wrapping a shawl about her shoulders and begging a couple of apples from Monsieur André, she left the quiet buzz of conversation in the servants' hall and went outside.

It had been raining all that day and at last it had stopped. It was a clear night, the sky littered with stars. Walking away from the house and trying to avoid the puddles, she followed the path to the stables, a path she often took when she found she had time to herself. Walking into the shadowy dimness of the yard where an occasional lantern attached to the walls cast an orange glow and filled the yard with shadows, the familiar fecund smells of straw and grain and warm animals and manure assailed her nostrils. There were several grooms who had their quarters over the stables which were quite extensive, for besides housing horses to ride, there was also space for carriages.

Going inside she smiled when she saw Bengal. His head reached out to her over the door of his stall where he was quartered. He whickered in welcome, pleased to see her.

'You can wait,' she said laughingly, bypassing him

and stopping by another horse. This was Merlin, a magnificent chestnut stallion. He belonged to Lord Jamie, the Montague heir who had disappeared in Spain. Stretching out his long neck, he took the proffered apple with obvious delight.

'Do you need help, Miss Napier?'

She turned and smiled when she saw Tom Anderson, the elderly head groom, coming towards her, a pitchfork in his hand. 'No, thank you, Mr Anderson. I just wanted some air so I thought I'd come and see the horses. I've brought Merlin an apple and Bengal too. See, Bengal is reaching for his.'

Having told him of her love of horses and her experience with them in India, Anderson gave her a conspiratorial smile. 'No doubt you'd rather be on his back than feeding him apples.'

'I most certainly would, Mr Anderson, but think of the shock and horror should the household—both upstairs and down—see Miss Araminta's maid riding hell for leather through the park.'

Anderson chuckled. 'They'd be no more shocked and horrified than they were when Lady Phaedra took to wearing breeches when she started working the horses. She's a firm believer that they must have regular exercise and she does know good horseflesh when she sees it. Aye, well, fed and watered they're all settled for the night so I'll bid you goodnight, miss.'

Lisette watched him go. He was going badly. With his arthritis he was not as able as he was. Holding her shawl with one hand Lisette offered Bengal the apple, smiling broadly when he greedily snatched it from her hand and began to munch. Reaching out with the other she stroked his nose, laughing softly when he tried to nibble her fingers, too wrapped up in her enjoyment to notice Ross's approach.

Returning from his club in Hatherton and reluctant to enter the house just yet, Ross was drawn to the stables and his horse. Being close to his precious mount never failed to soothe him. However, he was surprised to find Miss Napier stroking Bengal's nose. Ross's cool gaze took in the fetching scene. Standing in an orange glow highlighting her gleaming dark hair held in place by a black net, her profile was serene. With long black lashes shadowing her cheeks and a faint suggestion of a smile playing about her generous lips, she had a look of complete absorption on her face as she spoke softly to Bengal.

'And what brings you out here at this time?'

Lisette spun round and looked at him. She had not heard him approach and in that moment he might have been a figment of her imagination for he did not seem real. He had stepped, silently, from the dark shadows of the yard and as her eyes sharpened with the return of her senses she saw him clearly.

'Oh, Colonel Montague! You—you startled me.'

'Miss Napier! We seem destined to meet in the oddest places, do we not? But I'm sorry if I surprised you.'

'I came out to see the horses,' she replied simply. 'Miss Araminta is attending a dance at the Assembly Rooms in Hatherton. I felt like some air and I couldn't resist coming to take a look at the horses. Is something wrong?' she asked when she saw him staring down at her feet.

He felt compelled to point out the obvious. 'You are standing in a puddle.'

'Oh,' she said, following his gaze and seeing that she was and that the hem of her skirts was wet. 'So I am.'

'You appear to have a fondness for getting your feet wet.'

Knowing he was referring to the time he'd caught her dangling her feet in a stream, she laughed. It was a joyous sound, happy and full of the magic of youth and moonlight. It took Ross completely by surprise, and for a long moment he stared down at her incredulously, conscious of a swift flash of admiration.

'When I was in India there were times during the dry seasons that I would have given anything to see a puddle,' she confessed. 'Indeed, when it rained I often went outside to dance in them. You more than anyone should understand that—how it felt with the never-ending heat and drought all year round, except for the times when the monsoons came.'

He smiled, leaning against the stable door, which Bengal took as a cue to push his nose against his shoulder. 'I shall never forget,' he said softly. 'The summers are so hot that the air shimmers over the land in waves—it's often so hot it's difficult to breathe.'

'And the heat makes your flesh feel stretched so tight over your bones it hurts,' she murmured, closing her eyes and rubbing her cheeks with the tips of her fingers as if in remembrance of the hot Indian sun.

Ross lowered his gaze to her face, watching her fingers brush her skin. Though it may have been stretched tight in the tropical heat, there was nothing but softness to it now. Lust hit him with such unexpected force that he could not move.

Opening her eyes Lisette met his gaze. 'I never did mind the rain. I loved it.'

'As much as you love horses?'

She laughed again. 'Perhaps not as much as that. The rain here in England is especially nice. It's so gentle and the gardens look beautiful afterwards. The fragrance of wet grass and damp leaves is lovely.' She let out a breath in a deep sigh and he could almost hear her regret.

'But?'

'But it's not India. In India I would love the feel of

the rain on my face. I would often become soaked to the skin—which always roused my mother's wrath and she would scold me unmercifully.'

For the moment Ross could not form a coherent reply, for in some dim part of his consciousness, he could appreciate what she meant. But after what she had said he could not do much in the way of thinking. Standing close to him was a woman whose body he was certain was a hidden treasure, a woman whose hair was as black as jet, a woman whose eyes were the exact shade of warm amber, a woman who loved the fragrance of damp grass and leaves—and a woman whose innocent pleasure of getting soaked in the rain was proving as erotic to him as any aphrodisiac could be.

Recalling their kiss and her rejection of his suggestion that they take matters further, with all the discipline he could muster, he set his jaw and reminded himself of his position and hers. She worked for him, she was a servant, and there were rules about men of his stature getting too close to servants. But as his gaze remained focused on her face, he found it virtually impossible to think of her as a servant. To know her better, to spend time with her, was well worth the risk of being caught out.

'I get the impression that you are homesick,' he murmured.

Lisette met his gaze. His voice had deepened to a

husky timbre that plucked at her senses like clever fingers unlacing her stays. 'Yes,' she replied, 'I think I am.'

'Since you and I have much in common—'

'Only our shared love of India,' she was quick to point out.

'Which is a great deal considering the size of the country.'

'You will go back to your regiment?'

He frowned and shook his head, his expression hardening. 'I shall return in some capacity. No doubt I shall resume the rank in the service to which my seniority and my talents entitle me. I only hope that as a result of my promotion to colonel I will not be removed from regimental duty and set to work in an administrative capacity which often happens. Why do you smile?' he asked when he saw the corners of her lips twitch.

'Because I cannot imagine you sitting at a desk.'

Ross's vivid blue eyes, which had darkened to almost black in the dim light, captured hers. 'No? Then in what capacity do you imagine me?'

'Governing and controlling vast expanses of lawless territories, and with a lust for conquest without tainting your love and understanding of the country and its peoples. I imagine you leading your regiment into battle and claiming victory.'

What she said made him laugh. 'You are too generous, Miss Napier—you also have a fertile imagination.

I wish I could share it, but I suspect I shall not be permitted to return to my regiment.'

Her expression became serious. 'Then for your sake I hope you are mistaken.'

'Thank you. So do I. And talking about my love of India and your own, I would like to show you some of the art that I've collected on my travels and brought back with me. It's still packed in crates, but when I've unpacked it I would like to show it to you.'

Lisette quivered. She knew what Colonel Montague was doing, casting that spell of his again, with his dark-velvet voice and beguiling little smile. As simple and innocent as she was, she knew what game he played, and yet she could not understand why a person of quality would wish to tarnish their reputation by publicly associating with a maid.

She looked at him lounging against the stable door, two hunting hounds sniffing about his feet. In the dim light his face had a melancholy cast and he seemed to be totally indifferent to his inherited position. It was something Lisette rarely saw, but she recognised it instantly. It was something that could not be acquired or reproduced. It had to have time to develop, like a patina that told everyone you had no doubts about your place in the world or that you were concerned about others' perceptions of you.

The noise of the horses moving about in the stalls

brought her back to the present and she rubbed Bengal's nose to soothe him when he whickered loudly, tossed his head and banged his hoof against the door. 'The horses seem restless tonight.'

'The reason for that is there's a mare on heat. All the stallions start kicking their stalls and nipping the grooms—even the geldings start to misbehave.' Looking at her soft features, with tendrils of her black hair brushing her cheeks, desire still stirring his loins, Ross was tempted to say that men were like geldings when physical passion was denied them.

His explicit talk embarrassed Lisette and she looked away to hide her flaming cheeks. When he chuckled softly, clearly amused by her embarrassment, she turned and met is gaze. Shoving himself away from the door, he reached out and pushed a strand of hair away from her face, finding himself unable to pull his hand away. The skin of her cheek felt warm and soft beneath his fingers, and he wondered how a woman who had lived in the heat of India for most of her life could have skin as soft and fine as this. He touched his fingers to her lips, remembering their kiss. How could her lips feel as velvety as this? If anything, the feel of her flesh beneath his fingertips added to the awareness of sensuality he felt emanating between them.

'When I first saw you,' Ross said quietly, 'I had this strange feeling that we had met before. It was as if a moment out of time burned between us. But how could that be? I asked myself. Surely I would have remembered. How could I forget?'

Unable to move, Lisette was looking at him, her eyes wide with surprise, but in their depths, there was also something else, something that reflected what he was feeling. Remembering how it had felt to be held by him, to be kissed by him, desire was in her eyes and in the rapid wisp of her breath against his fingers. It was in the way she stood so still, tense and poised like a young deer about to flee. If he lowered his hand to her chest he would feel her heart beating as hard as his own. It moved a little in that direction before he drew it back.

In matters of the heart Lisette's judgement had always been clouded, but in those moments when all her senses seemed to be heightened nearly beyond all endurance, this feeling that she had only ever come across twice before—with this man in a raging river and again on the journey to Castonbury Park—robbed her of all judgement. Mentally, she was experiencing all of a woman's physical needs and longings and desires that could only be matched by one man—this man.

'It's time I returned to the house,' she said, backing away from him. 'Lady Araminta will be back soon and I have things to do.'

'My sister seems much taken with you, Miss Napier,' he said, reluctant to let her go. 'Indeed, she cannot stop singing your praises. But I feel that her broken betrothal—which I am sure you know all about since it is in her nature to confide in those close to her—has affected her and I'm not convinced she has recovered from it, though she denies it emphatically. She cannot remain at Castonbury forever and it's high time she had a suitable husband and a home of her own. I cannot return to India until I have seen that she is settled.'

Lisette glanced up at him obliquely, a little smile playing on her lips. 'Why, what is this? Are you to play matchmaker, Colonel?'

He grinned down at her. 'If that's what you would like to call it, then yes—providing she approves of the outcome and that she is happy.'

'Then it might be a very long time before you find you can return to India. At this present time your sister has her head firmly set against marriage to anyone.'

'We shall see. I work fast, Miss Napier,' he said, his gaze holding hers before lowering to her lips. 'But I am not concerned. There are a number of distractions I've already noted which will, I am convinced, make my stay worthwhile.'

The warmly mellow tones of his voice were imbued with a rich quality that seemed to vibrate through Lisette's womanly being. The implication of his words evoked a strangely pleasurable disturbance in areas far too private for an untried virgin even to consider, much less invite. As evocative as the sensations were, she didn't know what to make of them. They seemed almost…wanton. But then, the image of her meeting with him in India had been scored into her brain and had undoubtedly heightened her sensitivity to wayward imaginings. But she was not going to be intimidated. And yet, with her heart filled with gratitude and her desire for him overflowing, he seemed completely wonderful and omnipotent—a mighty defender who had charged to her rescue and saved her from drowning.

She looked at him obliquely, a smile curving her lips. 'I am intrigued, Colonel. I would not have thought there was anything at Castonbury of sufficient note to claim the attention of a gentleman of your…' She stopped herself, biting her lip, suddenly realising she was about to overstep her position. But he was not about to let her off the hook.

A well-defined eyebrow jutted sharply upward. 'Of my what? Inclination?' The rush of colour that flooded her cheeks answered his question. He smiled knowingly. 'Why, Miss Napier, what can you mean? Do pray enlighten me.'

Lisette met his challenging look and considered doing just that, but she said, 'If you don't mind, Colonel, I would prefer not to answer that. This conversation is not to my liking. It—it is not proper.'

Ross appeared to consider her words carefully, then

he stepped closer so they stood shoulder to shoulder. He looked down at her sideways, a wicked gleam lighting his eyes. His lips widened leisurely into a rakish grin as his gaze ranged over her. Though she had been leered at any number of times while strolling along the streets of London, this was an entirely different matter. Those warmly glowing blue orbs gave her cause to wonder if his expression would have changed even remotely had she been standing before him entirely naked. Indeed, she could almost swear from the way he was looking at her that he did have designs upon her person.

'Not proper? Very well, we shall speak of something else,' he said, while his eyes gave their message of seduction and his expression told her that this was only the beginning. 'I could be an avid pupil if you wish to teach me about plants and things in your spare time. After spending your time assisting your father with his work I expect you must have become knowledgeable about such matters.'

Despite her perfectly rigid resolve, Lisette's lips twitched. 'And pigs might fly, Colonel,' she returned. 'Not for one minute do I believe such trivia would be of interest to you. And besides, I am as ignorant of English botany as you are. I am here to take care of your sister. I have no time for anything else.'

'For which you have me to thank.'

Lisette looked into his eyes, into his face, and felt a

most peculiar shiver slither down her spine. 'You are not, by any chance, attempting to make me feel grateful—so that I'll imagine myself in your debt?'

His brows quirked, his mesmerising lips curved. His eyes—blue, intent and oddly challenging—held hers. 'It seemed the natural place to start to undermine your defences.'

Lisette felt her nerves vibrate to the velvety softness of his voice, felt her senses quiver as she registered his words. Her eyes locked on his as she struggled to think of some sharp retort, but none came.

Ross's features relaxed and he shook his head slowly. The last thing he wanted was for her to feel indebted to him in any way. From the very beginning he had been concerned by her situation and he had seen that there was more to her than met the eye. The undercurrents that surrounded her were considerable, running inexplicably deep. He had wanted to aid her, without letting on he was doing so. Pride was something he understood—he was sensitive to hers.

'I like you, Lisette. I desire you—which you already know.' His tone was softly earnest. 'And you know I mean that seriously.'

His words put her thoughts in turmoil. They looked at each other, neither of them speaking, their glances locked, speaking words which could not be heard but which both understood. Lisette's mouth was dry and immodest sensations were beginning to fill her body. She felt the heat in her face, and then the heat spread, filling every part of her at that nakedly desirous look. It was a look that was at once an invitation, a need and a certainty. He was as sure of her as that. But it could not be so. The feelings that assaulted her frightened her. She wanted him, desired him, but she also feared him—but more than that she feared herself.

For a while she had been carried away by the sheer pleasure of his company and by the soft aura of the night and the stables, and for that time she had allowed herself to forget the reality of her situation, but it was over. She was painfully aware of the gulf between her status and his—a maid was a servant, noble blood was noble blood. She did not belong there. Men of Colonel Montague's ilk were not for the likes of her.

She hesitated, searching for words, then she said, 'I know what you are saying but I have got to be sensible. We both have to be. I may be a maid, a domestic servant, but I am the daughter of a gentleman. You are a nobleman, successful, a man of wealth and position. With all that entails in time you will make a good marriage. It would be most unwise for us to form any kind of alliance. I could never be anything to you but your mistress. I am not looking for a protector. I may not have much, Colonel Montague, but the little I have I value. I have strong feelings for you—you know that—

but I have too much self-respect to be any man's mistress.'

He considered her apace, then nodded slowly. 'I could promise you ease and comfort.' He paused and tipped his head without releasing her gaze. 'Would that be a kindness or a curse?'

'Kindness or curse?' Lisette scoffed. 'Your wisdom escapes me. What you are asking of me is a sin. My upbringing, meaning the teachings of my parents, taught me the difference between right and wrong and I will not go against that. I will not be your mistress, nor anything else you think is appropriate for a servant girl. I'm worth more than that.'

'Along with everything else that draws me to you, I applaud your sincerity, Miss Napier.'

'I mean what I say. I don't like being made sport of, Colonel, but you obviously enjoy causing me discomfort. I am employed by you to take care of your sister's needs. My duties end there. It has to be that way.'

He nodded slowly, his blue eyes sparkling with humour. 'I can see you are a highly intelligent female, Miss Napier.'

'I'm glad you think so,' she answered, wondering where this unusual conversation was going to take her next.

'That was not a compliment,' he corrected.

Lisette looked at him with curious displeasure that

silently demanded an explanation for his remark. He answered as he reached out and touched her cheek with his forefinger, tracing its smooth, delicate texture.

'Were you less intelligent, you would not spend so much time considering all the possible consequences of belonging to me, and you would simply accept our situation along with the benefits attached to it.'

'Benefits? What benefits might they be?'

'Think of all the things I could give you. I would take good care of you.' Her eyes widened with indignation, but Ross continued with imperturbable masculine logic. 'Were you a woman of ordinary intelligence, you would be concerned with matters of normal interest to a woman, not torturing yourself about such subjects as the differences between us. Accept the situation now. It is inevitable.'

Lisette stared at him in disbelief. '*Situation?* Accept my *situation*?' she repeated. 'I am not in a "situation," as you so nicely phrased it.'

His eyes softened. 'I would never hurt you, Lisette. I promise.'

'Don't,' she said quickly, liking the sound of her name on his lips but she must not let it be. 'My name is Miss Napier and please don't make promises.'

Aware of her discomfiture Ross smiled, amused by it. One brow lifted arrogantly. He stood very close, totally commanding her vision.

'Why *there* you are!'

They both turned and beheld Nancy Cooper descending on them like a galleon in full sail. Ross frowned. The entire East India fleet wouldn't have been more unwelcome, but to Lisette, the maid's interruption was a godsend and saved her from replying to Colonel Montague's question.

'You are looking for Miss Napier?'

Despite his politeness, Lisette sensed his irritation, his annoyance, that Nancy's appearance had caused.

Nancy, a red-haired, white-faced kitchen maid, bobbed a curtsey, a rather sly, knowing smile on her thin lips. 'Indeed I am, sir. I'm sorry to drag you away,' she said to Lisette, 'but Miss Araminta has returned from the Assembly Rooms early and is asking for you.'

At that moment the carriage that had deposited Araminta and Phaedra and Aunt Wilhelmina at the door to the house swung into the stable yard.

'Then I shall come at once.' Bobbing a little curtsey, she uttered, 'Goodnight, Colonel Montague.'

Ross met her eyes. His smile still in place, he inclined his head. 'Miss Napier.'

Walking swiftly back to the house, Lisette sighed. Having left his presence the night seemed quieter, less colourful, less alive.

Nancy had to run to keep up with her. 'The colonel seems to have an eye for you, Miss Napier. It's not gone amiss.'

Her words and what they implied brought Lisette to an immediate halt. 'What on earth are you talking about, Nancy?' she asked crossly, not liking one bit what the maid was implying.

'I expect the colonel's like most men in that he's just as susceptible to a pretty face as the next man. I know this is your first position in a big house and I'm only saying this for your own good, but a handsome man like the colonel can pose a hazard to an innocent girl. They know the right words to entangle a gullible female mind, and I feel I should warn you about the risks you could encounter if you go on meeting His Lordship as you have tonight.'

Lisette almost staggered back, shocked by what Nancy had said. 'But I didn't arrange to meet him. We met purely by chance.' She put her hands to her burning cheeks, astounded by Nancy's insinuation. 'Oh, Nancy, I hope you don't think—but that's dreadful. I—I didn't think…'

Having worked in service since she was a girl and knowing what was what in a 'big house,' as she called Castonbury Park, Nancy scoffed at her naivety. ''Course you didn't. I know you like to see the horses, but be careful. With a face like you've got it's hardly surprising that you've caught the colonel's eye. But if you become entangled with a titled gentleman, you may well come to regret it. You could easily be sullied and then tossed aside, leaving you in a delicate condition with little hope of attracting a respectable husband. Affairs like that have a way of ruining lives. No man wants spoiled goods.'

As Lisette continued on her way, Nancy's words had made one thing clear. To protect herself from Colonel Montague's corrupting influence she would endeavour to stay out of his way. There was no chance she'd succumb to a handsome face and a devilish smile.

And yet if she had been in the privileged position of Miss Araminta, the sparring and fencing humour he deployed would have been most enjoyable. What fun that would be. But as she entered the house her frown deepened at the road down which her thoughts travelled.

Oh, yes, Colonel Montague was definitely corrupting.

As soon as Lisette entered Araminta's room she heard the wrenching sound of grief being poured into a pillow. Her young mistress lay in a crumpled heap of chiffon and silk on the bed sobbing her heart out. Alarmed by the distraught girl, immediately she went to her, sitting on the bed beside her.

'Miss Araminta! What's this all about? What on

earth is the matter? What has happened to make you cry like this? Oh, you poor girl.'

'Oh, Lisette,' she wailed, turning her tear-washed face up to hers. 'You can have no idea. Antony was there—at the assembly. I couldn't stay. I couldn't bear it. I just wanted to come home. I told Aunt Wilhelmina I wasn't feeling well.'

'You still love him, don't you?'

Araminta confessed that she did and that she had made a terrible mistake when she had broken off their betrothal, that it had all been a horrid misunderstanding. Lisette pointed out that the fact that Lord Bennington hadn't married anyone else might well mean that he still loved Araminta. Her eyes filled with renewed hope, Araminta said she would write to Antony and ask him to meet her.

'But he mustn't come here. Ross mustn't know. I'm sure he blames Antony for what happened—and he's right, it was Antony's fault. But I know Ross. If he knew how much I have suffered because of Antony's betrayal, he'd probably call him out. You can't imagine how awesome he is when he's angry.'

'Then perhaps you should think again before you write to Lord Bennington. Although, if you don't, he might think you don't care for him, after all, and return to Cambridgeshire.'

With that motivation, Araminta allowed Lisette to

coax her out of her finery and into her nightdress and brush her hair, as she did every night, looking compassionately now and then into the pensive face in the mirror. She talked to her soothingly, saying anything that came into her head. Her voice was dreamlike to Araminta, giving the impression that she was in some vague, slightly unreal world of hopeless and despairing resignation and yet behind her blank face her mind was slithering like a duck on a frozen pond as she tried to formulate a plan to get Antony back.

## Chapter Five

When Lisette finally left Araminta tucked up in bed mentally wording a note to Antony Bennington, she felt restless and confused following her encounter with Colonel Montague, so she went down to the kitchen for a cup of hot milk before seeking her own bed. It was relatively quiet with just the odd footman and maid passing in and out as they finished their duties for the night. They all had an early start.

Will Blackstock was in the servants' hall in conversation with Smithins, who sniffed and left when Lisette entered. After warming some milk on the stove she sat at the table with Will. She got on with Will—mainly because they had both spent time in India and always had plenty to talk about. He talked as he worked, rubbing the brass buttons on one of the colonel's military coats.

Fair-haired and cheekily attractive, he was a firm favourite with everybody. With his ready smile, sharp wit and the tales he told of his travels in India he had everyone enthralled. His devotion and loyalty to Colonel Montague was never in doubt, and he had a definite twinkle in his brown eyes whenever they lighted on Daisy, a pretty young housemaid.

Will and Lisette chatted amiably as she drank her milk, discussing the menus for the following day and the chickens which the kitchen staff had dressed earlier and were now residing in the larder awaiting Monsieur André's expertise to turn them into something quite delicious.

'Do you recall the markets in India,' Will said, 'when the livestock were brought in from the countryside—how the chickens were kept in cages and weren't killed until they were sold?'

'I do—very well—and the ducks and geese. Mother was always very good at bartering and invariably got them at a knock-down price.'

'How very primitive,' Nancy interrupted. There was a note of scorn in her voice. She saw Lisette as something of an upstart and was jealous of the attention Will paid to her.

Lisette looked at her. 'It's just a different way of life, Nancy.'

'A way of life that would not appeal to me. Nor could I understand it.'

'A person is always better off for understanding

something,' Lisette pointed out calmly. 'In my imagination life as it is in India will go on indefinitely.'

'In your imagination, water could go uphill and cats speak French,' Nancy retorted, and with a toss of her head she flounced away in a huff.

Lisette shot Will an amused, conspiratorial glance. 'Oh, dear,' she murmured. 'I don't think I'm one of Nancy's favourite people.'

'You're not the only one,' Will remarked. 'Mrs Stratton set her on after Christmas but she's too haughty for her own good that one—and lazy. If she doesn't start pulling her weight, you mark my words—she'll be out on her ear before much longer.'

Mrs Stratton walked in followed by Lumsden.

'Good evening, Blackstock—Miss Napier,' Lumsden said, his manner precise as always. Taking out his watch attached by a fob to his waistcoat he checked on the time. 'Mrs Stratton and I are to share a nightcap before I check to make sure that everything is locked up.'

'I'll just get some hot water from the kettle,' Mrs Stratton said, disappearing into the kitchen where André, always considerate to her needs, had left provisions for her late-night beverage. 'Have your usual tipple by all means, Mr Lumsden, but I'll settle for a cup of tea tonight.'

Having witnessed the brief show of intimacy between Lisette and Colonel Montague on the day following their arrival at Castonbury, Lisette was relieved that Mrs Stratton had made no comment on the incident. However, she was under no illusion that it had been forgotten and that from that moment her behaviour would be under the closest scrutiny.

Lisette liked Mrs Stratton. Her voice did not hold the superior tone one would expect of the housekeeper of such a large and noble establishment. She was a widow with one son, Adam. The last time he'd come home to Castonbury to see his mother it was to tell her that he'd left the navy and was to try his hand at business. Mrs Stratton had been horrified to learn that he'd given up a promising career. Disappointed by his mother's reaction, Adam had stormed off, vowing he would not return until he had made his fortune. Mrs Stratton was saddened that he had not been in contact since then, but she concealed it beneath her quiet demeanour.

'I trust you haven't forgotten that in the morning we are to make an inspection of the guest rooms, Mrs Stratton,' Lumsden said when she reappeared carrying a small teapot. 'It's so long since they were in use that we must make an inventory of things to be done to make them suitable for occupation.'

'Of course not. I made a note of it earlier—ten o'clock, I believe we said. And we must remember that should a certain lady arrive sometime in the future, there is a child to consider, so I think we should take a look at the nurseries.'

It was a topic much discussed with all parties taking sides. Only Lisette said nothing, which was not unusual. No one asked her opinion directly but as Miss Araminta's personal maid they believed she was privy to all the information they craved. Lisette knew no more than they did about this mysterious woman Lord Jamie was supposed to have married, but if she did she would remain silent out of loyalty to her mistress.

'If the rumour about the woman is true,' Nancy said, suddenly flouncing into the kitchen and almost bumping into Mrs Stratton, 'then what can he have been thinking of to marry a woman no one has seen? The duke's heir at that.'

'Well, I am inclined to sympathise with the young woman,' Mrs Stratton said, 'since I, too, was widowed and left with a child to care for. If she is indeed Lord Jamie's wife, then the child will be the duke's heir and it is only right that he is treated as such and comes to Castonbury. She must be given the shelter of this house. Now come along, Mr Lumsden. My tea is getting cold.'

Bidding goodnight to Will and Nancy, Lisette sought her bed but she couldn't sleep. She couldn't stop thinking about her meeting with Colonel Montague. He commanded her attention, filled her thoughts, almost to the exclusion of all else. His attitude, his appearance, his movements, that dangerous velvety voice—all reeked of seduction.

She told herself it meant nothing, that she shouldn't make too much of it, that it could simply be that he'd found nothing more scintillating at Castonbury, no lady more enticing, with whom to spend his time. Yet her heart leapt one notch, one rung higher up the ladder of irrational hope, every time he appeared in Araminta's room. When she finally succumbed to sleep he even followed her into her dreams.

Entering her mistress's room the following morning Lisette wasn't really surprised to see her seated at her escritoire penning a note to Lord Bennington. The housemaid whose business it was to make the fire was on her way out. On seeing Lisette, Araminta got up, having folded and sealed the note.

'I want you to do something for me, Lisette,' she said, handing her the note. 'I've written to Antony and would like you to take this letter and give it to one of the grooms. Ask him to ride to Glebe Hall which is outside Hatherton. He is to deliver it in person to Lord Bennington and wait for a reply.'

Against her better judgement, Lisette did as her mistress asked, but she could not quell the apprehension that gripped her or the feeling that she was colluding in something that would come to no good.

Returning to her mistress's rooms to inform her that she had done as she had instructed, her heart did a somersault when Colonel Montague strolled in every bit as handsome and imposing in his dark, brooding way as she remembered.

Lisette was putting away the brushes, the comb, the curl papers and ribbons which littered the surface of the vanity. The smile on Colonel Montague's face, curving those firm, fascinating lips, was more than enough to make her drop the comb. A blush came quickly to her cheeks, mounting high as she experienced the sensation of being stripped naked by his bright blue gaze. Picking up the comb she inwardly swore that she would not give him the pleasure of knowing how flustered she felt.

His broad shoulders were encased in a brown hacking jacket and his calves in shiny black boots. Taking an arrogant stance against the hearth, one hand resting on the mantel, in daylight his features were as hard edged as they had been last night. He watched her go about her chores with lazy interest, his predator's smile still in place.

But no matter how many distractions Lisette heaped on Ross, he was not immune to the change in Araminta this morning. Her cheeks were flushed and her eyes overbright, and as he listened to her extol the equestrian merits of the locality, she seemed jumpy and apprehensive and avoided meeting his eyes. He frowned with a mixture of curiosity and concern.

'You do not seem yourself this morning, Araminta. Are you feeling unwell?'

Araminta glanced almost nervously across the room at Lisette and then back to her brother. She laughed a little nervously. 'I confess I have a headache—probably too much wine at the assembly. A good gallop is just what I need to take it away. I'll go and see if Phaedra would like to accompany us,' she said, crossing quickly to the door. 'She'll be most put out if she knows we've gone riding without her.'

When she'd gone Ross looked at Lisette, a concerned frown etched on his brow. She bustled about, dropping objects onto the dressing table and floor—a sure sign the nervous maid was in a taking over something.

'What is wrong with Araminta? It is clear that she is not herself this morning. Has something happened that I should know about?'

'As she said—too much wine at the assembly,' Lisette replied. His eyes were probing hers, looking for answers. She bent her head over her task lest he saw the anxiety in her eyes.

'As I recall she came home early from the Assembly Rooms. You would tell me if there was something wrong, wouldn't you, Miss Napier? My sister is wilful, her conduct sometimes borders on inappropriate. It seems a weakness of hers to get into scrapes. If she is up to something you can be certain it will be something foolish and outrageous, so I would like to know about it before it happens.'

'It is not my place. I am here to see to the needs of Miss Araminta, not to divulge her confidences—if she had any, that is.'

'Is she up to something?'

Lisette looked at him direct. 'Colonel Montague, when you employed me you asked for my discretion and my loyalty. I will not talk to you about Miss Araminta.'

'Even though it is my wish?'

'Even so.'

'That is a shame. I have the greatest reliance on your judgement.'

'Then you are to be disappointed. You must forgive me if I tell you I have nothing to say to you on this matter.'

'And you are the most wilful woman I have ever met, Miss Napier.'

Ross relinquished his stance and moved to the vanity where Lisette was placing things tidily in the drawers. He stood behind her, his silence more eloquent, more powerful, more successful in impinging on her senses than Araminta's garrulous chatter. She didn't know why she felt apprehensive at his attention, for after his sister's warning not to take men's admiration too seriously, she would like to simply smile and accept any compliments they paid her. But Colonel Montague was a man who could not be ignored.

'Be assured that if there is anything wrong with my sister, I shall find out.' She looked at him before turning her head and lowering her eyes so she would not have to look at his penetrating eyes. His firm lips curved in a slight smile. 'I enjoyed our conversation last night, Miss Napier,' he said on a softer note, raising a hand and gently tucking a loose strand of her hair behind her ear, 'and I can't tell you what a pleasure it would give me to invite you to ride with us this morning.'

Lisette stilled, shocked, then raised her head. 'Don't do that!' A warm glow suffused the area he'd touched.

'You're frowning—you look cross.'

Drawing herself up and taking a step back, she turned and fixed him with a censorious look. 'That's because I am cross. I must insist that you refrain from speaking to me unless it concerns Miss Araminta.'

Inwardly Ross stilled. He looked down into her disapproving eyes, distracted by myriad emotions playing in her expressive eyes. 'Why? Do you not feel comfortable when you are with me?'

'Something like that.'

'Are we talking about the feelings that I arouse in

you, Miss Napier? Come, tell me. I am all eager attention.'

'If you must know, then yes, that is exactly what I mean.'

Suppressing his urge to smile, Ross smoothed his expression into an admirable imitation of earnest gravity. 'Oh, dear—that bad.'

Her eyes searched his, then her lips compressed. 'Last night I should have left the stables when you arrived. There must be no more conversations between us like that. I have no desire to bring censure down on myself. People will gossip and, should it reach Mrs Landes-Fraser, I will be dismissed.'

'Heaven forbid it would go that far. I apologise if my attention offended you, but I did not force you to yield to me when I kissed you.'

No, Lisette thought. In all fairness he hadn't. It was as if some spell had been cast over her and she had wantonly, willingly joined in her own seduction.

'Let us assume I am not your employer,' Ross said, his voice soft and provocative, his eyes preoccupied with her rosy lips. 'How would you react to my advances then, Miss Napier? Would you fall into my arms and allow me to kiss you to distraction?'

Her delicate brows drew together and amusement teased the corners of her generous mouth as she surveyed him, considering her answer. 'Based on what I already know of you, I might very well be tempted,' she confessed, unable to deny the truth since he seemed to know her thoughts so well. 'But the fact remains that you *are* my employer and that is the trouble.'

'And I feel compelled to point out that an employee should never contradict her employer.'

'Whenever I find myself in your company you forget yourself. Is your lofty rank supposed to intimidate me, Colonel?' she asked in her quiet voice, a surprising hint of anger in it that Ross had never heard before. 'Because if so, then you are mistaken. I am the daughter of a gentleman, and my parents brought me up decently.'

His eyes narrowed on hers. 'Your parents brought you up in India, where the climate is hot and allied to a different culture. That makes you inescapably different to other English girls. You can't change what you are.'

'And what am I?' she asked bitterly. 'Do you presume that because I am a servant, I'm fair game to be seduced?'

'I do not, and nor do I wish to seduce you—at least, not this minute. If I had wished it, it would already have happened.'

Lisette gasped at his arrogance. But the potency of his desire could not be denied. 'I will not let it happen. You presume too much where I am concerned, Colonel.'

The words were low, laced with contempt, bitter with

an emotion Ross could not place. 'Do not doubt my needs, Lisette,' he chided softly with a lusty stare, as if he could read all that was in her mind. 'Or my intention of having you.'

'You rate yourself too highly, sir. I belong to no man. Please don't speak to me like this.'

His chuckles sounded low and deep. Her face gave no sign of softening. Even so, its beauty fed his gaze and created in his being a sweet, hungering ache that could neither be easily put aside nor sated with anything less than what he desired.

'We don't have to speak at all if that is what you want, Lisette. For myself I would prefer not to.' His gaze settled on her lips. His eyes darkened and his hands came up to frame her face. 'Forgive me but I have to do this.' Then, tilting her face up, his descended. When his lips touched hers, Lisette couldn't have quelled the shudder that passed through her had her life depended on it. Stunned, poised to resist, she mentally paused. Soft but sure, bringing sweetness and pleasure, they covered hers, moving slowly, languorously, as if savouring her taste, her texture.

His kiss was slow and deliberate, yet there was nothing threatening or hurried in his lips' caress. Indeed, it was beguiling, luring Lisette's senses. Her lips were soft and hot, and he pressed his mouth to hers as if drinking in her heat. As her lips began to respond, in some part of her mind a warning bell began to ring, but she was long past listening. His lips felt and tasted just as they had before. Unable to resist the temptation to return the pressure, she parted her lips, slowly exploring the sensations of delight that infused her as his lips played against hers. Growing lightheaded, she rested her hands on his chest to steady herself.

She was sweet and pliant, her body pressing willingly to his. Taking advantage of her weakening, untutored response, Ross slid his tongue between her lips, slowly, with his customary assured arrogance, quite certain of his expertise and his welcome. But he held the reins of his desire in a grip of iron and refused to let the demons loose. Primal instincts urged him on—experience held him back.

She was giving a little more of herself every time they met; he knew it, but in her heart, deep in her heart, where no one could hear it or know of its existence, a small wordless whisper was beginning to woo her. His male body yearned to go on, to satisfy itself as it had always done. He was thinking like a man who is intent on seduction, and he supposed he was—but in the back of his mind was the thought that she was not the kind of woman to be rushed.

Her desire, her passion, answered his call and he knew she would be his after a little tender persuasion. But there was no need for hurry. She was innocent, naive, untouched, unused to the demands of a man's hands. He would not go too fast, otherwise she would turn skittish and balk and then he would have to work harder to win her back. Passion lay heavy, languid, between them. He let it sink into her senses so she would not forget, and next time he would savour her slowly and it would be sweeter, for the end was never in doubt.

Raising his head he looked down into her flushed face. Her eyes slowly opened, then she blinked, and stared straight at him. He couldn't stop his rakish grin.

'What are you doing?' she whispered as his head bent to hers once more. 'It would take some explaining if your sister should come in and see us.' At this thought a hand seemed to grip her heart and panic streaked through her. Neatly she slipped away from him. To her relief he straightened and drew back, but his confident smile didn't waver.

'A man can speak to the woman he wants any way he chooses,' Ross said, his male arrogance edging his voice again, his lips quirking in a mirthless smile. 'This will happen. I promise you.'

A cold shiver went down her spine. The idea that he was amusing himself, without any real intent, died, slain by the look in his eyes. It was intense. It couldn't have been clearer had he put it into words. She knew it was wrong, and yet what he promised was so wickedly exciting, like nothing she had ever experienced before. That she was deeply attracted to this man was undeniably true, but she must not go blindly, emotionally rushing into what might have many pitfalls and would end in tears.

'I am not regretful about our kiss,' he went on, 'nor will I regret having you when the time comes.' She glared at the arrogance of this statement, but Ross forged ahead with what he'd intended to say in a calm, philosophical tone. 'I could say that you are blameless in all this, that what happens is not your will—but mine. But that wouldn't be true, would it?' He knew that as soon as he asked the question he wanted her to assure him that he spoke the truth, that he didn't want her to deny that she'd felt all the things he had in their kiss, or that she wanted him almost as much as he wanted her. As if he suddenly needed to test her honesty and his instincts, he persisted, 'Isn't that right?'

Lisette didn't want to make it easy for him, nor to let him think she was so dazzled by his masculinity that she was almost drowning in her own pleasure as the wanton sensations ran through her body at his every touch, but she was unable to tell a lie.

'Yes!' The word burst out of her, without shame but filled with a thousand other feelings Ross couldn't identify.

'Yes?' he repeated, while a heady sensation of relief burst within him. 'Then I am not wrong.'

It was not the tone of relief in his voice that made her answer. It was, instead, her sudden memories of the way he had kissed her, memories of his incredible combined gentleness and passion. Added to that was the memory of her own urgent desire to experience more than his kiss, to become a part of him, at one with him, to expand on the exquisite sensations he was making her feel. She opened her mouth to utter a denial to his statement, but her conscience strangled the words in her throat. She had found glory, not shame, in their kiss, and she could not make herself lie to him and say otherwise.

'It was not my will for this to happen between us,' she answered in a muffled whisper. Dragging her mortified gaze from his blue gaze, she turned her head away and added, 'but once I was in your arms, it was not my will to leave them either.'

She had looked away, so she didn't see the new tenderness in his slow smile.

Forbidding herself to linger for fear of getting caught up in him again, she picked up one of her mistress's gowns that needed ironing and, draping it over her arm, she left the room.

Still smiling, Ross watched her go. Beneath her plain servant's garb, Lisette Napier was a natural temptress, alluring and provocative, with the slender body of a goddess, the smile of an angel and an unspoiled charm that made him smile whenever he thought of her. She was warm and lovely and as elusive as a butterfly. He couldn't get her out of his mind—the taste of her, the feel of her, the heady scent of her, wreathed his senses. He had given up trying to understand the reasons why he wanted her.

He did, and that was reason enough.

The following morning, pleased with a diversion from her duties, accompanied by Faith and Daisy, Lisette set off to walk into Castonbury village to purchase some yarns. It was a happy trio that sauntered along the High Street, pausing now and then to gaze into the shop windows and to watch a stagecoach deposit its passengers at the Rothermere Arms.

Unfortunately Mrs Hall's shop from which Lisette was to make her purchases was closed. In the bow window where an array of colourful ribbons and yarns were on display, there was a notice saying Mrs Hall had been called away and that she would be back within the hour. Faith and Daisy had to hurry back but Lisette said she would wait. Her companions left her sitting on a bench near St Mary's Church to await the shop's opening.

By the time she had made her purchases and started on the mile journey back to Castonbury Park, rain clouds were gathering. Heavy spots soon became a downpour. Finding shelter under a large oak tree she settled down to wait for the rain to abate.

In the distance a horse and rider appeared from the direction of the house. The rider's tall figure was outlined against the sky, a liver-and-white hound in his wake. It was Colonel Montague. Lisette was conscious of the sudden tension and nervousness in her as he drew closer. There was nowhere to hide. After their encounter the previous day, she didn't know how to behave towards him.

Holding her basket containing her small purchases in front of her, she drew herself up straight as he came closer, dismounted and strode towards her. He tossed his tall hat on the horn of his saddle, water dripping from his long riding cape. For one wild, unreasoning moment Lisette's life flared into vivid, lively colour. All the drab routine that had become her life faded away.

'Well, this is a pleasant surprise, Miss Napier,' he said, and there was a touch of irony in his tone. He bowed, smiling at her from deep blue eyes. A dimple in his cheek was deeply and wickedly cleft as he stood before her. The memory of their last encounter rose between them, intangible but strong. Taking a deep breath she tried to stifle her rising emotions. Colonel Montague somehow always caught her at her most vulnerable.

With an effort she said in a voice that she hoped sounded matter-of-fact, 'Good day, Colonel Montague.'

He raised one well-defined eyebrow, watching her. A faint half-smile now played on his lips as if he knew exactly what was going on in her mind. 'I never expected to see you here. What are you doing?'

'Exactly what it looks like. I am sheltering from the rain under this tree,' she replied primly, resenting his effect on her, the masculine assurance of his bearing. But she was conscious of an unwilling excitement, seeing him arrogantly mocking, and recklessly attractive. Here they were, just the two of them, together sheltering from the rain under a tree, in an atmosphere bristling with tension and subdued emotions.

Ross's eyes did a quick sweep of her lightweight dark grey dress and summer bonnet. 'I would advise you to wear something more substantial the next time you decide to walk into the village when rain is threatening.'

'There was no sign of rain when I set out. Unfortunately the proprietor of the shop from which I wanted to purchase some items was gone on an errand and I had to wait for it to open. Daisy and Faith had duties at the house and were unable to wait, so as you see, Colonel, I am quite alone.'

Ross gazed down into those brilliant amber eyes and that entrancing face. His decision to have her no matter how much trouble she put him to had now become an unshakable resolution. A slow, admiring smile drifted across his face as he said, 'Then you must forgive me if I take advantage of the situation and use the time to enjoy your company and to savour the anticipation of what is to come—although I am becoming heartily tired of the wait.'

'Then you will have to learn to curb your impatience, Colonel, for the weather is hardly conducive for a romantic tryst. If you do not agree with me, perhaps you should cool your ardour and step back out into the rain.'

Ross bit back a laugh, trying to keep his eyes off the alluring display of her breasts rising and falling beneath her gown. 'I observed you were not alone when you left the house. I saw the other two return without you.'

Lisette was not unaware of the possessive gleam in his blue eyes as they roved over her, or that he was bent on charming her again today. 'How observant you are, Colonel. Were you looking for me?'

'I was concerned.'

'Oh, I see. I suppose I should be honoured,' she said coolly, 'but as you see I am quite all right. I'm sure you have better things to do with your time than to come looking for me.'

'On the contrary. Your failure to show up with the other two gave me the perfect excuse to come looking for you.'

'And do you need an excuse, sir?'

'No, I don't.'

His devilish gaze that gleamed into hers touched a quickness within her, and she quickly averted her gaze. 'Had I known you were about, I would have sought a different tree—one with a trunk stout enough to hide behind.'

Ross grinned and stretched out a hand to smooth a strand of hair from her face. 'Ah, Miss Napier, do you fear me?'

Lisette straightened indignantly and pushed his hand away. 'It is only that I prefer not to be mauled and ogled as you seem to have a penchant for doing. Your eyes betray the path of your mind,' she accused him brusquely. 'It is rude to stare so openly.'

'I was admiring you.' The blue eyes glowed, and his grin was almost taunting. 'You are an extremely beautiful young woman, and like most men I always admire beauty.'

'You are bold, sir,' she scolded. 'I feel ravished every time you look at me.'

Ross's grin grew almost into a leer. 'You read my thoughts well, Miss Napier. Frequently I have fantasies of you naked in my arms.'

Lisette blushed scarlet. There was still so much of the girl in her at war with the young woman, and this man had the knack of bringing it quickly to the surface. 'It would seem that the kisses you stole from me have hardly cooled your lusts.'

'Not at all,' he confided lightly. 'Indeed, it has done much to stir them.'

When he would have come closer, Lisette placed her hand pointedly on his chest, stopping him in his tracks. 'Try to restrain yourself, sir,' she cautioned. 'I am returning from an errand to the village, not to seeking a secret rendezvous with you. Now I wonder if it is safe to stay until the rain has stopped. You seem never satisfied.'

Ross's eyes burned behind his dark lashes. 'Aye, you tempt me sorely, Miss Napier. But I would not wish you to get a drenching on account of my *lusts*.'

Lisette faced him squarely, meeting his gaze, even now feeling prey to that hawkish stare. 'Then will you behave?'

'Although your nearness tests me sorely, I promise I will try.'

'Thank you. That is kind of you.'

'Contrary to what you may think of me, I have been known to be kind on occasion.' Laugh lines appeared at the corners of his eyes, though he did not smile. 'But I confess I am not being kind just now.'

'Yes, I know, and it is not going to work.'

He tried to look innocent. 'What isn't going to work?'

'This blatant attempt to charm me into yielding another kiss—and other such tactics.'

'I know you are far too intelligent to be fooled by charm and trickery, Miss Napier. I use the only weapon I have.'

'Persuasion?'

'Temptation—if I can.'

For all her annoyance with him, Lisette knew it wouldn't be too difficult for him to tempt her into his arms. She was very much aware of everything about him, of the long, strong lines of his body, of the skin of his exposed neck, tanned and healthy. She tried to change her thoughts, finding her emotions unsettling. The dog that accompanied him bounded up and whimpered and sniffed about her feet. 'What a lovely animal,' she said, bending down. There was a note of affection in her voice as she patted the dog's head, fondling its ears.

Carelessly her hand brushed his when he grasped the dog's collar to drag him back. She felt a sudden stillness envelop them. Vividly aware of the damp scent of the wet grass, she was still overwhelmingly conscious of the man facing her. Confused, she straightened and looked away. She was irritated by the way in which he had skilfully cut through her superior attitude, the artificial posturing she had assumed to save herself from him. But the magnetic attraction still remained beneath all the irritation.

He cocked an eye at her; a sudden burst of light through the clouds flickered over his thick black hair outlining his devilishly attractive face. Then a full smile touched his lips. 'I imagine you are cross with me, Miss Napier—for taking advantage of you yesterday.'

'And the time before that,' she said with sudden impudent defiance as she tried to fight the power of his charm. He seemed amused as he studied her. She saw the twinkle in his eye, the twist of humour about his beautiful mouth.

'I don't recall you raising any objections to my kissing you at the time. There are more discomforting and less civilised experiences than kissing, Miss Napier.'

'And you would know that, would you, Colonel Montague?'

'I know that in a smart gathering of civilised beings, there run many dangerous and treacherous undercurrents, like dark, bottomless pools. The women, with their little jealousies and intrigues, have much warmongering amongst them, weaving webs of deceit.'

'And what are the gentlemen doing while the ladies are warmongering, Colonel?'

'Trying to better the next man, with their pious, self-righteous condemnation.'

Lisette was surprised at his speech, at the cynicism

of its content, then, seeing the teasing expression in his startling blue eyes, allowed the rich peals of laughter to escape from her throat.

'I do believe you jest with me, Colonel—quite an unexpected pleasure from one of such rank as yourself.'

He stared at her, liking the sound of her laughter. 'I am glad you see it as a pleasure, Miss Napier. You see I am not an ogre. You should know that by now.'

'I never thought you were.'

'And good manners would prevent you from saying so.'

'No, sir. The fact that you are my employer,' she replied candidly. 'Should I verbally abuse you in such a manner, I would find myself without a job, which is why, where you are concerned, I must tread with caution—even if you are unmannerly at times,' she added, the little smile playing about her lips mischievous.

Quite undaunted, a dazzling smile broke the determined line of his mouth and he stepped closer to her, looking down into her lovely, upturned face and capturing her eyes. 'Why? Because I stole a kiss or two? I never pretend to be anything other than what I am, but you, Miss Napier, are indeed a most attractive woman.'

Vividly conscious of her proximity to him, Lisette again placed a hand on his chest to hold him back before he could realise just how much he affected her. 'You're not going to kiss me again, are you, Colonel?'

Ross glanced down at the small, delicate hand laid upon his chest—heat was seeping through his clothes, desire already tightening his loins—and that with only her hand upon his chest. 'Reluctantly no—not unless you want me to. If so, I would willingly oblige.'

She sent him an admonishing look and dropped her hand. 'I have no doubt that you would, but no. It is not appropriate. Besides, it has almost stopped raining. I really should be getting back. Your sister will wonder where I have got to.'

'I will walk with you.'

'No—I would prefer it if you didn't.' She was quick to reply. 'Should we be seen together by any one of the servants, they would assume that I have caught your eye and that I dally where I should not.' She straightened her bonnet and stepped into the open. 'Now, I must be on my way so I will bid you good day, sir.'

Araminta was in a frenzied state of excitement as she paced her room waiting for the reply to her letter to Antony Bennington. It was just before luncheon when the reply was delivered directly to her. Tearing it open she held her breath as she read her beloved's words.

'Well?' Lisette asked, unable to bear the suspense a moment longer. 'What does he say?'

'Oh, Lisette, he wants to meet me tomorrow.'

'Where? Is he to come here?'

'Oh, no, that would never do. He asks me to meet him at the Dog and Partridge Inn on the Manchester Road.'

Lisette was more than a little scandalised to think that Lord Bennington should have suggested such a thing. 'And how far is that?'

'About five miles.'

'But you can't possibly. And anyway, it's out of the question that you go alone.'

'Of course I must. I refuse to have a groom tagging along watching everything I do and reporting back to Ross.' Araminta held the note to her breast and closed her eyes, whirling and twirling around the room. 'Oh, Lisette, just think. This time tomorrow Antony and I will be together. I can't wait to see him.' On seeing Lisette's frown of disapproval she scowled. 'I'm going, Lisette, and nothing you can say will put me off.'

Seeing the stubborn set of Araminta's chin, Lisette switched her tactics. 'Miss Araminta, please—think of your brother. What will he say if he finds out?'

Araminta hesitated, feeling the force of her brother's unwaveringly cold stare as if it were this minute focused upon her. She drew a long breath, then expelled it slowly. 'I am going, Lisette, and that is that. Not a word to anyone. I shall be back long before dinner. This morning's ride has given me an appetite. After luncheon I want you to get your bonnet and we will take a walk. I'm far too excited to remain cooped up in the house all day.'

Often when Araminta was on edge, irritable over nothing, bored and inclined to sigh with tedious regularity, Lisette would get their coats and bonnets and together they would walk into nearby Castonbury village to browse in the shops or climb the hills to take in the breathtaking views.

The terrain on the hillsides was often difficult, hostile to those unused to it, but Lisette loved it and felt the weight of her spirits lighten. She loved the freedom, the wind blowing off the moors and the scattered sheep and the rain that came from the west, the clouds breaking above the peaks that separated Derbyshire from Yorkshire.

The morning's rain had blown away, so it was windy but warm and sunny when they set out for their walk that afternoon. It had been Lisette's turn to choose the direction they would take today and she had chosen to walk round the lake. Araminta was in blue, the colour of speedwell, her bonnet perched on the back of her head, allowing the arrangement of her ringlets to be seen.

While they remained in full view of the house they walked as sedately as possible, but with the precincts of the house behind them, the decorum was thrown off. Picking up their skirts, they ran along the path before leaving it and winding their way through the trees. At one point, quite breathless, they stopped with their backs leaning against a tree and looked up through the branches that showed a spattering of blue.

'How lovely,' Araminta remarked, her eyes shining and her face flushed from her exertions.

'Why is it that running is considered most unlady-like?' Lisette said. 'Men run, so why not women?'

'I don't know, but it's fun. Come along, Lisette, I'll race you to the bridge.'

It was their girlish laughter ringing out from across the lake that drew the attention of the two riders. They were completely unaware that they were being watched by two gentleman on horseback who had been checking on the work being done in the park and paused on their way back to the stables to observe the two girls.

'That girl with Araminta, Ross. Who is she?' Giles enquired with a curious frown.

'Lisette Napier. Araminta's maid.'

'The girl from India?'

Ross glanced at him. 'You know?'

Giles gave him a wry look. 'This is Castonbury, Ross. Nothing is secret, as you know. Araminta tells me you both arrived at the same time in London.'

'True. We sailed from India with the East India fleet. She was on the *Portland*. Miss Napier's parents died of the cholera out there. Without means she was forced to seek employment.'

'She's an attractive girl. I expect there isn't a male servant either indoors or out who wouldn't like to get to know her better. By the way, I think you should know that Father received a letter from Alicia.'

Ross turned and looked at him. 'I see. Have you communicated with her since I saw her?'

'No. I meant to, but with Father being like he is, he forbade it until he has given the matter more thought. I've told him that we can't go on avoiding the issue forever. She isn't going to go away and something has to be done about the child.'

'What does she want?'

Giles gave him a wry look. 'Money. What else? She states that she is quite destitute and she will soon have to move out of her lodgings unless her situation changes for the better. Of course, she put great emphasis on the child, stressing that it isn't right that Jamie's son is being kept in abject poverty when he is heir to such a vast estate as Castonbury Park.'

'If she is indeed Jamie's widow, then she does have a point. On the other hand, until we hear from Harry you might be wise to stall her a while longer.'

'I know. And until Father agrees to it, I cannot give her a penny piece.'

They fell silent and continued to watch as Araminta

and Miss Napier headed for the bridge that spanned the narrow part of the upper and lower lakes. Suddenly the wind gusted strongly, loosening the bow that kept Miss Napier's purple bonnet in place and whipping it from her head.

'Oh, my goodness,' Lisette shrieked, decorum forgotten as she watched it soar into the air and be carried by the wind towards the lake. Indeed, even if decorum had been remembered it would have been ignored, for the sheer joy of running had her in its grip as she sprinted like a whippet towards the bridge with Araminta in pursuit of her bonnet.

The two girls paused in the middle of the bridge to look down with variable degrees of interest at the cascade of water that flowed from one lake to the next. The bonnet was bobbing about on the swirling water. Without thought, and certainly with no concern for what she was about to do, with the agility of a mountain goat, Lisette ran off the bridge to the water's edge. Kicking off her shoes and bunching up her skirts, she waded into the water towards the bonnet. Araminta followed, her face split into a huge grin of enjoyment, shouting her encouragement in a most unladylike way, wishing it were she who had the pluck to kick off her shoes to forge into the lake.

Ross and Giles stared in astonishment. Giles's face was a study of mixed emotions—incredulity and amusement, indicating that he'd never seen the like before. But as Ross watched Lisette wade towards the swirling water beneath the fast-flowing cascade, his expression turned rock hard as a suspended memory broke free and he recalled another time, another place and a raging river.

'Oh, my God! The little fool!'

His breath left his body and immediately he vaulted out of the saddle, already stripping off his jacket as he broke into a run, racing towards the bridge, more frightened than he had ever been in his life. In the space of one second, rage replaced his fear—rage that she had terrified him with her stupid recklessness.

Reaching out for her precious bonnet, the water from the cascade sprayed up in a shimmer into Lisette's face. As her fingers made contact with it, the wind was loosening the pins that held her hair in place, and she stumbled. Regaining her balance she turned to laugh in dismay as her skirts slipped from her clutching fingers, trailing in the water, her plait snaking loose and falling down her back.

'Goodness, it's cold,' she gasped. Reaching the bank she stumbled and slithered on the smooth mossy stones beneath the water. From nowhere a shadow appeared or so it seemed. She looked up, her eyes like stars in her face flushed with joyful laughter.

'What the hell do you think you're doing?' Ross demanded. With long, powerful strides he swooped down on her like Satan in his entire frightening wrath. The sound of her voice broke his angry reasoning, and with it went the terrible speculation, which for several moments had filled him with panic. It was as though something infinitely precious had been restored to him.

'You little fool! You stupid girl! You could have drowned.' Lisette lifted her head and blithely looked at him with that long, unblinking stare of hers, seeing the concern in his eyes. A smile was on her soft mouth, her colour gloriously high. But what Ross noticed, as he gazed at her, was the look in those liquid amber eyes. They were imploring him to soften, to smile at her. His mindless terror gave way and his expression softened.

Lisette stepped from the water, letting her skirts fall and slipping her wet stocking feet into her shoes. 'I'm sorry if I frightened you. I only went in to retrieve my bonnet. I wasn't in any danger.'

'With the amount and force of the water pouring into the lake from above, didn't you realise the current could have dragged you under?'

'It didn't occur to me,' she confessed, 'but I'm an excellent swimmer. I was perfectly safe and I don't think I did anything wrong.'

'Neither did the keeper's dog that drowned here some years back!' he said quietly.

'I'm so sorry about that,' she said, aware that Araminta

had frozen into stillness, her face a picture of bewilderment and alarm as she stared at her brother. Never had she seen him so affected by anything. 'I really am sorry if I frightened you. Truly I am.'

In silence, Ross gazed down at her smiling, upturned face. 'You're not afraid of anything, are you?'

'I'm not afraid of the water—or you,' she announced blithely. She was deeply touched by how alarmed he'd seemed. His voice had been hoarse with concern when he'd appeared in front of her, his face ravaged with worry as he had called her a little fool.

'I'm glad,' he said. 'I wouldn't want you to be.' He looked down at her dripping skirts, trying to ignore how delectable she looked with damp tendrils of hair clinging to her face. 'Go and change your clothes.'

## Chapter Six

When Ross had finally regained some of his composure, retrieving his jacket from where he'd tossed it, shrugging himself back into it he turned to his horse and swung himself up into the saddle.

Stupefied, Giles stared at him, thoroughly amused. It was unbelievable that Ross, who always had absolute control over his emotions, who treated women with a combination of indifference, amused tolerance and indulgence, could have been driven to such an uncharacteristic outburst of feelings by a mere maid. It was clear that Miss Napier's behaviour and imminent drowning had both alarmed and terrified him.

In stark contrast, instead of the haughty disdain one would expect to see on Giles's face, he had regarded Miss Napier from atop his horse with laughing admiration. In his opinion Ross's reaction had been a bit over the top. The water beneath the cascade wasn't deep and Giles didn't believe Miss Napier had been in any danger of drowning. Noting that Ross's eyes were still fixed on the young maid, rather than wait for an explanation he plunged right in.

'At the risk of intruding into your thoughts, Cousin, might I ask why you came down so hard on Miss Napier? As you tore yourself away from your horse, your thoughts appeared to be damnably unpleasant—in fact, the look on your face told me you were going for blood, no less.'

'I was,' he ground out in an attempt to conceal the terror that had almost consumed him when he feared she was in danger of being swept away. 'What a damned reckless and irresponsible thing to do—to go wading into the lake like that—after a bonnet!'

Giles gave him a laughing, sidelong look. 'Come now, Ross. When we were boys, did we not throw ourselves from that very bridge—times too numerous to count—into the cascade? We came to no harm—and I have to say that Miss Napier looked more than capable of taking care of herself.'

Ross threw him a black look. 'It can be hazardous. Even when the water looks calm there are eddies there. But I didn't realise you were being so observant, Giles,' he growled with a hint of mockery.

Giles's chuckling merriment could not be restrained and he laughed out loud. 'No more than you, Coz. After all, Araminta tells me that when she mentioned she was seeking a maid of her own, you were the one to recommend Miss Napier. I have to say that she has been blessed with the most incredible looks. With your reputation for the ladies—the dark and dusky maidens of India in particular, Ross—I can see perfectly well why you are attracted to her.'

Ross's frown was formidable. 'It depends on one's taste—which is something we never did agree upon—although,' he said with a reluctant smile, his mood returning to normal, 'I do agree that your Lily is quite perfect.'

Giles's features softened, as they never failed to do when his beloved Lily was mentioned. 'I agree with you absolutely.'

They rode on in companionable silence, following Araminta and Miss Napier at a steady pace. Ross turned his thoughts to what had just happened. It proved that Miss Napier's courage, her sense of adventure and of rebellion against the satin chain which bound her set her apart from her contemporaries. How many of the housemaids would have had the nerve to kick off their shoes and wade into the lake to retrieve their bonnet?

In fascination he watched the sway of the thick, shining black pigtail which hung down Miss Napier's back, and the movement of her hips as she walked over the grass with lithe, liquid movements—like a dancer, he thought…. In some far corner of his thoroughly distracted brain memories stirred and his pulse gave a wild leap of recognition.

And then, in that brief flash of time, like an arrow thudding into his heart, he stilled as troubled memories flooded back. An image drifted into his mind, of a girl in a star-spangled sari, a veil drawn over her hair—a shining black pigtail exposed to the sun.

Ross continued to follow her, his mind in turmoil, convinced there must be some mistake. There had to be.

'Wait,' he called. Both Miss Napier and Araminta stopped and turned to look back at him. Ross addressed his cousin but without taking his eyes off Lisette. 'There is something I have to say to Miss Napier, Giles. Take Araminta back to the house. I'll be along shortly.'

With a puzzled frown and no questions asked, Giles dismounted. Looking at Lisette, Araminta was about to protest when Giles took her arm, but after taking one look at her brother's formidable features, she allowed Giles to lead her away.

Alone now, Ross rode closer to Lisette, pulling Bengal to a halt just a few feet away. His eyes became fixed on her upturned face. She said nothing, nor did she move. She stood quite still, looking at him with wide, startled eyes.

'Tell me something. When your parents died I recall you telling me that you were living near Delhi.'

'Yes, Colonel, that is correct,' she replied, feeling slightly uncomfortable beneath his penetrating blue gaze. 'But I cannot see what that has to do with me wading into the lake just now.'

'Can you not, Miss Napier?' he said tightly. 'I can. Tell me, what did you do? How did you travel to Bombay—an English girl alone?'

'I travelled with others who were going south. Sometimes I walked and sometimes I was offered a lift in a bullock cart.'

'As an English girl?'

She looked at him, nervous now, clutching her wet bonnet to her chest. He remembered her. Suddenly her whole existence had shrunk, narrowed, until there was nothing but this moment—bright sunshine, the man looking down at her. 'No. For my own protection and to be less conspicuous I passed myself off as a native girl. In a land of many tongues and races, it was easier than I had feared to conceal my identity—and I speak both Hindi and Urdu.'

'How fortunate for you, and because of your colouring you resembled a native girl.'

'Yes.'

He was watching her now, his gaze intense. 'Did you travel south in a bridal party—in the retinue of the Rajah Jahana Sumana of the state of Rhuna, who had a daughter by the name of Messalina?'

'Yes,' she replied quietly.

'And when you left the bridal party, did you have to cross swollen rivers on your journey to Bombay?'

'All rivers in India become swollen during the monsoon. You should know that, Colonel.'

'But did you ever fall into a swollen river?'

With some consternation she looked away. 'Yes.'

'And how did you get out?'

'Someone—someone saved me.'

'A British officer?'

'Yes.'

'How did he save you?'

Lisette felt the net draw tight, felt paralysis set in as his predator's senses focused on her. It was as if the world stopped spinning, as if some impenetrable shield closed about them, so that there was nothing but her and him—and whatever it was that held them.

'He—he—'

Ross sprang from his horse and went to her, and taking her upper arms he stared hard into her face. 'He?'

She nodded. 'Yes.'

'And did the two of you by any chance spend the entire night marooned on a sandbank?'

She looked at him and searched his eyes, but couldn't read his thoughts beyond the fact that he was considering her. 'Yes,' she whispered.

'And in the morning you left your rescuer?'

'Yes,' she answered, her voiced strained. 'Yes, I did. It was unforgivable of me.'

'Why?' he demanded. 'Because you didn't thank him for saving your life?'

'Yes.'

He just stared at her. 'Well, well,' he said at length. 'So, it was you. I cannot believe that after all this time… I would not have believed it possible. Did it not occur to you how worried I might be, that I thought you might have been swept away by the river while I slept?'

Lisette's heart almost broke as she stared at him. It had never occurred to her that what had happened to her would affect him so deeply.

'Why did you go? Tell me that?' Taking her chin between his fingers, he forced her to look at him, the expression in his eyes suddenly grave. 'And do not play games with me. It is not kind, Lisette. Tell me.'

'I don't want to go over it. I can't.'

'I *need* to know,' he insisted forcefully. 'Can't you understand that? Not knowing what happened to you tortured me. I thought you were dead. It was not until I reached the bank and saw your footprints in the mud that I realised you were alive.'

'I'm sorry,' she cried. 'I didn't know. I left because I wanted to avoid any awkwardness—any questions— and…and you had made your intentions quite clear what you would demand of me later.'

'And what was that?' he asked softly. 'Remind me.'

'I recall you telling me you intended "bedding" me. I believe that was the term you used.'

'And you left me stranded because I said that?'

'You weren't exactly stranded. The river had fallen during the night and it was a simple matter to reach the bank.'

'As an English girl alone, I can understand why you disguised yourself as a native girl—easier that way, fewer questions asked—but did it not occur to you that as a British officer I was in a position to help you reach Bombay safely?'

'No—no, it didn't.' Tears filled her eyes. It was the one reaction Ross was not prepared for and it not only disconcerted him but left him feeling helpless. 'I was alone. I did not wish to draw attention to myself. When I left Delhi I was desperate. My parents were dead. I thought I would die of grief and loneliness. Messalina— she was my friend and was to journey to Bhopal to marry a prince. She suggested I travel with her part of the way. Her father was always kind to me and he agreed.' Gazing up at him a sorrowful look entered her eyes. 'On the dock—in London—you didn't know me.' A tear trailed down her cheek. Ross was ashamed because he hadn't recognised her, but he had never forgotten the Indian girl whose life he had saved—and thank goodness he had. 'I didn't expect you to.'

'No, I didn't, but I knew as soon as I laid eyes on you that there was something familiar about you—I just couldn't remember. How could I? The night we spent in the middle of the river was pitch-black, and when I'd seen you previous to that, I truly thought you were a native girl. My abiding picture of you was from the first time I saw you with the bridal party. I thought you were the Princess Messalina's sister.'

'She doesn't have a sister.'

'I didn't know that. Only seeing you from a distance I never saw your face. You talked to those in your own party and I did not have reason to address you. I just looked at you, sitting with the princess, wearing costly silks over your dark hair, the lower half of your face veiled. And then I moved on. I did not see you again until the river.'

'Then—just now when you called me back? How did you know?'

'You have a way of walking that is distinctive—like a dancer. It suddenly came to me who you were. Why in heaven's name didn't you tell me who you were, Lisette?'

'When we met in London I almost did, but something held me back. Later, when you suggested that I work for your sister, I considered it prudent not to remind you. I wanted the work rather badly, you see. Knowing who I was could only complicate matters between us.'

Ross was suddenly aware of a disturbing mixture of emotions that he did not wish to analyse just then. 'Go and change, Lisette. We'll talk about this later.'

Backing away from him she gave him one last look. 'Yes. If you will excuse me, Colonel, I have duties to attend to. You sister will be wondering what has happened to me.'

'As I did on the night you left me.' His eyes darkened with memory. Lisette saw the warm glow within their depths and was suddenly afraid that because of that night his attempts to seduce her might become more intense.

'Nothing happened between us, Colonel. Let us just say we became caught up in the moment. You saved my life. I am grateful to you and that is all,' she said, pressing home her point with calm reason. 'It was nothing.'

'Obviously.'

'We both survived, didn't we?'

'Yes.'

'Well, then, there is no reason why we have to mention it again, is there?' she demanded with a soft, beguiling smile.

She had neatly managed to put him in a position of either agreeing with her or else, by disagreeing, admitting that she had been more to him than a flirtation in the middle of a raging river.

Ross let her go, trying to come to terms with what

he now knew—that she was the woman he had risked his life for. Coincidence or fate, the knowledge put a whole new slant on his relationship with Lisette Napier.

The following morning Lisette rose to the sound of howling wind. Heavy rain clouds raced across the sky and a yellowish light seemed to shroud the land. She begged and pleaded with Araminta to cancel her assignation with Lord Bennington, but the girl remained deaf to her entreaties.

And so Lisette watched her go and waited in a state of acute apprehension for her to return. The day wore on and the rain played havoc with her nerves. Lightning streaked across the sky, illuminating the entire room, and thunder boomed until the windows shook. Lisette closed her eyes and prayed Araminta would come back soon.

When the gong sounded for dinner she jumped. Araminta still hadn't come home. That was the moment she was no longer able to sit and wait passively. Worried for her safety—fearing she might have been thrown from her horse in the storm and be lying in a ditch somewhere, Lisette did the only thing she could. She made her way to Colonel Montague's room feeling as if she were going to her execution.

Ross was about to go down to dinner when there was a small tap on the door.

'Who is it, Blackstock?'

'It's me,' Lisette murmured, moving towards him, a worried look on her face.

Lisette was the last person he'd expected to see and he sensed quite rightly that she had come on behalf of his sister and that it had nothing to do with what had transpired between them the day before.

Looking from one to the other, Will hesitated. When Ross gestured with his head that he should make himself scarce, he nodded and went out with a knowing smile. Will had sharp eyes. Nothing much escaped him, and he knew the colonel had taken a bit of a shine to Miss Napier. Not that there was anything wrong with that, and not that anything could come of it mind—with their difference in status—but there was no harm in a little dalliance to pass the time, if the lady was willing like.

When Blackstock had left, Lisette hesitantly broke the news to Ross of Araminta's assignation with Lord Bennington. As he listened she observed his reaction, saw his jaw clench so tightly that a muscle began to throb in his cheek. Gradually his face became so outraged that fearing he might lash out at her she took a step back.

'And you say she went alone—without even a groom in attendance?'

'Yes,' Lisette whispered.

Ross stared at her, his eyes boring into her. In frigid silence he accused her of complicity and treachery. He swallowed the oath that sprang to his lips, swallowed the wave of anger at the thought that Lisette had allowed Araminta to go galloping off alone to who knew where for a liaison with Antony Bennington.

His temper, a true Montague temper, was never a wise thing to stir. Right now it was prowling, a hungry wolf seeking blood. If anyone had harmed his sister, that equated to an act of aggression against him, and the experienced soldier concealed beneath the veneer of an elegant gentleman reacted and responded appropriately.

His eyes narrowed to dark blue shards. Lisette lowered her head. 'Look at me, damn it! Where did they arrange to meet?'

'At the Dog and Partridge Inn on the Manchester Road.'

Unable to quell the cauldron of emotions that were seething inside him, his fury escaped him—it vibrated around her. 'This is insane!' His anger scorched her. 'You knew what she intended and yet you let her go?'

'No,' she cried as he began tearing off his jacket. 'I tried to stop her—I begged her not to go, truly, but her head was set. She refused to listen to reason.'

'You do not have the slightest concept of the importance of appropriate behaviour. If you had you would have tried harder to dissuade her or come to me. *I* would have talked her out of it,' he flared, stalking to his dressing room and returning with the first riding jacket he could lay his hands on. Thrusting his arms in the sleeves he dragged on his boots over his evening trousers. 'I *knew* she was up to something yesterday. That girl hasn't a grain of sense or propriety, jaunting all over the countryside in this weather. I swear I'll strangle young Bennington with my bare hands if any harm has come to her.'

Lisette went with him to the door. 'Is there anything I can do, anything…?'

'I think you've done enough,' he snapped. Suddenly he turned and faced her. 'Does anyone else know about this?'

'Just the young groom who rode to Glebe Hall to deliver the note to Lord Bennington.'

'What was his name?'

'Jacob.'

'I'll speak to him.' He walked on. 'Instruct Lumsden to offer my apologies to Aunt Wilhelmina for our absence at dinner and say that we have made other arrangements.'

'What will you do?'

Turning to look at her, his expression became more forbidding than before. 'Find her, and when I do she will feel the full force of my displeasure. That I promise you. My compliments to you, Miss Napier,' he reprimanded contemptuously, 'on your duplicity, your deceit and your disloyalty.'

Lisette's heart wrenched with pain at the unfairness of the accusations he flung at her. 'Colonel, please,' she implored, taking a few hesitant steps towards him. 'Your sister deeply regrets separating herself from Lord Bennington and desperately wants to make amends.'

Ross started towards her, his expression threatening. 'If Araminta wanted to see him, then she should have approached me. I would have dealt with the matter myself and paid young Bennington a visit, which would have been the appropriate action to take. What she has done goes way beyond the bounds of propriety,' he uttered scathingly.

Lisette began talking faster as she automatically backed away. 'But you must try to see it from her perspective—'

'Must?' he interrupted scathingly, his eyes hard and contemptuous. 'I think you are getting above yourself, Miss Napier. If you are wise,' he said in a soft, blood-chilling voice, 'in the future you will avoid me very carefully, and if you collude with my sister in anything as outrageous as this again, then you will find yourself looking for another position. Is that clear?'

In stunned silence Lisette watched him stride swiftly along the landing and bound down the stairs. She felt frozen inside, her mind blank. Upon her soul, she had never been spoken to in such a harsh and brutal way. Unable to form any coherent thought she left the colonel's room, too dazed, too numb to think or feel, but she could hear over and over again, the words Colonel Montague had so cruelly flung at her—*duplicity, deceit and disloyalty*...and dismissal.

Like a moth blundering in the lamplight, she stumbled her way through the maze of the house's many corridors, her only instinct guiding her to the refuge of her own bedchamber. Once inside the privacy of her room, she closed the door behind her and clamped her hands over her ears, but it was a futile gesture. She could still hear the colonel's words ringing in her ears, muted only by her own sobs as her heart fractured into tiny pieces.

Thunder clouds, dark grey and menacing, raced across the sky and a leaden curtain of drenching rain descended on Ross. Shrouded in his greatcoat and gritting his teeth, by the time the family sat down to dinner at Castonbury Park, he was heading in the direction of the Manchester Road, his horse's hooves pounding the muddied ground.

It was dark when he returned with a remorseful Araminta. Waiting in the basement hall, her back against one of the columns, having pulled herself together but with a vestige of pain still lingering, Lisette watched them enter. Colonel Montague was wearing a caped greatcoat and the wind had ruffled his hair. With the light behind him he was a dark silhouette made even larger by the capes of his coat spread wide by his broad shoulders. Shrugging it off he handed it to a footman.

Not until she moved did Ross notice Lisette. His voice was as cold as his eyes. 'Take my sister to her room. She is to stay there until further notice.'

Without a word Lisette turned from him and accompanied her distraught mistress down the length of the hall. Colonel Montague's voice suddenly halted her.

'Miss Napier, wait.' Araminta went on ahead. Lisette turned back to face him. He came close and stood looking down at her. 'I trust you are aware of the seriousness of this and that you will not utter one word to anyone about Araminta's transgression.'

Deeply offended and angered that he thought she would, Lisette stiffened. 'I will not.'

'In the meantime,' Ross said, with cold practicality, 'Araminta must socialise and act as usual—as if nothing untoward has happened. It is my hope that everyone will be blessedly unaware of this day's debacle and that lurid versions of her activities are not already spreading like wildfire from Derbyshire to London. If the story of the episode at the Dog and Partridge is circulated, she will be ruined.'

'All that sounds rather harsh and unfair to me—that society can be so judgmental,' Lisette uttered tightly.

Her ignorance of English protocol and the behaviour of society brought a mocking smile to Ross's lips. 'You have lived too long in India, Miss Napier. If a scandal ensues, in the eyes of the *ton* Araminta will be seen as a shameless wanton, soiled and used and unfit company for unsullied young ladies, gullible young heirs and polite society in general. But as things stand, love him or hate him, Araminta will marry Antony Bennington. I insist on it. Do I make myself clear?'

'Perfectly, Colonel.' Lisette was too tired to argue or protest further. Colonel Montague's actions were what one would expect if a man had compromised his sister. 'Now if you will excuse me I will go and attend to her.' Dipping a stiff curtsey and lowering her eyes lest he saw the anger there, she turned and left him.

Lisette chafed at his harsh reprimand. She could hardly believe he was the same man she had met in India, the same relentless, predatory seducer who had taken advantage of her, who had held her clasped to him while his hungry mouth devoured hers. It was as if he were two people, one she could like and one she feared and mistrusted—with excellent reason since he had threatened to dismiss her.

On reaching the landing Lisette met Phaedra coming from the drawing room where she had been taking coffee with her aunt Wilhelmina.

'Good heavens,' she said, 'was that Araminta who

just scooted past me? She's extremely wet,' she remarked in sympathy. 'We wondered why she wasn't at dinner. One of the grooms said she'd been gone all afternoon. Don't say she was lost in the rain all that time.'

'No, she—she came upon a shelter in the woods and stayed there until the rain let up a little while ago.' It seemed the wisest thing to say. Since no one knew of Araminta's assignation with Lord Bennington, Lisette had every wish to avoid a scandal, which would surely ensue should anyone find out. 'Excuse me, Lady Phaedra. I must go and prepare Miss Araminta a bath.'

On entering her mistress's rooms, Lisette searched her strained face. 'Are you all right?' she asked concernedly, proceeding to help her out of her damp clothes.

Araminta nodded, pulling her arms out of her sleeves. 'Yes, Lisette. Although Ross was extremely angry.'

'I expect he was.'

'You told him where to find me.' Her words were more of a statement than a question. Lisette was relieved there was no hint of accusation.

'When you didn't come home I feared you might have had an accident. I had to do something.'

'It's all right. I really should have listened to you. Still, it's done now. The most important thing is that Antony still loves me and assures me that everything will be all right. Ross insists we marry as soon as it can

be arranged. I think he's afraid my indiscretion will get
out and create a scandal.'

'Which I imagine would be most unwelcome for the
Montagues after everything that has happened.'

Lisette did not see Colonel Montague again for two
weeks—whether it was by chance or his own choosing she had no idea, but she strongly suspected it to be
the latter.

Alone, she was carefully laying out the dress
Araminta would change into for the afternoon when
she came in. Colonel Montague was behind her, carrying some small packages. They'd taken the carriage
into Castonbury to do some shopping. With a bottle of
lotion in her hands, Lisette stopped what she was doing,
watching as Colonel Montague placed the packages
on the bed. When he turned to face her he studied her
with the casual interest a man might assume when he
meets for the first time a woman he does not consider
particularly attractive and therefore hardly worthy of
his attention.

Lisette wanted to leave, but she knew she was
trapped. His tall, powerful frame barred her way to
the door, and his expression was like granite and as
forbidding as it had been since that fateful day of
Araminta's fall from grace. She had no choice but
to remain. Her pulse pounded as she looked at him.

Their gazes locked—a tremble ran the entire length of her body.

'Miss Napier! I trust you have not been colluding with my sister in any more undesirable escapades.' His voice was sharp, without any hint that his attitude had softened towards her.

'Ross,' Araminta chided, coming quickly to her maid's defence. 'Lisette had nothing to do what happened between me and Antony, so will you please refrain from being horrid to her. I will have nothing said against her, do you hear? None of it was her fault.'

Ross cocked a mocking, amused brow at Lisette. 'You are asking me to be nice to someone who not only colluded in what you did but also encouraged it.'

The unfairness of his accusation brought Lisette's head up and, on meeting his, her eyes flared. 'I most certainly did not. I tried extremely hard to dissuade her. Miss Araminta will testify to that,' she said, keeping the anger and hurt boiling inside her tightly shut down. If he expected her to squirm beneath his anger and contempt he would be disappointed. She was not going to weep or run begging for forgiveness—not that she had done anything that warranted forgiveness. She would not let herself be bullied. She was learning not to let her face show her feelings.

'Lisette is quite right,' Araminta retorted. 'You are being unkind to me and discourteous to Lisette. What

I did was wrong. But I do love Antony and that cannot be wrong—and what do you think, Lisette?' Araminta said, almost bubbling over with excitement. 'Ross has given his permission for Antony and me to marry as soon as it can be arranged—here at Castonbury, in the chapel. Isn't that wonderful?'

Lisette smiled at her. 'I'm so pleased for you—truly. I hope you and Lord Bennington will be very happy together.'

'We will be. How could we not? Since our betrothal was of many months' standing before I foolishly broke it off, Ross sees no reason for us to wait—and then he can go back to India. Is that not so, Ross?'

'It is, but not until there's word from Harry,' her brother replied. 'Hopefully when he contacts Giles he will have news about Jamie.'

'Good news, I hope,' his sister said, beginning to tear open the packages to inspect the items she had bought in Castonbury village. 'Poor Uncle Crispin. It must truly be awful not knowing if your son is dead or alive. And then there's the woman who claims to be Jamie's wife… What a muddle it all is.'

'And nothing for you to worry your head about, Araminta. You have quite enough to occupy your mind with your forthcoming betrothal party. You might like to go into Buxton for a new ball gown or wedding gown or something.'

Araminta's eyes lit up and she reached up and kissed his cheek affectionately. 'You are so good to me, Ross—the best brother in the whole world. Oh, how I shall miss you when you go back to India. Now, Lisette. I have not forgotten that it's your afternoon off so run along now. If I need help to dress I'll get one of the other maids to help me.'

'If you're sure.' Placing the bottle of lotion on the dresser, Lisette went towards the door. Colonel Montague was standing in her way. 'Excuse me, sir,' she said tightly.

He raised enigmatic eyebrows as his eyes met hers and he stepped aside, polite, incurious, totally indifferent to her as a female, he would have her believe, but in his eyes there was a shadow that did not quite conceal his innermost thoughts and his secret emotions.

His total lack of concern gave him away, for a man who had held a woman in his arms cannot but help retain the memory of that moment. Something remains and the studied blankness of his expression showed how hard he was trying to hide it. It was still there, that bond between them, pulling at them, tormenting them, no matter how Ross Montague tried to hide it.

'After a year of mourning, I think the time is right to invite people in again, Ross,' Giles agreed when Ross approached him about a wedding party for Araminta.

'Your father must be consulted, of course. Will he allow it—or even consider it?'

'I think he will. Until we know what has happened to Jamie we cannot mourn him, and the official period of mourning for Edward is over. I can see nothing wrong with putting on a party for Araminta, and I'm delighted she's going to marry young Bennington, after all. As the eldest son of the Earl of Cawood his credentials are impeccable and she would be a fool to allow him to slip through her fingers a second time. Go for it, Ross. A few new faces about the place will be a pleasant change. Will his parents be travelling up from Cambridgeshire for the event—and his delightful sister, Caroline? She's quite a beauty as I recall—just had her first Season.'

'As to that, I wouldn't know. I imagine they will all come—although because they are close friends of the Lathams, I expect they will stay at Glebe Hall.'

'I'll speak to Father about it—although he's so out of it at times I doubt he'll object, or even notice for that matter.'

'Thanks, Giles. I'll see it won't be a crowded, animated affair but it will do for Araminta. As long as she marries Antony Bennington she will be perfectly happy about it.'

Having finally received a reply from her father's lawyer, Mr Sowerby, in Oxford, Lisette had much to think about and consider. So it was on her afternoon off that she climbed halfway up to the high peaks where she could be alone with her thoughts. As she walked past the stables, although she kept her eyes averted, she was aware of Colonel Montague in conversation with his cousin, Lord Giles. She felt his eyes on her, following her, but she did not look back. His attitude, his cruel, angry words, his threat to have her dismissed, had reminded her of her humble position—that she was a servant and therefore dispensable.

Her initial reaction had been violent hurt and she could not, even now, truly suppress it. After her efforts that had sent her fleeing from India, she'd thought she'd conquered hurt. She'd been wrong on that score.

Climbing upwards through the park, she noticed three bored gamekeepers with dogs. They watched her pass with an admiring interest that she was in no mood for. Walking on she left the woods behind, emerging onto an open hillside. Climbing higher and walking round the sheep that looked at her with curious stares, she eventually found a suitable place to sit in the shade of a stone barn and read her letter once more.

Mr Sowerby had written to offer his condolences over the demise of her parents and went on to inform her that her father, who had been well rewarded for the work he had carried out in India for the university, had left her a substantial legacy of five thousand pounds. Lisette was astounded. She didn't know anything about any money. Her father had never spoken of such things to her. But to suddenly find that she was a wealthy young woman in her own right and that she need not fear for her future again, was such a wonderful feeling she could not believe it at first.

Fixing her gaze on the horizon, she made her first decision about her future. She would leave Castonbury Park. She could not stay here. To be near Colonel Montague, to continue being his sister's maid, knowing the disdain with which he regarded her, was an intolerable prospect.

But where else could she go? What could she do? She had done nothing but help her father with his work and for a few short months she had been a maid. For the first time she began to wonder if there were other possibilities for her future. She decided it was time to stop believing she had no choices in her life. It was time to begin deciding her own destiny. Perhaps it was even time to have a bit of fun. She would remain until Araminta married Lord Bennington. Araminta would then leave Castonbury Park—and maybe she could fulfil her dream and return to India.

Having watched her walk away from the house, Ross had been unable to resist the temptation to follow her. For the first time he saw her with her hair unbound. It was black and shining and moved like waves on a beach as she walked. He had not been alone with her since that day she had come to his room to tell him about Araminta's assignation with young Bennington. He had treated her badly, said harsh things he did not mean, things he knew must have hurt her, and he wanted nothing more than to make amends. Hopefully the gift he would present her with would go some way to aiding his cause.

Silently he approached. He paused and studied her, seated on the grass with her arms clasped around her drawn-up knees watching a scatter of magpies scuttling about the remains of a dead rabbit in the tussocky grass down the slope. Her gaze shifted to a shallow, slow-moving stream which, when it reached the valley bottom, would wind along the valley floor. The sun was warm on her face, the air sweet, and she breathed deep of it into her lungs, leaning back against the stone wall.

She wore a light floral printed dress with a demure white fichu tucked into her neckline, her slender arms concealed in three-quarter-length sleeves. Staring at her delicate wrists and long fingers made him long to know her touch on his bare skin. For long uncounted moments, Ross simply looked, let his eyes drink their fill of her soft curves, of the shining gloss of her unbound hair, of her intrinsically feminine expression, the simplicity of her pose. He felt the surge of emotions that gripped him. He didn't know why he'd been so furious with her when she had told him of Araminta's assignation with young Bennington. After all, it wasn't her fault, but for some reason he had been incensed.

But he had come to regret his condemnation of her, for Araminta's disgraceful behaviour was her affair and had nothing to do with her maid.

Lisette could feel his presence all around her. She did not look round since she had known he would come. He was dressed in breeches, an open-necked shirt beneath his jacket and knee-high riding boots. Without a word he moved to lean beside her, crossing his arms over his broad chest, and they stared out over the splendour of the wide, wild open hills and bracken-clad moorland together.

'How did you know I would be up here?' she said at last, carefully folding Mr Sowerby's letter and putting it in the pocket of her dress.

'Because I followed you. Araminta mentioned it was your afternoon off—remember? And when I saw you walk past the stables and head for the woods, I thought you might like some company. I was about to ride into Hatherton.'

'Then why didn't you? Why did you follow me?' She did not look at him but continued to gaze at the broad expanse of moor that had entered her heart the first time she had seen it, like a child settling in its mother's lap. 'What is it that you want from me?'

'You.' That was the moment Ross realised how true this was. His attitude to love had always been of the easygoing, take-it-or-leave-it variety, and now he found himself stunned by the force of his desire. Never had he wanted a woman so much, and never had he felt less sure of his ability to get what he wanted.

'I will be no man's plaything, Colonel.'

'If I wanted a toy I would buy one, Lisette. I wanted to talk to you and to apologise for my behaviour when you came to tell me about Araminta—and again when I saw you earlier. I was boorish, I know.'

'Boorish? You were downright rude. But then, you are my employer and entitled to speak to me how you see fit if you consider I have done wrong,' she said with more than a hint of sarcasm, 'even to go so far as to dismiss me should my *duplicity*, my *deceit* and *disloyalty* not meet with your approval.'

'You are wrong, Lisette,' he said softly. 'I should not have spoken to you like I did and I'm sorry if I hurt you. Not one of those words applies to you. It was unforgivable of me. My temper got the better of me.' He smiled grimly. 'I should try singing from Aunt Grace's hymn sheet.'

'What do you mean?'

'That I should be firm to the servants without being

severe, kind without being familiar, to converse with reserve and distance of manner and be particularly careful to maintain respect for their feelings.'

'Goodness, I have much to learn about my superiors as well as my own kind.'

'Why did you come up here and why did you seem unsurprised to see me? Did you expect me to follow you?'

She ignored his question and asked one of her own. 'Why did you want to talk to me? What have you and I to say to each other?'

'I told you. I wanted to apologise.'

'You could have done that at the house without following me all the way up here.' She pushed her hair back from her face and looked at something in the distance, as though it didn't really matter what he said.

'I want to talk about us, Lisette. About you and me.' His words were spoken quietly and did not take her by surprise.

'There is no us. There never can be.' She sighed deeply and turned for the first time to look at him, having to tilt her head to look up into his face. 'You are a titled gentleman, a man of some importance and wealth, and I'm just a maid employed to look after your sister. If Mrs Landes-Fraser was to see me up here with you she'd have me out of Castonbury Park in a snap.'

'My aunt is not your employer.'

'No, and you are not my master. No one owns me,' she told him, getting up and brushing down her skirts.

'I do not play the game according to society's rules, Lisette. I write my own. That is something you will have to come to terms with.'

'And why should I do that? We can never mean more to each other than what we are now. You are Colonel Lord Ross Montague while I am a mere maid, a domestic—the lowliest of the low. You belong to a place like Castonbury Park and I belong in your sister's boudoir as her maid. You are soon to return to India. We are too different—worlds apart, in fact.'

'Why?' he demanded.

'Because we are.'

'Defend your argument.'

She inhaled sharply, feeling as though she was getting nowhere. 'I've told you why,' she said on a weaker note. 'I cannot be more explicit—and we are different in our values.'

'How? How are we different?' he persisted.

Her eyes snapped and she almost shouted, 'Because you are who you are and you are too eager to judge. I have just suffered your outrage at first hand...and your indifference—'

'I am never indifferent to you, Lisette.'

'Don't interrupt. I suffered your indifference for some unwitting transgression.'

'For which I have apologised.'

Emboldened by his attentive, angry stare, she forged on. 'Perhaps you can be satisfied with a clandestine relationship but I need more than that—and I do not mean riches or rank. I fail to be dazzled by all that.'

'Because you feel that may only make me want you more,' he uttered quietly. 'What is it going to take for you to let me hold you—kiss you?'

'I don't have a price, if that is what you mean. I have no interest in money or jewels. I am not for sale.'

Ross smiled and moved closer. 'Well, well, Lisette. It seems you have a temper. I knew there was more to you than meets the eye.'

'Why are you so interested in me?' she cried. 'There are plenty of other girls you could have—who are far prettier than I.'

'Your question is simple to answer. It is because I don't want anyone else. I want *you*.'

'For what purpose?' Lisette exclaimed. 'Oh, but of course—to warm your bed. That's it, isn't it?'

'More than that.'

'Why?' She just wanted to hear him say, *Because I love you*—to say those words—but not if it wasn't true.

'Because I do,' he answered, refusing to say it.

'This is not about what *you* want. Is that all you care about?'

He studied her irate face for a second, then he began

to laugh softly. 'You are so adorable when you're angry—do you know that?'

'What?' She was bemused and growing flustered as he drew closer.

'I have just one question for you,' he murmured, staring into her glorious amber eyes, 'and I want you to answer honestly.'

'What?'

'Do you want me?'

She stared at him, and when he reached out and brushed her cheek with the backs of his fingers, she quivered. 'I—I… Oh, don't do that. Please don't…'

Ross realised the effect his caressing fingers were having on her senses, but he responded with a questioning lift to his brows. 'Why not?' he asked, running his fingers down her neck. 'You like me to touch you.'

'I—' she began, uncomfortably aware of the knowing look in his eyes.

'Yes?' he prompted.

Lisette swallowed hard and turned her head away, telling herself she must be strong. 'I don't know—exactly,' she admitted. All she knew for certain was that, for just a moment, she would have liked to be in his arms.

Suddenly he laughed and took hold of her hand. His

mood had changed. 'Come, Lisette—we will continue this conversation later. But first I have a present for you.'

Totally bemused, Lisette followed him to the other side of the barn where two horses were tethered side by side. One was Bengal, the other a beautiful white mare she had often favoured with an apple. Puzzled, she looked up at Colonel Montague.

'You did not come alone?'

'Oh, yes.'

'But…I don't understand.'

He grinned roguishly. 'Knowing of your passion for horses—and that you have not had the opportunity to ride since you left India, which must be torture in itself, I thought you might appreciate a gallop.'

Lisette stared at him, unable to believe the marvel of what he was offering. 'But…how can I? If I am seen atop a horse out of the Montague stable—have you any idea how I will be made to suffer?'

'Don't think of it, otherwise it will spoil our ride.'

'But…the risk if we are caught…'

He grinned. 'I'm prepared to risk it if you are. It will be well worth it.'

She returned his smile, too excited with anticipation of the ride to care.

'Let's get you into the saddle and we'll be away. To

have ordered the groom to fit a side-saddle onto the horse's back would have raised eyebrows, so you will have to ride astride.'

She laughed, thrilled by the prospect of being back on a horse. 'I ride no other way.'

## Chapter Seven

Lisette sat tall and straight-backed in the saddle; her shoulders were slim and square, her head erect instead of submissively bent as becomes a gently nurtured woman. But to Ross riding beside her as they rode among the green-clad hills, her plain servant's garb seemed to emphasize her femininity far more than the graceful folds of a lady's velvet habit. The straight lines of her body showed the swell of her breasts and her slender waist and rounded hips.

The mare was galloping at full stretch, and it was doubtful anyone could have turned her—but Lisette made no effort to do so, as she crouched over the saddlehorn with her weight thrown forward and without any idea where they were going.

At first she worried Ross with her recklessness, bent so low over her horse's neck with her face almost buried in the dancing mane, riding as no lady should and astride. But his fears were soon dispelled. She was one of the most skilled riders he'd ever seen—man or woman—light and lovely in the saddle. He gave a shout of laughter as Bengal thundered over the hard green turf alongside her. Riding at breakneck pace, Lisette took each jump with an effortless, breezy unconcern for style that Ross had never seen before. He grinned approvingly. There was jubilant simplicity as she soared over each jump, at one with her mount—confident, trusting and elated—its tail floating behind like a bright defiant banner.

They had been too occupied to pay much attention to how far they had ridden. Dreading the moment when she would have to dismount, they slowed their horses to a walk.

'I never knew a woman could ride like that,' Ross exclaimed with an admiring laugh. She was smiling broadly, her generous lips drawn back over perfect white teeth, and her colour was gloriously high. 'I think it's time we turned back.'

The horses wandered forward unchecked, pausing occasionally to crop a mouthful of grass and moving on again while their riders were content to go with them. Coming to the brow of a hill they paused and looked down the slope at parkland which rolled away into the distance. Lisette's eye was caught by some sort of encampment with an assortment of brightly painted caravans and carts. Some of them had a shabby appearance. Dogs roamed and several piebald and skewbald ponies grazed nearby. While children played, men and women stood about talking and others sat around a fire where ribbons of smoke spiralled upwards out of the embers. Swarthy skinned and with shiny black hair, they had a foreign look about them. Gold earrings glinted in some of the men's ears and brightly coloured scarves were tied loosely around their necks.

'Who are those people?' Lisette asked curiously.

'Gypsies.'

'Are they trespassing?'

'No. They have permission to set up camp in the park. They always come at this time of year to help with the harvest.'

'Are they harmful?'

'As a rule, no. They're hardworking people and always behave themselves. They abide by the law of the land while they are here. Their help is invaluable.'

They rode on. On reaching the barn where they had started from, Ross swung himself out of the saddle and went to assist Lisette, who was most reluctant to get down.

'Thank you so much,' she said, taking a moment to rub the spirited mare's wet muzzle against her palm. 'It was wonderful to be back on a horse again. I can't tell you what it means to me. I had a horse—she was called Silva. She was so beautiful.'

Ross moved to stand behind her. 'What happened to her?'

'I left her with Messalina.'

Placing his hands on her waist and drawing her hair aside, Ross kissed her nape. 'Well,' he murmured, his breath warm on her flesh, 'since you don't want money or fancy jewels from me—and to present you with a horse would raise more than a few scandalised eyebrows—I shall have to give you a present you will approve of.'

She trembled, casting about feebly for her ability to resist him. 'Please—please don't do this. I really must be getting back....'

'Why?' he breathed, his whisper fraught with wicked seduction, taking her earlobe gently between his teeth. 'It's your day off, remember. You have all the time in the world—and so have I.' He turned her to face him and drew her into his arms.

'This is how we held on to each other that night, isn't it?'

'Yes,' she whispered.

'I have a confession to make.'

'What is it?'

'I knew that night that if the river had risen, neither

of us would have seen the dawn. We would have been washed away like so much flotsam.'

'I know. I was so afraid. If I hadn't had you to hold me...'

'We shared a moment in our lives known only to us—binding us together like nothing else can.'

Keeping one arm securely around her waist, with his free hand he lightly traced his finger down her cheek to her chin. He gazed at her lips, at the soft rose-tinted curves he was beginning to know so well. Their shape was etched on his mind, their taste imprinted on his senses. 'I came up here because I wanted to be alone with you, Lisette.'

Lisette's entire body began to vibrate with a mixture of shock, desire and fear. It was one thing to be kissed by him in the middle of a raging river, but here, with absolute privacy and nothing to prevent him from taking all sorts of liberties, it was another matter entirely. Struggling desperately to ignore the sensual pull he was exerting on her, she drew a long, shaky breath.

'Why should you think I wanted to be alone with you?'

His relentless gaze locked on hers. 'Because I remember how it felt to hold you in my arms that night in the river.'

'It was both dangerous and foolish.'

'Foolish or not,' he murmured, 'I wanted you. We

wanted each other. I want you now.' Lisette made the mistake of looking at him, and his deep blue eyes captured hers against her will, holding them imprisoned. 'Neither of us has anything to gain by continuing this pretence that what happened in India is over and forgotten. When I kissed you in Araminta's room it proved that it wasn't over. I've remembered you all this time, Lisette—and I know damn well you remembered me.'

Lisette wanted to deny it but couldn't. 'Yes—all right,' she said shakily, 'I never did forget you. How could I?' she added defensively. 'I would have drowned if it had not been for you.'

He smiled and his voice gentled to the timbre of rough velvet. 'Yes, you would. Now, come here.'

'Why?' she whispered.

'So that we can finish what we began that night.'

Lisette stared at him, fear mixed with violent excitement. 'How?'

Lowering his head Ross lightly touched her lips with his own, feeling the heat, the compulsion, that surged in each of them. He held from pressing down on her lips, content for one timeless moment simply to touch and be touched, but not denying it. The beauty of the fragile moment stretched, their heightened awareness washing over them.

Curiously breathless, Lisette quivered. A small, insidious voice in her mind urged her to enjoy this time they were together, that she was entitled to some stolen passionate kisses if she wanted them. Another voice warned her not to break the rules of convention and leave him. But it was too late. She was already losing the battle to resist the desire that engulfed her whenever they were close. It was an effort to raise her heavy lids. At that moment her mind emptied itself of all thought. She was proud, but she was also young and sensual.

A blankness took over and with a soft sigh she relaxed against him, warm and trusting as he began to kiss her neck, teasing her senses into glorious awakening for him, her power to push him away fading fast. When he raised his head she offered him her mouth and he claimed her lips immediately, his arms going round her, and she revelled in his embrace despite her earlier determination not to let this happen. She closed her eyes tight to concentrate on the sensation. His mouth moved against hers, and it seemed natural to part her lips. Her mouth and body had suddenly become extra sensitive, so that she could feel the slightest touch.

At length he ended the kiss and held her fevered stare. At that moment they smiled into each other's eyes like equals. When he took her hand she did not resist as he led her inside the barn where he removed his jacket and dragged her into his arms once more. His lips found hers, finding them eager, warm, parted and moist. She clung to him, her arms about his neck.

His shirt was fine lawn. Through it she could feel the heat of him.

Their bodies fitted together, and her very softness tensed his muscles, her curves fit against him, their mouths fused, moving, caressing, their tongues touching. He put his hand to her head, entwining his fingers in her hair which fell in a shining black mane of living silk down her spine. She lifted her chin and his lips slipped beneath it and along her jaw. He was murmuring her name as he kissed her breasts through her gown, and then, eager to view her beautiful body unfettered, his hands went to the tiny buttons of her bodice which slipped open and the ribbons of her chemise needed no more than a tug to release them. The bounty he'd captured, their softness filled his hand, and lowering his head he took the hardness of her rosy nipples in his mouth.

His lips burned and Lisette gasped with sheer pleasure. He pushed away her dress and slipped it from her shoulders. Her chemise soon followed, bearing her aching breast fully to the soft light, the warm air and his attentions. His hands moved with infinite care as he began to remove her clothes, pausing now and then to caress and to fondle, roaming above her stockings and venturing above her garters, meeting bare skin. When there was nothing else to remove, swinging her up into his arms he carried her across the barn and laid her down on a pile of hay, a lovely bed, soft and ready for them.

Lisette watched as he stripped himself of the covering of civilisation to reveal his beautiful male body, brown and hard and eager. That was the moment she was made to realise that there was no going back, no escaping what was to happen and at last she accepted it.

Joining her in the hay he gathered her to him, her breath feathering his cheek as her fingers lightly touched him, sliding, gliding over his flesh, cindering his will.

'Show me,' she breathed. He was all heat and shockingly hot hardness. 'Show me what to do.' She wanted to know all of it.

Her words vanquished the last of Ross's resistance, the last remnant of caution. She was exuding something else besides the fragrance of flowers. It was as if some part of her, hitherto hidden or held back from others, was being offered to him. He wanted her with every fibre of his being, and she wanted him. Those demons that drove him urged him on, lending their talents to achieving victory in the most satisfying way. Reaching down he caressed her legs, his hand slowly moving up her inner thigh. Lisette gasped. All thoughts beyond this place, this moment, this man, fled. Forbidden pleasure turned to bliss as his lips kissed every part of her and his knowledgeable fingers explored those secret places known only to her.

They beguiled her until a delicious tension coiled so tightly inside her it broke loose with a vengeance. His face was a mass of concentration etched with passion as he intimately learned all about her, filling his male senses with her feminine secrets, driving her to a sensual excitement with practised ease. She melted, sinking into the soft hay, moaning, arching. In that moment, totally aroused, he could have taken her. She was his to do with as he willed. She was his instrument. Her body and, more alarmingly, her soul were fully open to him.

Ross felt her surrender and inwardly smiled, satisfied that she was taking all he lavished on her. He held her for one aching moment, and then he covered her and thrust powerfully, deep into her body, breaching her maidenhead. She cried out and he held still for just a moment, before his demons claimed him and drove him on, far beyond thought and reason.

Lisette clung to him, holding tight as their passion took flight, every sensation new, battering her overloaded senses. She thrilled to each new intimacy, determined to feel it all, to know the sheer hard delight of his body anchoring her, to glory in the hardness that filled her, claiming her, to sense her vulnerability in her nakedness, to revel in the shameless excitement that swelled and grew, then flooded her—more powerful than desire, deeper, more enduring than anything she had experienced in her life. She gave herself up to it, sharing it through her hungry kisses, through the worship of his body. And then he let go, allowing his body to do what came naturally and driving them both over the edge as the explosion broke over them.

Breathing heavily, their bodies damp with sweat, Ross felt the shudders rack him. Lisette felt, deep inside her, the strong ripples of his release, and then he became still. It was only then that he came to his senses, reminding himself of the inevitable consequences of what he had just done.

'Lisette?' he whispered, bracing himself on his arms and looking down at her. 'Open your eyes and look at me,' he commanded quietly.

Her lashes fluttered and he stared down into the warm amber of her eyes. 'Did I hurt you?'

She swallowed and shook her head, fighting down the wanton urge to plead with him to take her again, to beg him to love her not just with his body but his heart also, which was what she wanted more than anything in the world. In a few short minutes he had broken down every barrier she had erected against him, battered down her defences and left her weak and eager for him as if she'd been a naive girl.

'Then why the sad face?' he murmured. 'You do... want me, Lisette?'

'Yes,' she admitted in a fierce, suffocated little voice. 'But…I don't *want* to want you.'

A sound part groan, part laughter escaped him as he shoved his fingers through her lustrous hair, imprisoning her face between his hands. 'And I want you,' he told her, kissing her flushed cheek, 'more than you will ever know.'

'You shouldn't.'

Placing his finger beneath her chin, he tilted her face to his. 'I told you that I do not play the game according to society's rules, that I write my own. In bed or out of it, I consider you my equal in every way, Lisette. Never forget that.'

Moments later, Ross swept his hand along her thigh as she pressed alongside him and nestled her head within the crook of his arm. 'You are very lovely,' he murmured, dragging his gaze away from her shapely legs long enough to give her a smile. 'Truly, my love, I've never seen the equal of your perfection.'

Returning his smile, Lisette ran her fingers through the fascinating feathering of dark hair covering his chest. 'You are far from imperfect yourself, Colonel.'

Frowning, Ross tipped her face up to his. 'Ross. My name is Ross, Lisette. Considering our long acquaintance—not to mention what has just transpired between us—I find it ridiculous that you call me "Colonel."'

'Very well. Ross it is—but only when we are alone.'

His gaze did a slow admiring sweep of her body stretched out alongside his. 'I want to see you again. When I can—when you can. No one need know. It could be here—or somewhere else.'

'But people would talk. It wouldn't be good, for me or you.'

'Who has to know?' he replied, and Lisette could see gentle laughter in his eyes. 'It will be good to fade into the background from time to time. You didn't mean this to happen,' he went on, and his voice was stronger, deeper, more persuasive with every word. 'But we couldn't help it. We're two of a kind. We recognised it in each other. I'm glad.' He took a deep breath. 'Has anyone ever told you how utterly beautiful you are without your clothes?'

With her hair streaming loose and a shamefaced smile, she pressed her brow against his lean cheek, saying, in a breathless pretence at reproach that was nothing of the kind, 'Only you. You really are the most sinful man I can imagine.'

As he kissed the top of her head, he answered, 'And you the wildest woman I know—so, a good match.'

With a deep sigh of contentment Lisette settled against him. 'I suppose we should be getting back.'

Ross's arm tightened about her. 'We will—but not just yet.'

At the insistent urging of his knee, she lifted a slender limb and laid it over his hip, allowing his thigh to encroach between hers. Somewhat in awe of her handsome lover, she admired the steely bulges of his shoulders and the taut ribs, the manly nipples. She began to brush kisses over the ridges and hollows. Ross watched her, amazed by her gentle passion.

When she curled into his side, he tried to come to grips with reality. With his arm holding her close, he couldn't explain what had happened to him. All he knew was that no other woman had ever been like this. He was the first man she had known and he knew it and triumphed in it. It therefore came as no surprise to discover, as his sated senses cleared, that he was once again possessed of an urgent desire.

His need evident to Lisette, she sighed and stretched, lifting her arms above her head, deliberately displaying her proud breasts for his hands to cup, and it began again, this time slowly, lingeringly, exploring each other's bodies, kissing and smiling until he lay over her, plunging into her again and again until she wept with rapture and great joy of what he did to her and he groaned as though he were in agony.

Clearly, with his skill as a lover, he could take her to the heights of desire. He devoured her and she knew that nothing would ever be the same again. She felt beautiful, feminine and absurdly happy at this moment. How delightful that coupling with a man could do that to a woman. It was an extraordinary thing, she thought as she went falling into a white-hot haven of pure sensation, until he pushed her over the edge of oblivion.

As they began to replace their clothes, the late-afternoon sun had moved round in the sky and the light in the barn was dusky but they were reluctant to leave this moment, this time, this wonderful thing they had discovered together.

Ross had made love to many women but had loved none of them. He knew the difference now and the ecstasy he had just experienced with Lisette was an awakening for him. He'd thought he knew it all and he hadn't—until now.

He wanted her—in his bed and in his life. There was no doubt of that fact, no room for manoeuvre or negotiation. Her loveliness had flowered and blossomed in his arms, and his masculine desire for her was intense. He had the kind of feelings for her that a man can only feel for one special woman, though what the hell he was to do about it he didn't know and at this precise moment he didn't give a damn. She was his, she belonged to him—he could tell it by the expression in her eyes, by her lack of surprise when he'd appeared.

Lisette was well aware of the startled looks they drew as the group of keepers and one red-haired female on the other side of the lake took note of them together, Ross leading the two horses by the reins.

'I anticipated this. It is exactly what I hoped to avoid,' she told him. 'I had reservations about agreeing to walk back with you and shouldn't have agreed to it—and to make matters worse I believe that is Nancy Cooper, one of the kitchen maids, talking to them.'

Ross was not unaware of the curiosity that rippled among the keepers as they walked side by side, and he could only imagine how the rumour mill would soon churn. He was an old hand at dabbling in scandal and as a rule he always ignored it, but if their affair was made known it would be too distressing, too upsetting, for her to withstand.

'Forgive me, Lisette. I should have paused to consider the possible repercussions that would occur if we were seen. I should have let you walk back alone.'

'It's too late now. Nancy Cooper has ears as big as a rabbit and through practice she can move from a key-hole with the lightning speed of a weasel. Be assured, before the day is over the whole of Castonbury Park will know we have been together.'

'I sincerely hope that will not be the case. I prefer to keep what is between us private for the time being.'

There was something in his voice that bemused and unsettled Lisette. In the time it took them to reach a place hidden from prying eyes, she had time to think about it, to dwell on the consequences of what she had done, to the realisation that a man who has marriage on his mind will speak of it. Ross Montague had not and she marvelled at her own naivety in believing that he would. She flushed hotly when she recalled how she had sighed and melted and moaned in his arms, and though she did not deny that she loved him and always would, she should not have allowed him so much liberty.

Slowing her steps until she had stopped altogether, she turned and looked at him. '"For the time being," Ross? And what then? You are soon to leave Castonbury. Until that time what are we to do? Do you intend taking me whenever you fancy—expect me to lie down for you for an hour's pleasure? Is that why you followed me—trapped me up there on the hill?'

'Trapped you!' A wicked gleam appeared in his eyes. 'You were as willing as I was and don't deny it. What is it you want, Lisette?'

Shaking her head she turned away. 'Nothing, Ross. I don't want anything from you that you are not prepared to give willingly.' It was a bitter pill to know that though he was able to marry her, for nothing but his family stood in his way at this present time, he would not. He had decided that this was how it would be. Had she really thought he would marry her? Had she really been that naive and stupid in thinking that he loved her enough to make her his wife?

Ross stared at her, trying to comprehend her thoughts. Did she expect him to marry her, was that it? It was a measure of the deep feelings he carried in his heart for her that he had already begun to consider the idea of making her his wife. She had become a necessity in his life, like food and water, but at this time it would be socially impractical to bring it about.

She was lovely and gracious, and in fashionable gowns she would hold her own in any society, but until Araminta's wedding was over and because the Montagues were on tenterhooks awaiting communication from Harry with news of Jamie, he would prefer not to add to the family's worries by announcing his affair with his sister's maid.

Reaching out he cupped her chin with his hand which moved on and gently caressed her warm cheek. 'Be patient, Lisette. I am trying to avert scandal—goodness knows the Montagues have had their fair share in the past and this is not the time to create another.' He thought he saw a sheen of disappointed tears in her wide amber eyes. She was badly hurt, he knew it, but at present there was nothing else to be done.

Feeling the tide of pain rise in her, Lisette stood for a moment. If he was indeed the man of courage she believed him to be, he would have been prepared to fly in the face of prejudice and hypocrisy his family and his social equals would have turned on him. But he was not prepared to do that and the realisation was overwhelming and hurt her deeply. Her heart was in shreds as the battle for common sense and her love for him fought tooth and nail for dominance. Managing to claw back some of the self-esteem he had stolen from her, she knew what she had to do. She would not beg him to marry her and it was some measure of her strength that her pride came to the fore.

'You are quite right not to want a scandal at this time,' she said, drawing herself up straight and calmly meeting his piercingly blue gaze. 'If our affair—or whatever you care to call it—should become known, it would certainly create one. It would alter my relationship with my employers and they will look at me with different eyes. I will be considered to be getting above my station, which, after all, is the lowest it could be.'

His eyes passed lovingly over her face and a smile curved his lips. 'An adorable servant, Lisette.'

She smiled a bitter smile. Not adorable enough, it would seem, she thought. 'It is in my best interests that it is kept between ourselves—as well as your own,' she added as if it were an afterthought and his concern for his own well-being not on the same level of importance as her own.

'I'm glad you understand. For the time being I believe it is the most sensible course to take. Get used to the idea, to the knowledge that you are very special to me, that I will make a decent life for us both, that I will take care of you and that you have nothing to fear. What we feel for each other is quite unique, that is evident, and all it needs is time—and we have plenty of that.'

Lisette looked at him, wanting to sink against him, to be held to his chest in strong arms which would tell her he loved her. To sigh and melt and feel again that languorous magic drift through her...

'Yes, you're right, of course.'

When they parted, walking back to the house she gave herself up to her thoughts. Had she been seduced, beyond recall, not by Ross but by *her* desire for him? She knew in the depths of her heart that it was a most pertinent distinction. This desire was of the kind that had trapped women since time began into loveless unions. She had every reason to distrust the emotion, to avoid it, to reject it.

But she could not—perhaps before today, but now this rogue emotion was too strong, too compulsively within her, for her ever to be free of it. But this in itself brought no sadness, no pain, and indeed if the act itself could illicit such power and joy, such boundless excitement, such pleasure that she was addicted to it, then given the choice she would have the experience rather than live the rest of her life without it.

Having made her decision she was aware of a kind of peace stealing over her. But like a dark cloud coming over the sun, she knew this small sense of peace and happiness she had felt so briefly in Ross's arms could not continue—not in the face of what was real.

Ross began visiting Araminta's room more often. He began to waylay Lisette whenever he could. Sometimes when she was going to and from the kitchen he would stop her for no reason at all other than to hear her voice. Having stressed his desire for secrecy, Lisette could not believe how he flirted with danger and ran the risk of being caught dallying with a servant girl in a house that bred scandal.

He came up behind her and wrapped his arms wordlessly about her. On turning, her heart almost stopped when she saw his lazy, dazzling white smile that swept slowly across his handsome face, and the way his vivid blue eyes crinkled at the corners. He kissed her softly, gently, his lips travelling across her face to the corners of her eyes, smoothing her cheek, before releasing her and allowing her to go on her way.

But this happy state of affairs could not last. With sly hints and insinuations from Nancy Cooper, gradually the other servants began to take notice of the attention Ross paid her, and not only to notice but to disapprove. Some accepted the situation they suspected existed between the colonel and one of their own—after all, there was nothing new in one of their lordships having an eye for a pretty maid as long as they were discreet about the liaison. But some of the more strait-laced were horrified that a servant should be guilty of such an atrocious error of judgement, a wicked deviation from the accepted code of conduct, and to be allowed to get away with it.

Her fears that Nancy Cooper had done her worst were realised when Mrs Stratton summoned her into her sitting room early one evening before dinner. Mrs Stratton's sitting room was a comfortable room with a good fire in the grate. There were deep, comfortable armchairs on either side and a table on which stood a white china teapot with cups and saucers to match. Lisette liked this room. It was so warm and welcoming as a rule, but not today. Mrs Stratton, who always treated her kindly, was seated at the table, and by her blank expression and cool manner, it was clear she had something to say. She did not invite Lisette to sit down.

'Is anything wrong, Mrs Stratton?'

'It depends how you define the word *wrong*, Miss Napier. I felt I had to speak to you. It has been brought to my attention that you and Colonel Montague share a…relationship.'

Lisette suppressed a bitter smile. 'I see Nancy has already given you her version.'

'I abhor gossip and I will not have it in the servants' hall.'

'It is a rumour, Mrs Stratton, no more,' Lisette said, hating the falsehood but she could hardly tell the house-keeper the truth. But how could she look Mrs Stratton in the eye after this lie?

'In my experience all rumours have a ring of truth about them. Two days ago you were seen walking down from the hills together.'

'That is correct, Mrs Stratton. There was nothing furtive about our meeting. It was my afternoon off and I went for a walk. I encountered Lord Montague. We walked back to the house together, that is all. Having come from India, we share a common interest.'

'I am sure that is true, but it has been noted that it was not the first time he has sought your company. Indeed, I recall seeing the two of you together myself on your arrival at Castonbury, which I chose to over-look at the time. Your position as Miss Araminta's maid requires a certain code of behaviour which I am not at all convinced you share.'

'I do understand the need for such a code.'

'I am relieved to hear it. It is a part of my duty to pro-tect and encourage virtue, especially in the unmarried girls of the house. I am in a position to establish rules, Miss Napier—those rules apply to everyone.'

'I know that, Mrs Stratton.'

'A word of advice, Miss Napier. One must carefully avoid all reproachful, familiar terms when speaking or ministering to the family. This is one rumour I would prefer to keep below stairs. Should it reach the ears of Mrs Landes-Fraser I doubt she would be as lenient as I. Many a servant has lost a comfortable home, and a mistress a useful assistant, by forming unsuitable relationships—that goes for upstairs as well as below stairs. You will do well to remember that a maid is more interested in retaining a good position than her employer is in retaining her, and that no matter how the maid might strive to achieve it, she can never be her employer's equal. Do you understand what I am saying, Miss Napier?'

Lisette took a deep breath and lifted her head. 'Oh, yes, Mrs Stratton.' And Lisette did understand. She understood perfectly well.

'Miss Araminta speaks very highly of you. It is important that you guard your good name. Whatever the truth of it, there is nothing more detestable than defamation, so if you wish to remain as her maid, then you must avoid it.'

'I will bear that in mind.'

'I understand you had little experience when Lord Montague employed you as Miss Araminta's maid.'

'That is true, Mrs Stratton.'

'Well, then, I hope you understand you were very fortunate to be given this position.'

'I do.'

'Very well, Miss Napier.' Standing up she smiled and her expression softened. 'Colonel Montague is an attractive man—indeed all the Montague men are very handsome—there's little wonder some of the maids have their heads turned. But I must remind you that it is fitting for every servant to maintain a good character—they have nothing to depend on but their good name. But you are a sensible girl. I think you know what happens when a servant behaves improperly with their master.'

A wave of colour mounted Lisette's face. She bit her lip and lowered her eyes. There was a constriction in her throat and there was a feeling inside her of…what? Shame? Regret? She didn't know, but she didn't like it. Her voice sounded very small as she answered. 'I take your meaning, Mrs Stratton.'

'What Colonel Montague does in his spare time,' Mrs Stratton went on, 'which is private and not for us to comment on or wonder at, is his own business. But when one of the servants becomes involved it is my duty to speak out.'

Lisette smiled. 'I do understand, and I will give you no reason to have to speak to me again.'

'That's all I ask. Attend to your duties.'

As Lisette closed the door to Mrs Stratton's sitting room she asked herself what she had done. The enormity of her transgression hit her. The housekeeper had implied that a maid who crossed the line was in danger of finding herself in a delicate situation. Please God it hadn't happened to her.

The days passed and the smooth flow of life at Castonbury Park was to be temporarily disrupted by the arrival of a small party of guests to celebrate the marriage between Araminta and Lord Antony Bennington. Such an occasion would be a useful tool in their avowed endeavour to convince the world that the Montagues were not on their uppers as some people thought.

It was an exciting time for the servants, especially for the maids. With the guests would be coachmen, grooms and perhaps the odd footman. There was speculation, too, among the menservants about the numbers of ladies' maids who would accompany their mistresses, to ensure they looked their best at all times.

As preparations got under way, beneath the frenetic rush ran a sense of gathering excitement. Mrs Stratton gathered the household staff to warn them about forming hasty liaisons with the servants of the guests. It was one thing for a maid to fall pregnant to one of the Castonbury menservants—many marriages had started that way—but it was quite another to bring a man to the altar who lived many miles away and would probably deny all responsibility.

The servants were also reminded that the esteem in which the Montague family was held would suffer if they did not work hard to ensure that this party was deemed a great success.

With her marriage to Lord Bennington only three weeks away, eager to get started on her bridal trousseau, Araminta gave herself over to the seamstresses who travelled from Buxton. Amid swirling bolts of fabric bringing a riot of colour of every imaginable shade to the room, not only was she to be fitted for a new wardrobe for her new position, they were to make her wedding gown. With Araminta standing for what seemed an eternity on a raised platform, smiling and expressing her pleasure and stating her preference, she was measured and pinned and tucked and turned.

Never had Lisette seen the like. She looked around at the dizzying array of chiffon and gossamer, sumptuous silks and soft batistes, embellished with gold and silver.

Not until Araminta had left with Ross to visit Antony Bennington at Glebe Hall was Lisette able to restore order to the room. She was in the dressing room repairing a seam on one of Araminta's gowns when they returned. Wanting to get it done she carried on sewing.

She lifted her head when she heard Ross saying, 'Will

you mind going to live in Cambridgeshire, Araminta? It's important for me to know you will be happy there.'

Then came Araminta's voice answering, 'When I am married to Antony I will be content to be wherever he is. His parents are perfectly happy about the marriage and relieved we have put that unpleasant business behind us.'

'You mean the broken betrothal.'

'Yes. They are hoping very much that Antony's sister, Caroline, will make a good match too.'

'They must know someone who'd be right for her.'

'As a matter of fact they don't, but I do. I was thinking that over in the carriage on the way home.'

'And?'

'I realised I do know someone—a man who will meet her father's lofty criteria. I am in no doubt that he is the right man for her.'

'I am sure her father will thank you for that. Who is he?'

'You.'

The word hung on the air while Ross almost choked on a hearty laugh. 'Araminta, I am *not* a candidate!'

'Why not? You would be perfect.'

Lisette froze, her heartbeat suddenly too rapid and loud in her ears. It wasn't admirable, eavesdropping on anyone's conversation, but she couldn't force herself to move.

'You know, Ross,' Araminta went on, 'Caroline is exceedingly pretty, irresistible and charming and would do very well for you. The family also have connections with India which should appeal to you—I believe her uncle invested heavily in the East India Company. Now you are a colonel and you may be given more sedentary duties, you really ought to be thinking of settling down.'

'I have been thinking along those lines myself so cease your worrying.'

'What? A wife and children?' she asked, her voice excitable at the prospect.

'Precisely. I have thought about my responsibilities. To marry well, to ensure that I have at least one son, to make the future as secure as possible for my descendants, have become the primary duties of my life. I have postponed them in favour of my regiment for too long.'

'Oh, Ross, I'm so glad. Caroline is exactly the sort of wife you should have. I do so worry about you. I can't wait for you to meet her and to introduce you to the Earl and Countess of Cawood. Now go and get ready for dinner while I seek out Phaedra. I promised I would give her a full account of our visit to Glebe Hall.'

The door opened and closed again. Stunned by what she had heard, her cheeks burning and drowning in humiliation, with trembling hands Lisette dropped the work into her lap. All the fears that had engulfed her following her interview with Mrs Stratton returned with a vengeance. She sat there for a long time as the quiet of the house settled about her, feeling the burden of her lowly state more than she ever had before.

To marry well, Ross had said, for was that not expected of him, how he had been raised to think?

She had believed that when Ross took her into his arms, he had been mastered by the same attraction, and suffered the same irresistible revelation, as she had herself. She had been foolish to confuse physical desire with love. Just because a man made love to a woman with such fierce intensity didn't mean his heart was engaged. She had merely served to distract a man who, for the sake of relieving his boredom, had seduced her—and because she had known no different she had given herself gladly.

What had she done? How could she have allowed such a thing to happen? She had let herself be borne away on a tidal wave of passion. She, Lisette Napier, had succumbed like some overheated village girl, to the coercive, compelling force of Ross Montague's masculinity. For a brief eternity nothing had existed for her but him. He had drowned her reason with his kisses, playing upon her virgin senses as a master musician plucks the strings of a familiar violin, arousing her body with such skilful tenderness and breaking down every barrier of her reserve. He had made her a willing, hungry accomplice to his lusts, and for that she despised him.

It made her sick with grief and horror to think that she had been simply a toy for him. Had she snatched up the reins of her own life only to hand them over to the first man capable of putting heat in her belly? The memory of their kisses and caresses which, not so very long ago, had been so sweet, now burned her like a red-hot iron. Utterly overcome with shame and jealousy of a woman she had not even seen, a woman who would tempt him if she had the irresistible charm Araminta had spoken of, with a sick yearning in her heart she covered her face with her hands and began to cry as though her heart would break.

At some point she made it to her room to be alone with her wretched thoughts. With her back pressed against the hard wood of the door she was no longer crying, nor was there present in her that dreadful feeling of humiliation. In its stead there was a white flame of anger. It was a new emotion and was burning her up inside. It had a strength all its own, a separate mind of its own, and it was telling her what to do. She couldn't face him—not yet, not until she managed to collect herself and her battered emotions.

## Chapter Eight

During the following days Lisette went out of her way to avoid Ross. When he visited his sister she would disappear into the dressing room and wait until he had left before emerging.

Putting the finishing touches to Araminta's toilet, Lisette glanced at her mistress in the looking glass, thinking how pretty she looked in a gown of lavender silk, with dozens of small buttons fastened up the back. Araminta was excited because Lord Bennington and his good friend Roland Latham were to dine with them this evening, along with his parents, Lord and Lady Latham from Glebe Hall. Mr Seagrove and his daughter, Lily, were also invited.

'What an exciting time this is,' she enthused. 'I really can't wait to marry Antony. After the wedding breakfast, Aunt Wilhelmina has decided that something must be done to entertain the guests. There will be dancing afterwards in the salon. The salon was always used as a ballroom in the past and is not used nearly enough nowadays. Aunt Wilhelmina thought that several people who do not live very far away and will not have to be accommodated should be invited.'

'That will be nice,' Lisette replied quietly, preoccupied with her thoughts and not really listening. 'What jewellery were you thinking for tonight?'

'The diamond necklace, I think, Lisette. Here, I have it already.'

Lisette draped it round Araminta's neck and fastened it securely, saying quietly, 'There is something I wish to say, Miss Araminta. It's only right that I tell you now.'

'Why, what is it, Lisette?' Araminta asked, admiring the necklace in the mirror. 'You do look serious.'

'I—I have heard from my father's lawyer. It would appear that he has left me a small legacy.'

Araminta met her eyes in the glass and smiled broadly, genuinely pleased for her. 'Why, that's wonderful.'

'Yes, it is—only I've decided that when you marry Lord Bennington, I won't be going with you to Cambridgeshire. I intend to resign my post.'

Araminta swung round on the dressing stool and looked straight up at her, disappointment clouding her eyes. 'But— Oh, Lisette! I will be so sorry to lose you.'

She stiffened and gave her a sharp look. 'Has something untoward happened to you?'

'No, not at all,' Lisette hastened to assure her, hoping she sounded convincing. She could not bear it if Araminta learned she had overheard their conversation and Ross's eagerness to become acquainted with Caroline Bennington.

'Must you leave?'

'Yes. My mind is made up.'

'But…what will you do? Where will you go? You told me you have no family of your own.'

'That is true. I've decided to go back to India. I don't know yet what I will do. I'll decide when I get there.'

'I see—well, what can I say? You have clearly made up your mind.'

'Yes, yes, I have. But, for the present, I prefer no one else to know.'

'Not even Ross? I should tell him what you intend.'

'No—please. I would rather he didn't know—at least, not yet—not until I've made my plans. I will tell him myself when I am ready.'

'You know, Lisette, I did think that you might have feelings for Ross—not that anything could have come of it.'

Lisette straightened up, once more reminded of her lowly station. 'No, Miss Araminta,' she uttered stiffly. 'Colonel Montague is your brother—my employer. That is all he is and all he will ever be. We may have a shared interest in India, but nothing more than that.'

'Of course not. I—I'm sorry, I didn't mean to imply anything or give offence—but I shall be sorry to lose you, truly.'

Lisette's expression softened and she smiled. 'Yes. I shall be sorry to leave.'

Lisette was leaving Araminta's rooms when she saw Ross's imposing figure walking towards her. He was elegantly attired in evening clothes, the dark fabric of his coat moulding his powerful shoulders.

Ross smiled when his eyes lit on her, thinking she looked so fresh and lovely, it almost took his breath away. He found her slender body more than capable of arousing him. The sudden tautness of his own body whenever he came near her proclaimed louder than words how much he was attracted to Lisette, and how difficult he was finding it to control his physical reactions to her. Their lovemaking had been unique in his experience, satisfying him totally yet leaving him longing for more.

When she was close that tender spot at the curve of her neck looked so appealing that when she was within reach, throwing caution to the winds, he gave in to the urge to taste it. Lightly grasping her arms, he planted a swift butterfly kiss on her silken skin.

When she gave a start and pulled away, he grinned with quick, boyish warmth. 'Where have you been hiding yourself? I've missed you, Lisette.'

He thought she had simply been startled by his intimate gesture, but Lisette visibly stiffened at his words. She didn't seem at all pleased to see him. When she quickly averted her gaze, his grin faded.

Lisette had been startled by Ross's brief caress. Casting a nervous glance around her to be sure no one else had seen his kiss, she turned away from him. The words she had so unfortunately overheard were still spinning in her mind. Ross wanted only what she could give him—the means to slake his physical lust. He had done that. She wouldn't humiliate herself further by letting him know how much she craved his kisses, his touch.

'I have not been hiding,' she replied stiffly, forcing the words past the tightness in her throat, trying not to be intimidated by his towering masculine presence. 'I've been kept extremely busy of late—as I am sure you will understand.'

Her tone, her very posture, was cool and aloof. Ross peered down at her, trying to read her expression. He was puzzled and frankly astonished that after all the exquisite passion she had shown him, she had suddenly turned cold. Her response disturbed him, as had the way she'd flinched at his touch. He wasn't sure what had happened, but he didn't like to consider the possibilities.

The corner of his mouth twisted wryly in a gesture that was not quite a smile. 'You do not look pleased to see me. I presume our relationship gives me the right to speak to you privately.'

'This is not the time.'

He regarded her darkly, his gaze narrowed and assessing. 'Then do you mind telling me when it is the right time?'

'There isn't one. It is best if we do not meet again like this while the house is full of guests.'

'Lisette, would you mind telling me what is going on?' She wasn't merely objecting to seeing him, she didn't appear to want to at all. 'Is there some problem I don't know about?'

Lisette managed to return his gaze briefly. 'Problem?' she asked quietly. 'I don't know what you mean.'

A muscle flexed in his jaw. 'The way you're behaving—so stiff and formal. I thought after...'

'Am I being stiff? I didn't realise.' If she sounded cool, perhaps even haughty, then she was glad. Glad that Ross couldn't see what an effort it was to be so close to him.

'I think you do. I am glad to find you haven't lost your tongue,' he commented, a wry note in his voice.

'Of course I haven't. It's where it's always been.'

'You are angry. I can see it in your eyes.'

Lisette's heart slammed against her breastbone and all her new-found confidence was in danger of deserting her. There was something in his eyes, something in his voice, that hurt, that made her remember the woman she had been before she had met him, a woman blissfully unaware of how heartbreak felt. She drew a deep, steadying breath. That woman was gone, and the woman who had taken her place was not going to feel any pain because of him.

'Surely you did not seek me out to comment on my eyes.'

He searched her face, hesitating a long moment before he replied. 'Would you like to meet me later? Somewhere private where we can talk.'

'No,' she replied.

'No? What do you mean, no?'

'I won't meet you. I fear I have so much to do that I shall be quite weary later. I shall retire as soon as Miss Araminta is in bed.'

'I see.' His eyes began to flash quietly and his face hardened.

'Please excuse me.'

She walked on, thinking that she'd managed to cover her hurt well—until she reached her room and couldn't stop her tears.

Ross watched her back as she walked away, tempted

to go after her. Instead he went to find Giles. Together they would greet the guests due to arrive shortly.

The evening was a pleasant one for everyone except Ross, who was quietly seething following his encounter with Lisette. Sherry was served in the drawing room as the guests arrived, though most of the gentlemen preferred to take a glass of brandy to crisp the stomach before dinner. Antony Bennington, Lord and Lady Latham and their son, Roland, a handsome brown-haired young gentleman who had been at school with Antony, were the first to arrive. In their early sixties, Lord Latham was a tall angular man, his wife small and on the plump side.

Antony's parents, the Earl and Countess of Cawood, due to arrive in the next few days, were to stay with the Lathams at Glebe Hall.

Ross was both proud and delighted with the way Araminta greeted their visitors with charm and self-assurance. It was almost as if she had suddenly matured, as if tonight marked the end of her life as a girl and the beginning of her life as a wife. He noted how Antony watched her, too, with adoring eyes. With the incident at the Dog and Partridge Inn behind them, Ross had no qualms about Araminta marrying this tall, fair-haired young man.

The conversation was merry, with Ross, seated next

to Araminta, and Giles at the end of the table outdoing each other in telling tales of their experiences in India and Spain. Araminta, too, was in high spirits as she quipped across the table with her adored Antony and Mr Seagrove and Lily on Giles's right, who wanted to know how preparations were progressing for the wedding.

'You will officiate, Mr Seagrove?' Wilhelmina said. 'Araminta has a notion to be married in the chapel here at Castonbury Park'

'I shall be happy to, Mrs Landes-Fraser. Here or at St Mary's in the village—it will be an honour. It is only fitting that Araminta should be married in the family chapel. I hope it won't be too long before I can officiate at my own daughter's wedding.' He twinkled a smile at Lily.

'It won't,' Giles said, giving his betrothed an adoring look.

Ross had fallen silent, content to listen to what was being said. Becoming distracted, he reached for the glass of wine Lumsden had placed before him, looking at Lily. He imagined another young woman seated at the table, with hair as black as Lily's, though her eyes were amber and her skin golden. Despite her lowly rank Lisette was undoubtedly a lady, regal in her bearing and possessing the unconscious grace of a true thoroughbred. For Ross she represented everything most desirable in a woman. The thought was pleasing to him, but he knew his family would think differently and refuse to countenance even the idea of such an association with a girl they would consider lowlier than a vicar's foundling daughter.

He was deeply troubled by Lisette's cold attitude towards him earlier. What the hell had gotten into her? Whatever it was he intended to find out.

Ross was leaving his rooms the next day when he saw Lisette carrying some clean linen to his sister's room. Ross was unable to resist a moment in which to question her about her behaviour the previous day and to recapture that enchantment they had known in the barn.

'Lisette!'

The blood drained from Lisette's face when she saw Ross bearing down on her with a look of wrath. Letting out a small cry she turned to retrace her steps, but before she could do so, his hand was planted on her elbow.

'Don't you dare,' he warned. 'Come with me. We are going to go somewhere private where we can discuss what the hell this is all about.'

She twisted free, scorched by his touch. 'Don't,' she exploded, her body shaking with wrath. 'Why guard my sensibilities now when you've made a laughingstock of me since the day we met. Why stop now?'

He caught her elbow and none too gently drew her into his bedroom and closed the door behind them. Relieving her of the pile of linen he deposited it on a chair.

'What do you think you are doing?' Lisette tried to push past him but taking her arm he pressed her back against the hard wood of the door. 'Let go of me, damn you,' she cried, trying to prise his arm out of the way. Being so close to him caused her heart to pound with wild confusion and her foolish body to react much as it had when they had made love. In fact, her burning re-action to him was even worse now. His smell was that of pure, potent masculinity, and when she planted her hand on his chest to try to push him away once more, she felt the heat of his body through his clothes.

'Such language,' he drawled, his eyes glittering with reproach as he refused to release his hold. 'This is no way to greet your lover, Lisette.'

He looked much too large and darkly threatening to Lisette. 'You are not my lover,' she retorted, her magnificent eyes shining with tears of humiliation and wrath.

'Lisette,' he chided softly. 'You are mine. Do not doubt it.'

'The devil I am! I belong to no man—and you should not have dragged me in here. I have things to do.'

'They can wait.' A glint of wicked intentions passed

behind his eyes. Staring down at her in chilly, fierce reproach, he lowered his head, his lips hovering close to hers.

But Lisette wouldn't allow it. While she still had some small vestige of sanity she had to end this madness. Though her treacherous female body was ready to arch itself to accommodate his, gathering all her emotions into a tight, hard knot of pride, she struggled free.

Ross eyed her warily, unable to understand what had got into her, so sure had he been in his belief that her need must be as great as his and she would soon respond to his warm, moist mouth and searching hands.

'Please don't do this,' she said, her voice trembling with fury. 'How dare you think you can drag me down whenever the fancy takes you. I'm not some—some loose woman who'll lie down for you as you seem to think.'

Her words pulled Ross up sharp and he just stared at her. 'Well. Well,' he said at length, unable to believe all his romantic plans were being demolished. 'It seems I've found myself a little spitfire. The perfect servant, eh? I knew there was more to you than meets the eye.' His brows creased. 'My desire for you is hard driven, Lisette. Do not push me away. What is this about, and why have you been avoiding me?'

It was his voice that made her want to lay her head against his chest and weep, that beautiful deep voice, and his face—that harsh, handsome face she adored. It was as though she had been living all these weeks in a fantasy world, a world where dreams would come to fruition if she was only patient, a world where his loving had lulled her into a false belief. How could she have been such a credulous fool? To give in to him now would be to sacrifice her independence, which, she realised now, she had fought for and won, even if it was only as a servant, and little by little would be completely possessed by him, completely absorbed, and it terrified her,

'Please don't ask me—don't question me. Let it be enough when I tell you it is over.' Lisette meant it. She couldn't let him see how desperately she was in love with him, how her heart yearned for a reciprocated love, not this one-sided affair where all the emotion seemed to be on her side, and where all his tenderness was simply borne out of a man's natural lust for a woman. 'What we did should never have happened.'

His brows snapped together in an ominous frown. 'Are you saying you regret what we did?'

Lisette swallowed painfully and nodded, averting her eyes. 'Yes,' she lied. 'Yes, I do. Now let go of me.'

'Did I displease you? Is that what all this is about?'

In a voice fraught with emotion, she said, 'How can any woman be displeased with you? Looking as you do and with such impeccable credentials, I have no doubt you are the dream of every woman living in Derbyshire.'

'Is that the way you feel about me?'

Lisette groaned within herself. If only he knew how her heart ached for him, he wouldn't even consider asking that question.

'Let me look at you, Lisette,' he cajoled gently, but when she complied by lifting her head, his brows gathered in perplexity. The tears glistening in the long silken lashes were difficult to ignore. Laying a lean hand alongside her cheek, he gently wiped away a droplet with his thumb. 'What is troubling you so much you feel the need to cry?'

Embarrassed because she couldn't contain her emotions, she responded with a frantic shake of her head. 'I'm not.'

His hand moved to the tender column of her throat, and he came to marvel at the rapid pulse he felt beneath his palm. She was far more upset than she wanted to admit. 'Then why are your lashes wet? If they aren't tears, then what would you have me believe they are?'

Lisette recognised the threat of her emotions welling forth in greater volume and tried to turn her head aside, but his hand, gentle yet unyielding, remained on her throat, refusing to allow her to escape his close inspection. She could do nothing but submit to his probing gaze.

'Please, Ross, let me go.'

'I will when you tell me the cause for your dejection,' he bargained gently.

Forcing his hand away she walked to the centre of the room and whirled on him, her hands clenched into fists at her sides. 'Why can't you let it be? Why do you have to keep chipping away at me? I've said all I want to say on the subject. I really don't want to talk about this now. My tears have nothing to do with what happened between us.'

'On the contrary, Lisette. I think what we did is at the very heart of your despondency, and if you'd care to enlighten me, I'd be most grateful.'

'No,' she uttered sharply. 'The fact is that I have changed since…' She cast her gaze downward to avoid his eyes. 'I dislike the situation and I have decided that it would be for the best if we put it behind us. Henceforth you may go your way without giving me a thought. I want no more of it. *Indeed*, I can bear no more of it.'

'You're not being rational,' Ross argued striding towards her. Reaching out a hand, he rested it gently upon her forearm as he sought to calm her. 'I must get to the bottom of this. I have no intention of ending our relationship unless I have reason to believe that your contempt for me—if that is indeed what it is—is beyond the measure I can bear. Come, my love. You'll feel different if you just let me hold you.'

'No, I won't! I'll feel exactly the way I do now!' she cried, throwing off his hand. 'Except that I will hate myself a little bit more.' Her voice broke with emotion as she demanded, 'Please! And don't call me your love. I'm not your love—nor have I ever been.'

'Lisette, for pity's sake—be reasonable,' Ross pleaded, and tried to draw her towards him.

'I'm freeing you from any commitment you may feel towards me,' she declared resolutely, shrugging free. 'As far as I am concerned there is no more to be said. You have to understand that it is finished between us!'

Elevating a dark brow and folding his arms to restrain his hands from touching her, he continued to gaze down at her. His eyes narrowed, because he could not link the figure standing before him with the lovely young woman who had loved him with such passion— a transition had taken place.

'Do you think that making love to you meant nothing to me, you foolish girl?' he said abruptly, his lips curling in slight mockery. 'Do I look like a man who is playing games? The hell I am! How dare you dismiss me without any sort of explanation? Exactly whom, Miss Lisette Napier, do you think you're dealing with?'

Lisette fought the urge to shrink from his show of bluster and forced herself to sound as calm as possible. 'I know precisely who I'm dealing with. That's the trouble. We do not suit, Ross. We have been fooling ourselves.'

'Why?' he demanded.

'Because we are too different. We have been through this before. I don't want to have to go through it again.'

'And neither do I.'

'Why do you want me?' she cried. 'There are plenty of women prettier than me in your world.'

'I don't care about them any more than you care for my status. I want *you*,' he added, even more decisively as he began prowling towards her.

'For what purpose?' she exclaimed. 'Wouldn't it be best to find a woman who doesn't work in your household?'

He shrugged, dismissing her question. 'I don't care about any of that. It is you I want. You are the most delightful lover any man could be fortunate enough to take to his bed.'

Lisette clamped her jaw and glared at him, his casual remark raising her ire to the fore. 'And that is precisely what I am—your lover, Ross, and I will be your lover no longer.'

'Lover? Good God, woman! You make it sound as though I chose you as I would a decent hunter—because you had a beautiful face and figure and the kind of nature that would suit my purposes admirably. I didn't *choose* you, Lisette. What man in his right mind would choose a woman whose acquisition creates nothing but problems? The truth of it is that I was attracted to you from the first. I couldn't help myself.'

'So you admit that by association I will bring you nothing but grief, which is what I have been saying. This is why it cannot go on. I cannot believe I let you do what you did to me, but all I can do is pray for forgiveness for my lapse from grace. Now will you allow me to take my leave or do I have to shout for help?'

She threw back her head and Ross was alarmed to see not only rage but what looked like a mixture of contempt and...was it anguish? His jaw hardened. He unfolded his arms and his long, lean, handsome body rose to its full height.

'Very well, but may I ask what has brought about this temper you are in?'

'*Temper*? I wasn't in a temper until you dragged me into your bedroom.'

'How else was I to speak to you?' They wanted each other, they both admitted that with brutal honesty, so why the hell were they glaring at each other with what seemed to be hatred? They were both free and could do as they pleased so why was she making it so complicated?

'Why are you going over this again?' he asked, and even as he spoke his mind his senses were bemused by the way the light from the window shone in the blackness of her hair neatly coiled into a chignon in her nape. The heat of her anger had also put a flush beneath the creamy smoothness of her skin and her amber eyes blazed at him from beneath the fine arch of her brows. 'I thought we'd had all this out. I have told you it is not important.'

'It is to me.' Lisette felt her heart contract with pain, and tremors seemed to flow into every part of her body. She loved him so, she knew that now, more than her own life, and yet it would soon be over and she would never see him again.

'Don't struggle like this, Lisette. Don't fight me. I am not your enemy. I want nothing more than to help you—to love you.'

'That's the trouble, Ross. That's how I got into this—this dilemma.'

He looked at her sharply as a thought struck him. 'Are you with child? Is that what this is all about?'

She almost laughed as she stared at him. After the talking to Mrs Stratton had given her, she was amazed at having escaped the consequences of her transgression. 'There will be no child, Ross.' What she would have done faced with such a predicament she had no idea. At least now she could move on. 'I can't afford you! Your *help*, as you like to call it, has cost me my reputation and my good name.'

'And for that you blame me?' His eyes were colder than an icy winter sky and there was a thin, white line about his mouth. He watched her, his anger fierce and knife-edged, hating her, loving her, wanting her. His voice softened for a moment, since he adored the very ground she walked on, but when he put out a hand to restrain her she shook him off and backed away.

'I am not blaming you. All I am saying is that it should not have happened—*I* should not have let it happen. Whatever you have to say to me I don't want to hear it. I don't want you to come near me again. Ever. Get on with your life and I will get on with mine.'

His nostrils flared, and he responded with a violence to match her own. 'You dare to speak to me like that! You forget, Lisette—'

'Forget! Can I ever forget that this is pretence? Can I ever forget your noble birth or your military rank? Yet I do dare to say that what we had is over. I am no lady, but I have been your equal in love, and for this I dare to tell you how I feel.'

He stalked towards her, tall, formidably muscular. He stared at her, intensely, the hard lines of his jaw and cheekbones starkly etched. 'Don't do this, Lisette. A word of warning. If you send me away I won't come back. I'm not a man to beg.'

'Don't threaten me. I will not be threatened. There is a saying, Ross—we live and learn—and I have been very slow to learn, lacking in experience you understand. But if I have learned anything at all, it is never to make the same mistake twice.'

'Damn you, Lisette.' He thrust his face, which had become hard and uncompromising, into hers, his rage growing, his frustration at her unwillingness to listen boiling inside him. 'Since you are clearly not as enamoured of me as I so foolishly thought, I trust you will not object if I find someone more amenable.'

'Do that, and I wish you joy in her.'

'Oh, I assure you I shall.' His voice was mocking and his eyes gleamed sardonically, though he was still white-lipped with anger. 'And you can go about your business carrying that pride and bloody determination on your shoulders for all I care.'

'Leave me alone,' she said, turning away. She did not want to hear any more for she could feel her weak woman's body straining towards him, yearning to give in, to lean against his strong male body, to have him enfold her in his strong arms. 'I have nothing more to say to you.' Picking up the linen she strode out of the room.

To Ross she looked like a young queen, with her head held high and proud, her body moving with unconscious grace. He watched her in silence, feeling the familiar, hot need for her rising in his loins, the longing he'd felt for days to seek her out and gather her into his arms and lose himself in her. He went back into his room, but he was unable to shake off the image of a tempestuous beauty with blazing amber eyes and a face alive with fury and disdain. The picture became etched on his mind along with a voice that trembled with emotion. She'd actually looked and sounded as if she meant everything she'd said to him, and he was still puzzled as to the reason why.

As Lisette walked away from him, it was strange, but all the anger had gone from her. There was a coldness in her, an empty coldness. All the strength seemed to be draining out of her. She did not feel the need to cry, but a great need to sleep, to shun this life and dream that she was back in India with her parents, with her days filled with simple happiness and pleasures—before she had ever come across the man called Ross Montague.

There was great excitement and rushing about as more guests began to arrive. The housemaids were given the lowly task of ensuring the fires in the guest bedrooms were kept alight, coal scuttles replenished and hearths kept clean. They were also to ensure that washbasins were emptied and cleaned, water jugs kept filled and hot water carried upstairs for baths. The footmen who weren't employed doing other duties did the heavy carrying.

It was a particularly busy time for Lisette. Not only had she Araminta to take care of, she was called on to stand in and wait on some of the other ladies who had come without their maids. Once they left their rooms to partake in the celebrations, her duties became far less onerous.

Everything was planned and when the first of the guests arrived, a happy feeling of excitement pervaded the house—an unusual feeling nowadays because of the time spent in mourning two of its sons.

In the domestic quarters the air was heavy with the smells of cooking and there was a din of clattering pans and shouted orders. Monsieur André, his darkly handsome face flushed with heat and hurry and wearing a pristine white apron, was preparing dinner at a huge table with the aid of half a dozen young kitchen maids.

He was hailed as a genius by everyone upstairs and downstairs. He could cook an egg in fifty different ways. He was considered economical because he could produce an inexhaustible variety of dishes without any waste of ingredients, and the elegance and piquancy of flavours which are necessary to stimulate the appetites of all. His attention was chiefly directed to the stew pan, in the manufacture of stews, fricassées, fricandeaus and the like.

Overseeing this apparent chaos from a gallery, which was reached by a servants' corridor from the main part of the house, was Mrs Stratton. She stood watching the frenetic activity with an unperturbed expression, satisfied that everything was in order and perfectly organised to her experienced eye, and that the guests' meal would be ready on time.

In the servants' hall Lisette accepted a glass of Madeira from Mrs Stratton. She was seated at the table from which the servants' evening meal had been cleared away, with her workbox beside her and her sewing in her lap.

Suddenly the door swung open with a clatter as a couple of young footmen carrying a tray loaded with plates and cutlery marched in. They looked very handsome in livery of knee breeches and silk stockings. Becca, a young scullery maid, took one of the trays and carried it to the sink.

'Are they a pleasant lot?' she asked, not really interested, for being a scullery maid she never got to see any of the guests.

'They're all the same to me,' Sandy, one of the footmen replied. 'Lady Kate's just turned up,' he said, placing an untouched pyramid of grapes on the table and giving Faith a teasing wink. 'I see she's still got Miss Fisher in tow. Smithins will be delighted, I don't think! She breezed in and strode after her mistress as if she owns the place.'

A pained look crossed Mrs Stratton's face. 'Oh, dear! No change there, then.'

'Fat chance,' Sandy said, popping a succulent green grape into his mouth, which earned him a frown of disapproval from the housekeeper.

'Lady Kate was expected back today or tomorrow so I've had a fire lit to warm the room. I'll go up and see her when she's settled. I doubt she'll want to join the guests so I'll prepare her a tray and have Daisy take it up—unless Miss Fisher comes down for one.' Getting to her feet she fingered the keys on her belt. 'Are the ladies in the drawing room?'

'They'll soon be coming out, Mrs Stratton.'

She looked at Lisette and Faith. 'In that case, you two will be needed upstairs by your mistresses.'

Picking up her workbox, going ahead of Faith, who stopped to have a word with Sandy the footman, who was her beau, Lisette left the kitchen and began the long walk to her mistress's room. It had been another long day and it wasn't over yet. The servants were all very tired, but they still had the task to finish clearing up after the guests and the family, and it would be a long time before some of them went to bed.

She climbed the narrow flight of carpetless stairs used only by the servants. It came out on the top of the main staircase. Closing the door behind her she paused and looked over the banister to the bottom of the grand staircase. Some of the ladies were taking coffee in the conservatory to the right of the stairs.

She was about to move on but paused when Ross appeared. She knew she should go about her business but she had never seen such fashionable, glittering ladies and gentleman. Her gaze remained fixed on Ross. As she looked down at his lean, undeniably elegant form, her feet remained glued to the top of the stairs.

He was talking to Caroline Bennington, who beamed up at him. This young woman Araminta would so like to become romantically involved with her brother was incredibly lovely. Golden haired and with sparkling green eyes, her small and slender form attired in a cream silk gown, any man would have to be blind and insensible not to be drawn to her.

Ross was holding a glass of champagne in his hand—the same hand that not so long ago had caressed every inch of her body, and his lazy white smile was as devastatingly attractive as ever. Attired in formal black evening clothes with a white waistcoat and frilled white shirt, he looked quite splendid.

Suddenly, as if he could feel her gaze, he looked up and checked at the sight of her looking down. His eyes looked straight into Lisette's and she felt a tremor of alarm as he contemplated her. Unaware of the storm that was raging in the young maid's breast, he inclined his head ever so slightly before placing his hand beneath Lady Caroline's elbow and steering her into the conservatory.

Recollecting herself, Lisette melted into the shadows.

* * *

Staring fixedly ahead, concentrating on what Caroline was saying proved difficult, because Ross couldn't stop thinking about Lisette. Whenever she was in a room with him, he had trouble keeping his eyes off her. When she was absent, he couldn't seem to keep his mind off her. He'd wanted her from the moment she'd jumped in front of his out of control horse.

No, he thought, he'd felt something for her even before that—from their meeting in India, when he'd thought she was an Indian girl, wearing a star-spangled sari. He loved her intelligence and her unaffected warmth. He loved the way she felt in his arms, and the way her mouth tasted. He loved her spirit and her fire and her sweetness, and her honesty. My God, that he should feel this way about her, that he should love her! After a succession of meaningless affairs, he had finally found a woman he wanted, a woman who wanted only him. He'd known that from the very first and his instinct told him she hadn't changed, no matter how much she proclaimed otherwise. He was so stricken with the innocence of her, that he could not rouse himself to seek relief in someone else's bed.

In the days before the wedding, the house party rode and hunted and jaunted off to nearby Castonbury village and further afield to explore the delights and drink the waters at the spa in Buxton. The evenings were filled with sumptuous feasts cooked by Monsieur André, brilliant conversation, cards and for some of the gentlemen a game of billiards.

It was a beautiful sunny morning for the wedding. The ceremony was conducted in the thirteenth century church which stood in its own grounds at the back of the house. It contained monuments and effigies which reflected the ancient lineage of the Montague family.

Since it had been impossible to invite some of their friends and omit others, and because the family was only recently out of mourning, the decision had been made to limit the wedding guests to immediate family only, which avoided offending the sensibilities of friends and made it a quiet, intimate affair. But the villagers had conspired amongst themselves to gather together and waited in the grounds of the church to see the bride and groom as they emerged as man and wife.

Araminta had insisted that Lisette be among the privileged servants to occupy the back of the church to watch the ceremony. Having straightened the bride's train and handed her her bouquet of pale pink roses, trying hard not to look at Ross, whose presence was like a tangible force, powerful and magnetic, Lisette hurriedly took her place between Lumsden and Faith, who was craning her neck so she wouldn't miss the moment when Miss Araminta entered the church beneath the chevron-moulded arch.

The duke and Mrs Landes-Fraser, Lily Seagrove and the bride's cousins, Lady Phaedra and Lady Kate, occupied the box pews in the chancel to watch the proceedings. The groom and his best man faced Reverend Seagrove, waiting patiently for the bride to appear.

'Here comes the bride,' Faith whispered when the music soared.

Like everyone else, Lisette was caught up in the moment. Every head turned to look at Araminta as she walked slowly down the knave, her hand tucked into her brother's arm.

'Oh, isn't she simply beautiful?' A woman sighed.

'Exquisite. And did you ever see such a gown?' whispered another as the bride passed the south transept which housed an alabaster tomb chest with lifesize figures of a knight and his lady. 'All ivory gauze and silver lace... Oh, and just look at her bouquet.'

Lisette paid little attention to the comments of those around her—had she not dressed the bride in her finery? She was staring at Ross as he walked his sister slowly down the aisle, his tall, muscular frame moving with that easy, natural elegance already so familiar to her. His attire was simple but beautifully cut—light grey trousers, a plum-coloured cut-away coat, black satin waistcoat and crisp white neck linen. As he walked, smiling and bowing his dark head to those he passed, for one unwelcome instant Lisette felt the barbs of envy pricking her heart when his eyes seemed to linger for an exceedingly long moment on Lady Caroline Bennington.

But for the whims of fate, Lisette thought bitterly, she might have been the one to receive his admiring gaze. It was almost as if she had suddenly and cruelly been made aware that the prize to which her own soul had secretly aspired had just been handed over to someone else.

The ceremony went smoothly, and when Reverend Seagrove announced Araminta and Antony were now man and wife, a collective sigh went through those present, joyous smiles dawned brightly and eyes misted with tears.

When the wedding breakfast had been cleared away, the company rested and readied themselves for the evening's festivities, a steady stream of luxurious conveyances, mostly containing local gentry, began to arrive at the house, waiting to pull up before the brightly lit facade to unload their passengers.

'It looks like a Grecian temple,' one female guest was heard to remark as she was led by her escort up the immense stone steps and entered the house through the great north portico to be confronted by the marble hall designed to be no less impressive than the exterior. Pinks and greens had been chosen for the ceiling, with panels of military trophies and arabesques.

The gown of duck-egg blue trimmed with lace slithered over Araminta's head. The neckline was extremely low, showing off the tops of her small white breasts. Lisette stood back to cast a critical eye over her handiwork. Then she smiled and stood back to admire her mistress.

'You look a picture, my lady. Your husband will be quite dazzled by the sight of you. I doubt he'll allow anyone else a dance.'

'Oh, I do hope so, Lisette. I'm so excited,' she said, dancing to the door but hurrying back when she remembered her reticule. 'Wish me luck,' she breathed before whirling about and rushing off to find her new husband.

Watching her go, a pang of envy wrenched Lisette's heart. Lisette was just twenty years old—her birthday had come and gone. She was young. How she wished she could go to the ball, to laugh and have fun—to dance in Ross's arms.

But it was not for her.

When the dancing was under way, several of the servants found their way to the salon to take a peek at the gentry enjoying themselves. It was a beautiful room, a high-domed rotunda, contained behind the triumphal arch of the south front. Like the marble hall it rose to the full height of the house with rosettes carved on the dome. Lisette stood on her tiptoes among the jostling press in riveted curiosity, trying to peer over Daisy's head to see through the crack in the door to the brilliantly lit salon. What she saw took her breath.

'Heavens,' she breathed, never having seen the like.

Splendidly dressed couples were dancing the waltz on the wooden sprung floor, and urns and plinths were placed in alcoves. Red silk damask chairs and settees were designed to echo the curves of the walls, ringed just now by a colourful array of local belles and beaux.

Catching sight of Ross dancing with Lady Caroline Bennington, Lisette's heart sank. His dark head was bent close to the lady's beautiful face—whispering pretty compliments, no doubt—and she was simpering and pouting and fluttering her eyelashes with all the vivacity of a born flirt. Lisette felt the pain in her chest where her heart lay—the bitter pain caused by the malevolent pangs of jealousy. *He doesn't even know I'm here*, she thought. Abruptly she closed the door and gave her attention to finding her way back to the kitchen and ignoring her sinking heart.

## Chapter Nine

The servants had their own special celebration. Several bottles of sherry had been brought up from the cellar to toast the happy couple. When Lord Giles and Colonel Ross Montague strode into the kitchen, they could see that already several glasses had been drunk. Normally the household staff conformed to a rigid, centuries-old hierarchy, with the head butler and the housekeeper at the pinnacle of it, but it was obvious to the two gentlemen that the consummation of liquor had been something of an equaliser.

Their appearance in the servants' hall caused quite a stir. Lisette's gaze riveted on Ross the instant he came into view, and the sight of him had the devastating impact of a boulder crashing into her chest. She had not expected him to appear among them and wondered what all this was about. Of late she had made sure he only saw her from a distance—she had learned the art of disappearing when he was about and in a house the size of Castonbury with its hidden corridors used by the servants to remain invisible, it wasn't difficult.

Standing across the room between a chambermaid and a laundress, with servants in their various household uniforms in front of her, gave her a chance to study him. The overall expression of his masculine face was one of intensity and precision. Looking at him now—and she could see she was not the only one—with his thick black hair, deep blue eyes and tall, athletic physique, Ross Montague was magnificent. Lisette seemed to forget all about telling him to leave her alone, and she found herself falling under his unfathomable spell much as she had experienced before.

'We are not here to disrupt your festivities,' Ross intoned, 'in fact, quite the opposite.' As his gaze swept the room, as though his brooding eyes and deep velvety voice could mesmerise any unsuspecting victim, he was like a snake charmer Lisette had once seen in the bazaar in Delhi. 'We hope you are all enjoying yourselves.' He turned to Lumsden. 'Have some champagne opened for everyone to toast the happy couple, will you, Lumsden? Carry on.'

When the fiddler began scraping a sprightly tune, becoming caught up in the moment, Giles laughingly gathered a surprised Mrs Stratton in his arms and began waltzing her around the floor to the amused delight of everyone present. Joining in the spirit of the occasion, footmen and maids alike grabbed a partner and joined them.

The company neatly under his control, Ross glanced oh-so-casually at Lisette, a discreet glimmer of devilry in his eyes. Lisette shook her head at him in bewilderment, wishing she could melt into the background and slip through the door into the passage beyond, but he was not going to let her escape. His wicked smile in answer to her thoughts and his slight, private nod merely seemed to say to her, *Oh, no, Lisette, you're not going to escape me now.*

Obviously he'd decided that both he and she were wasting their time on differences, and he was playing an amusing game designed to either divert her or discomfit her entirely, she wasn't certain which. He deftly steered his way towards her. Watching him, Lisette could not help admiring his bold, confident walk, as if he could march through fire and not get burned.

When he finally stood in front of her, the subtle scent of his tangy cologne wafting over her, her nerves had wound taut, coiled tight in her stomach. She was deeply and embarrassingly conscious of every eye in the room focused on her. She wanted to say something but she now found herself tongue-tied.

'Miss Napier. My sister would like to share her happiness with everyone at Castonbury, which is why we came down. She also insisted that I dance with you.'

He stood very still. Lisette lowered her eyes. Had she not done so she might have seen the flicker of victory in his eyes and then the sly satisfaction that curved his lips. Knowing she could not possibly refuse, she allowed him to lead her into the dance, where he swept her up into his arms.

'You should not have done this,' she whispered.

'No?' he murmured, both raven eyebrows arching high now. 'And why not, pray? I could think of no other way of getting you to come to me.'

'But…you sought me out?'

'And you could not refuse to dance with me.'

'Yes, I could.'

He smiled with mild amusement. 'And regretted doing so. You should have gauged by now that I am capable of removing obstacles in my way.'

'You shouldn't have singled me out. As if things aren't difficult enough for me. Already I am the subject of gossip. My life will be impossible now.' He gazed down into her eyes with that same thoughtful expression she'd noticed before. He seemed to peer down into her very soul.

'I'm sorry our affair has had adverse effects on your standing, Lisette, but what is life without a little danger?' he countered, flashing her a dangerous smile. 'We have both had our share.'

'Yes, indeed. And you expected me to dance with you as a reward for rescuing me from a raging river?'

'My dear, Lisette. If I had done it for the reward,' he murmured, his warm breath caressing her face and his hand tightening about her waist, 'I promise you, I would be asking for more than a dance.'

The sheer wickedness of the slow lazy smile he gave her made her catch her breath against the tightness of her buttoned bodice. All of a sudden she longed to be rid of it, rid of all her clothing, when he looked at her that way. Her strong determination to distance herself from him, which she thought had worked when they had last spoken days ago, was completely overwhelmed by his palpable expertise, and she thought again of what it was like to have him make love to her, to caress and kiss her body into insensibility—and she was tempted.

Looking down at her, all soft, entreating woman in his arms, drugging his senses with the sudden familiar scent and feel of her, he remembered the one time he had made love to her—how could he forget, for it had been the most wildly erotic, satisfying sexual encounter of his life? He had marvelled at the heady, primitive sensuality of her, real and uncontrived.

'Come to me later, Lisette.' His voice was low and husky, his eyes compelling with his need.

Until this moment Lisette had felt strong in her determination to abide by her decision to steer well clear of him, but she was so happy to see him, so achingly thrilled to have him this close, and so much in love with him, that nothing else seemed to matter. Yet the words he used sent a chill coursing along her spine. She struggled to free herself from the trance-like state induced by the intoxicating closeness of this strangely irresistible man and the touch of his hand holding hers, filling her with conflicting emotions.

'But I said…'

'I know what you said and why you said it, and now I want you to forget it,' he murmured in the lazy, sensual drawl that always made her heart melt.

'But I don't want—'

'Yes, you do,' he said, wanting to give her a shake to make his full meaning sink in. She met his gaze and he smiled, content in his belief that he had measured the weakness of her character in the strength of her passion. 'There is no gulf between us that cannot be bridged. What we feel for each other cannot be denied. You *will* be mine tonight. We both know it, so do not fight me, Lisette,' he said softly, his voice a caress. 'I know you too well. I know how you feel.'

'Please leave me alone,' she whispered, her cheeks hot, her pulse racing as she tried to control her emotions.

'I'll *never* leave you alone.'

He spoke softly, holding her with his gaze, knowing that she, too, was a victim of the overwhelming forces at work between them. She stared back at him, and he was sure he heard a soft moan escape her.

Lisette wished she were alone with him, away from all these people with their knowing eyes and judgemental looks. She wanted to fling herself into his arms and kiss his mouth, his face, his neck, as if nothing in the world existed for her but him. Shocked by the unladylike drift of her imaginings, she warded off the wayward thoughts before she could complete them. She studied his lips for a second, then shook off the shiver of awareness that ran through her body. And then the dance ended. Releasing her, taking her hand, he lifted it to his mouth and pressed the palm against his lips.

'Later, Lisette. I *will* see you later.'

Then he turned and with Giles left the hall, satisfied that Lisette would do as he asked.

In the beginning he had deeply resented her decision to avoid him. He had seethed with frustration each time she disappeared as he approached, simmered with inept rage whenever she left a room rather than remain in his company for a moment. But tonight she would come to him in his rooms—and if not he would go to hers.

Leaving an excited yet apprehensive Araminta to await her bridegroom, Lisette went to her room without any conscious effort or awareness of doing so. How long she sat beside her bed she didn't know, but when at last she got to her feet, she felt strangely calm. She would go to Ross. In two days she would leave Castonbury. She would leave Ross. Would it be so wrong of her to want just this one night?

Stepping quietly from her room she negotiated her way to the west block. Arriving at the room she sought, she stood looking at the door when suddenly she froze. She couldn't go in. Would the joy of being together for just a short while be worth the agony of parting? Had she not been lucky to avoid the consequences of their last tryst—surely this would be tempting fate to try it again? Would it not be better if they stayed apart, not to see him at all? Blindly she turned on her heel and retraced her steps.

Ross heard a sound outside his door. As a soldier trained for war, he'd developed the faculty of detecting the slightest out of the ordinary sound and coming instantly alert. Immediately he crossed to the door and looked out, just in time to see the figure of a woman disappear round a corner. His instinct told him it was Lisette. Without hesitation he hurried after her.

Knowing she was being followed, Lisette found herself in the massive Marble Hall she had first seen on her arrival to Castonbury Park—a room meant to overawe and to establish a sense of Roman grandeur, rising to the full height of the house and recalling the open atrium at the centre of a Roman villa. But now, in the dim silvery light, eerie shadows draped the walls. She paused, looking around.

About her the great house lay slumberous, the cloak of night temporarily disturbed before settling back like a muffling shroud. And then she heard the soft footsteps of someone who walked quietly towards the hall. Silently she slipped behind one of the twenty alabaster fluted Corinthian columns that dominated the room, holding her breath and standing as still as the cold, blank-eyed statues that occupied the niches about the hall. The footsteps came to a stop just a few feet from where she hid. She shrank back, flattening herself against the cold column, thinking he might hear her heart beat. But then he moved away, the sound of his footsteps tapping on the inlaid Italian marble floor, leaving her in silent darkness.

Or so she thought, for she was unprepared when she slipped from her hiding place to find herself face to face with Ross. A silent moment passed as his eyes settled on hers. They seemed to draw her towards him.

'Come to me, Lisette.'

Closing the distance, placing her hand into his palm, suddenly became the easiest, most natural thing she had ever been asked to do. He looked down at her and stared into her eyes before allowing his gaze to travel, slowly and lovingly, over every inch of her face. Without relinquishing his hold on her hand he led her back to his room. Lisette crossed the threshold and he shut the door. She walked into his arms, wrapping her own around his waist and placing her cheek on his broad chest.

The curtains were drawn against the night, and the room, so spacious and elegant, was warm and secure against the things that lurked outside. There was a silver moon but it did not intrude into the golden glowing room. A mother-of-pearl-and-gold clock ticked on the mantelshelf. Everywhere was rich comfort, even the hound lying in front of the fire was accustomed to sleeping on a thick pile of Turkish rugs.

The logs crackled in the fireplace, carried up by one of the footmen from the stack behind the stables. One spat as the sap within it dripped into the flames, eliciting nothing more than a lift of the dog's ears.

Ross tilted her face up to his. His eyes were a dark sapphire blue in a tanned face and his eyebrows were raised in quizzical enquiry. 'Why did you run away?'

'I suddenly got cold feet,' she answered, looking up at him.

Ross couldn't blame her. If he was honest, from the very first he'd set himself up with his attempts at masterful manipulation. 'I want you, Lisette, you know I do, and I know you want me.'

As he studied her, words rang in her head. The prize

wasn't the same as what he habitually lusted after. This time he wanted a great deal more and he knew why. It was because Lisette was different, because in her heart she carried the same things he did. They were like two halves of a broken coin waiting to be mended.

He'd known the first time he'd laid eyes on her, the instant he'd held her in his arms and kissed her. They fitted together, and he'd known instinctively, immediately, on a level deeper than his bones. He wanted all of her, not just the physical her, but her love and devotion and her heart. He wanted it all. He would settle for nothing less than that.

'Why did you make me come to you?' he breathed.

Leaning back, Lisette tipped her head to one side. 'It has not escaped my notice that you have been otherwise occupied.'

'My darling,' he chuckled tenderly, 'you are the only female alive who would bring up Caroline Bennington at a time like this.' Sighing quietly he cupped her face in his hands as if it were a precious thing, kissing her mouth in such a way that the sweetness, the tender honesty of it, swelled her heart. 'Caroline means nothing to me. Believe it, Lisette, for it is true.'

Lisette closed her eyes and no longer wondered what had drawn her to this man. Initially she thought it might be his compelling good looks and his powerful animal magnetism. She had convinced herself that it was so, that the strange hold he had over her was merely his ability to awaken those intense sexual hungers within her. Now she realised this was just the tip of an iceberg, that the truth lay in its hidden, unfathomable depths. What she felt for Ross Montague went far beyond either physical or romantic love.

'Ross.' Her mouth murmured the word against his.

Without taking his mouth from hers he lifted her in his arms and carried her across the room. Placing her on the bed he knelt beside her and with slow, deliberate hands he undressed her, loving every inch of her naked body before gathering her up and nestling her against him with what seemed to be perfect content.

She knew it was wrong, and yet she felt it couldn't be. Did she care? Did it matter that she was a servant when his mouth and his hands and his powerful body were demanding of her what she knew only she could give him? No, she thought. She loved this man. She wanted him and it was enough.

Ross shrugged out of his clothes and lay beside her, in no hurry. His manner implied this would be as good as it had been before, the firm flat muscles of his body pressing against hers, the exploration of his hands on her skin, the sweeping caresses that set her purring and glowing, but when he entered her she felt the heated frenzy come upon her which demanded that she be possessed by him. She cried out and so did he, while all about them the great house and the servants slept and the lovers were unheard.

And then she slept, her head resting on his chest, his arms about her, his lips against her hair. But Ross did not sleep, for his thoughts were occupied with how he was to keep this beloved woman in his life. Before he closed his eyes he knew there was only one way and having reached his decision he was content.

Before dawn Lisette sat up and her loveliness struck him. Her raven-black hair tumbled about her round, peaked breasts and her graceful shoulders and back. Without a word she slipped out of bed and fumbled into her clothes, smoothing back her flowing hair and securing it in a knot in her nape. Then she leant over and kissed him.

'I must go before anyone is about.'

'Yes, you should. We will talk later,' he murmured, his body sated, his spirit quietly joyous, caressing her cheek.

Lisette left him then, his kisses still warm on her lips. With the house slowly stirring to life, she moved swiftly back to her own room with a heavy heart, for it was as though he had taken the spring of life within her. The thought that she would not be with him again tormented her, and she could not bear a day, a month, let alone an eternity beyond that, without him. The weight of it, her love, was almost more than she could bear. Her heart ached with the desolation of it and with the loss that must come next.

When Smithins appeared in the breakfast room and issued a summons to Giles and Ross for them to attend His Grace in his rooms, they were surprised. He had become such a solitary person of late he seldom disturbed the males and females of the household or saw them except when it suited him—avoiding everyone except Smithins and the Reverend Seagrove when he came to call.

Ten minutes later they stood before him seated in his chair. It soon became clear that he wished to speak to them on a matter of grave importance, for not even the dedicated Smithins was allowed to remain.

His Grace fixed his rheumy eyes on his son and nephew. The death of two of his sons had left him feeling tired, old, ineffectual and useless, but Jamie's son had given him something to think about, something to fight for, injecting new life into him. He sat straight in his chair, and when he spoke his voice was more controlled than it had been in a long time.

'There is something that you should know right away—something I have decided concerning Jamie's wife and the child.' He said it quietly, but the room was hushed and waiting for something which would not be pleasant when it came. 'Young Crispin is my heir so he is my responsibility. I am trustee to the estate and therefore his guardian, so it is for me to make some sort of provision.'

'There is still an element of doubt that Alicia is telling the truth,' Giles said, sitting opposite his father and indicating for Ross to do the same. 'We have no proof that Jamie married her. Until we hear from Harry I suggest we do not commit ourselves to anything.'

'And what happens to the child in the meantime? He cannot be ignored—and nor would I wish to.' His voice was high, every word stressing his indignation. He cast Giles a stern look. 'Since Jamie was taken from us, on my request you have assumed the position of heir apparent well, Giles.'

'Of course, but you know it is a position I have never coveted.'

'I know that and Jamie's son will relieve you of the responsibility. The inheritance issue can no longer be ignored. We cannot disclaim that young Crispin is Jamie's child and we must recognise him legally, not only to give him his name but to have papers drawn up with the utmost speed. We have the same blood running in our veins. No class or legality can wipe out that fact. I am thinking of taking certain steps with regard to the child and having him brought to Castonbury.'

'And the mother?' Ross asked, conscious of a sudden feeling of unease creeping over him. His uncle Crispin believed in his right to ride through the heritage of the Montague family, and when he had his mind made up about something, he would not allow any obstacle to stand in his way.

'Some provision will be made for her.' The duke stared at his nephew for a moment, then he said, 'You have met the woman, Ross. Tell me, how did you find her?'

'Likeable and civil—given the circumstances.'

The duke's face twitched. 'The circumstances?'

'She is a poor widow with a child to raise alone. It cannot be easy for her.'

'Did you see the child?'

'No, I did not. But I believe she is a good mother and she spoke fondly of her son.'

The duke made a sound in his throat and after a moment he muttered thickly, 'I wish to see him. The child is my grandson, my heir, and I want him to be brought up as such. If what you say is correct and the mother has no means of supporting him, then I'm sure she could be persuaded to let him go.'

Unable to believe he was serious, Ross studied him in cool silence, noticing for the first time that there was an infuriating arrogance about his uncle, his thin smile, and even the way he was sitting in the chair. 'Let him go? What are you saying?'

'It is my will that the child should be removed from her.'

Giles was staggered by his father's words and deeply shocked by what he intended. 'We cannot do that. She will not part with him.'

'Why not? She will be amply compensated. Arrangements will be made for her and an offer to place her in some comfort elsewhere.' His voice was impatient. 'The child is being brought up in poverty and I will not allow it to go on. I could take her son away from her by the simple matter of going to the law.'

'Are you saying that you would remove the child by force?'

'If necessary. Possession is nine-tenths of the law, don't forget. If the child was out of her reach for a time, then she might be brought to her senses through argument and discussion. Of course, she could take the matter to court under the heading of abduction—'

'Or kidnapping,' Ross interrupted, absolutely astonished at what his uncle was planning to do.

'She couldn't afford to do that. The law has ways and means, and if I decide to make it a legal matter she wouldn't have a leg to stand on.'

'I know what you are saying, Father, but it is not right. It is not right to separate a child from its mother.'

He came back at Giles sharply. 'Right? Of course it's

right. The child will have everything he could wish for and nursemaids to look after him.'

'Nursemaids are no substitute for a mother,' Ross pointed out.

'I second that,' Giles said. As children he and his siblings had been kept in deferential awe of their parents. Indeed, they'd seen little of them. As babies they had been given over to the care of wet nurses and later cared for by nursemaids and nannies, with just the occasional duty visit from their parents. If what Ross said was true, then young Crispin's closeness to his mother was surely better than that.

Banging his hand on the arm of his chair, the old man's eyes swung to Ross, madness and desperation in their milky depths. 'Who is this woman anyway? A nobody by all accounts. A woman who had to work for a living before she married Jamie. She is not fit to call herself the Dowager Marchioness of Hatherton. I will not acknowledge her. I am still a powerful man. I have ways and means to get what I want, and a position such as hers offers me numerous ways and means.... You understand me?'

Both Giles and Ross understood him—and with the understanding their fear grew. He was right; he had the power to take the child from Alicia. Of late he had become possessed of only one idea, and that was to have Jamie's child under his care. He had even gone to the extraordinary lengths of ordering Mrs Stratton to have all the nursery floor redecorated, setting the whole household agog. It was plain to both his son and his nephew that His Grace would have his grandson by fair means or foul.

'The courts don't always do what is expected of them,' Giles pointed out.

There was a slight constriction in His Grace's throat. He moved his thin blue lips, one over the other, then looking at Giles with hard eyes, he said, 'Which is why it would be wise to have this matter settled once and for all—quietly and without fuss. I want you to send a letter to this woman, informing her that I wish to see her—and her son. I expect you to respect my feelings.'

Giles nodded. 'I will write directly.' His father was still very much the master of the house and the family and his wishes must be obeyed.

It was a deliriously happy, shiny-eyed Araminta who greeted Lisette on her first morning as a wife. In fact, she was so caught up in her own happiness she failed to notice her maid's unusually quiet manner. It was when Araminta went to join her husband in the breakfast room to bid farewell to the guests who would be departing after breakfast that Mrs Stratton appeared to inform Lisette that Mrs Landes-Fraser wished to see her.

Lisette knew why she was being summoned into the presence of the great lady. She expected the worst.

Mrs Landes-Fraser gave Lisette a cold stare. Normally she never interfered with the hiring or dismissal or discipline of the household staff. She usually left that sort of thing to Lumsden and Mrs Stratton, but her loyalty to the Montagues was never in doubt, and if anyone threatened any one of them her stoic nature turned to steel and she became a lioness defending her cubs.

Her instinct told her that this extremely beautiful girl was such a threat. However, she grudgingly admitted that she was certainly presentable. She had the colouring, the carriage and the neck most young women of class would envy. She drew herself up, looking down her long patrician nose, making no bones over her disapproval. In her day all young ladies had known the rules, had been inducted from birth in the rituals of their world. But this young woman was from a different world entirely.

'I understand you wish to see me, ma'am.'

'Most certainly. You can be at no loss to understand the reason. Your own conscience must tell you. A report of a decidedly vulgar nature has reached me.'

She went on to berate Lisette on her unacceptable conduct, leaving Lisette in no doubt that her employment as Miss Araminta's maid was indeed at an end.

'The Montagues are descended from a noble line,

Miss Napier—respectable, honourable and ancient. It is clear you have a clever head on your shoulders so you will know what I am saying.'

Standing straight and proud, Lisette raised her head and looked the superior lady in the eye. If she'd had any hopes at all of forming some kind of life with Ross, then Mrs Landes-Fraser's voice now attacked them with the cutting knife of reality.

'Perfectly.'

'Then if you have any sense of propriety and delicacy you will walk away.'

'I am aware of the embarrassment I must have caused and I would like you to understand that I am not aiming to claim anything more than an acquaintance with Colonel Montague. You need not trouble yourself that I will take advantage of our encounter. Colonel Montague has done nothing wrong. I assure you his sterling reputation is constituted by a keen observation of all the proprieties and a more than ordinary measure of honour. I hold him in the highest regard. I understand your concern, ma'am. I will leave at once.'

Without another word, with her head held high, Lisette turned and walked away. After packing her few things together she went to say goodbye to Araminta.

Araminta was astounded by Lisette's disclosure. 'You and Ross?' A smile curved her lips. 'I have to say that it comes as no great surprise to me. I knew from the very beginning that my brother showed an unusual interest in you. Why else would he have suggested that you be my maid?'

'You…don't disapprove?' Lisette asked tentatively.

'As a bride I feel so happy today that I would like everyone else to feel the same as I do, and if you make Ross happy, then why should I mind? It certainly explains why he was reluctant to encourage my sister-in-law into forming any kind of relationship. But must you go so soon? Please, Lisette, wait for Ross to get back from Hatherton.'

'I cannot. I am doing this for Ross. It is because I love him that I have to leave.'

'But—but if you love each other, he surely will ask you to marry him.'

'He has made no indication that he will. He must think of his future. One day he will meet someone he will be proud to introduce as his wife and to bear his children.'

'No, Lisette. If you loved him you would not put him through this torment.'

Lisette turned to go. 'Just ask him to forgive me.'

She next went to say goodbye to members of the staff who had become her friends—others slanted their eyes in her direction, all judging her, all condemning her.

Faith was genuinely upset by her dismissal and

hugged her close. 'I'm sorry you're leaving, Lisette. I, for one, will miss your friendship sorely.'

'And I yours, Faith.'

'Whatever the truth of it, if it makes you feel better, Nancy with that treacherous tongue of hers has also been dismissed. She was idle and lazy to boot.'

'It doesn't make me feel better, Faith. But it doesn't matter now.'

'I am sorry for your situation, Lisette.'

Lisette smiled and embraced her friend. 'You are very kind. Be happy, Faith, and don't wait too long before you marry your Sandy.'

'I won't. Now you'd better go. John is waiting to take you to Buxton in the carriage.'

On arriving in Buxton, Lisette boarded the coach for the first stage of her journey. She intended travelling to Oxford to see Mr Sowerby and then on to London where she would book a passage on the first available ship bound for India. Clinging to a lifeline, she felt her life, which had slipped precariously since she had left Ross's bed, right itself for a moment in the emptiness of her heart which held all her love for Ross Montague.

Ross arrived back hardly half an hour before sunset. His happiness shattered the moment Araminta told him what had transpired. Entirely unprepared for the announcement, incapable of any kind of rational thought, what he felt at that moment was raw, red-hot anger. The possibility that Lisette might leave at once had never occurred to him. Araminta saw the colour drain from his face and a white line show about his mouth.

'What time did she leave?'

'Midmorning. I'm sorry, Ross. There was nothing I could do. You know what Aunt Wilhelmina's like. She draws blood. Why must she be so savage?'

'That's Aunt Wilhelmina. She's never more righteous than when she's in the wrong.'

'But she isn't, is she? At least not to her way of thinking. She saw Lisette as an obstacle that had to be removed and was adamant that she should go immediately.'

'It wasn't Aunt Wilhelmina's business to take Lisette to task.'

'She likes to hold all the reins. But Lisette had already decided to leave before that.'

Ross stared at his sister with eyes that were almost black with anger. 'Leave? Why in God's name did no one think to tell me?'

'I wanted to, but Lisette was adamant that you should not be told.'

'How did she seem when she left?'

'Upset—although she tried not to show it,' Araminta said quietly, remembering how she had wanted to go to Lisette and clasp her hands and bring comfort to her in some way, for her eyes had looked so deeply sad, entirely lost.

'You say she intends to return to India?'

'That's what she told me.'

'She cannot afford it. She does not have the means.'

'Apparently her father left her a legacy—his lawyer wrote to her informing her of the fact. She no longer has any need to work for a living. Ross, what do you propose to do?'

'Go after her,' he said tersely. 'It's too late to do anything today.'

Araminta looked at him steadily. 'It's true, isn't it? You and Lisette… You've fallen in love with her, haven't you?'

Ross smiled bitterly. 'Is that such a bad thing, Araminta? Or are you of the same opinion as Aunt Wilhelmina and consider her too far down the scale of things to marry the nephew of the Duke of Rothermere?'

'I'm not sure that sort of thing matters much to me. I have your happiness at heart, you know that, and if you and Lisette love each other, then I am content.'

'I would love her however, whatever, whenever, dear sister.'

'As much as that.'

'More than that.'

'Then find her. Antony and I are to leave for Cambridgeshire the day after tomorrow. You no longer have to worry about me. Go after Lisette, find her and marry her and take her back to India. It's what you both want.'

With the knowledge that Ross was to leave Castonbury the following morning, it was a subdued family that met in the drawing room before dinner, with only the duke absent. Seated next to her husband on one of the four huge blue damask sofas that matched the walls, Araminta, who was already missing Lisette and dreading the moment when she would have to bid farewell to her beloved brother, was noticeably quiet. It was inevitable that the dismissal of her maid was raised, and by Ross, who was furious that his aunt had taken it upon herself to dismiss a member of his household's staff.

'I'm sorry I did not get to speak to Miss Napier, Ross,' Kate said, seated next to Phaedra. 'I would have liked to meet her.'

'I'm sure you would, Katherine,' Mrs Landes-Fraser remarked, 'and no doubt you would have made her your bosom friend, which would have been ridiculous— laughingly so—and given her ideas way above her station.'

'In other words, Kate,' Phaedra chipped in, 'Aunt Wilhelmina is reminding you that ladies of our social position are allowed to visit the deserving poor, to take broth and blankets to the old and infirm who would be obligingly grateful, but not become friends with them.'

'Precisely,' her aunt uttered coldly, taking a sip of her dry sherry.

'There's more to charity work than feeding them broth, Aunt Wilhelmina,' Kate said. She gave Ross a conspiratorial glance, noting that his jaw was clenched tight, his chin jutting and ominous as he struggled to remain calm. He bore little resemblance to the laughing, gentle man she remembered before he'd become a soldier and gone to India. Today, he was an aloof, icy stranger who was regarding Aunt Wilhelmina with glacial eyes and every word he spoke had a bite to it. 'Did you meet Miss Napier before she became Araminta's maid, Ross?'

'We met in India. I saved her from drowning in a flooded river.'

'How very romantic,' Phaedra commented.

Ross omitted to mention that at the time he'd believed her to be a native girl and that he'd failed to recognise her when he'd encountered her in England.

Mrs Landes-Fraser sniffed disdainfully and tossed her head, the feathers in her purple turban swaying precariously. 'An encounter she has clearly taken advantage of—a schemer if ever there was one.'

Fury ignited in Ross's eyes and he had to struggle to subdue his temper. 'A schemer—' he retorted, then he bit back the rest of his words, clenching his jaw so tightly a muscle jerked in the side of his cheek. 'You're wrong about her. She's not hard enough or brittle enough or ambitious enough to be accused of scheming. Lisette is without guile or greed. She is a rare jewel and I am going to marry her.'

'Then you will be making a grave mistake,' Mrs Landes-Fraser said in glacial tones. 'In suitability she will be on a par with the maids in the kitchen.'

Ross's eyes darkened with anger. 'Say no more. Lisette will never be on a par in any way with the kitchen maids. She is the daughter of an academic, a highly intelligent man and a gentleman. My decision to marry her does not stem from a flash in the pan.'

'Your ideas are quite unorthodox and I can see it's no use arguing.'

'No, it is not.'

'Then I am most disappointed in you and I cannot pretend otherwise. I cannot imagine what Crispin will have to say.'

'I don't think Father will have much to say on the matter,' Giles remarked, his expression grave. 'At this present time his mind is taken up with other things—namely Alicia and his grandson. Having the child brought to Castonbury is his one thought and concern.'

Kate gave him a sharp look. 'And is it true that Father intends to offer Alicia money in the hope that she will go away so he can raise the young boy himself?' she asked.

'So it would seem.'

'That is quite atrocious and I, for one, will not stand for it. I cannot understand this irrational hostility he has for a woman he has never met—a woman whom I hope will speak for herself.'

'Having met her I am sure she will,' Ross remarked. 'If my opinion of her is correct, she will not be parted from her child.'

'I sincerely hope not and Father is quite mad to suggest such a thing.'

'He has shown irrational tendencies of late, which, when all is considered, is understandable. I assure you I shall do all in my power to dissuade him from this action. I have written to Alicia inviting her here,' Giles informed them. 'You will be able to judge for yourselves when she arrives.'

'Then I suppose all we can do is wait for her to turn up,' Mrs Landes-Fraser said stiffly. 'I don't expect you will be here to welcome her, Ross.'

'I shall be leaving tomorrow. I am content that Araminta is in good hands and that you, Giles, have things at Castonbury under control. As for Alicia—I shall write to you. I shall be most interested to hear how things turn out. As far as Lisette is concerned, I think I have made my intentions clear, Aunt Wilhelmina,'

Ross said. 'I have thought deeply on it and I will not welcome any interference in my personal life. If anyone feels the need to try to dissuade me from forming any kind of alliance with her, then I will not listen. The matter should be left to me and Lisette—and fate.'

'And Miss Napier...what does she say?' she enquired.

'I have yet to find that out.'

'But the girl will be halfway to London by now.'

'She is returning to India. If I fail to meet up with her on the road, then I shall do so in London.'

## Epilogue

With money of her own Lisette had purchased some dresses that made her look less like a servant and more like a young lady of substance.

She stood at the rails as the ship got under way and she watched London slip away. She did not come up on deck again until they had reached the English Channel. It was much the same as the ship she had sailed on from India with a mixture of ordinary citizens and soldiers, but now the soldiers on board were returning from leave to take up their duties with their regiments.

The swaying deck beneath the creaking and flapping of canvas was a patchwork of shadows and vivid orange-coloured light from the oil lamps. A burst of laughter added itself to the noises of the night and Lisette turned to see a group of men who had imbibed too much liquor over dinner and were in high spirits. Smiling softly she turned away, drawing the shawl tighter about her shoulders when the cool wind blew off the water. The sun had set and the moon had risen, hanging pale and large above the shining levels of the Channel like some enchanted Chinese lantern.

There were footsteps and someone stopped behind her. She turned. It was Ross.

Lisette stared at him, feeling her heart give a joyful leap. Her mouth was dry and her eyes were burning. She couldn't believe that he was standing there—handsome, dark and authoritative in his scarlet and gold regimentals. His face was inscrutable, and after a long moment, with a groan he pulled her roughly towards him, wrapping his arms around her, and with a raw ache in his voice, he said, 'You little fool. You adorable, beautiful little fool. Did you really think you could escape me—that I would let you go?'

Lisette was startled. She had expected cold rage, for him to chastise her for leaving him, not this. Never had she known a man so perplexing. 'Ross! I think I must be dreaming and any minute I will wake up and find you aren't here.'

'I assure you I am flesh and blood. If you love me, Lisette, at least say you are glad to see me.'

The dryness was going out of her eyes, the moisture was filling them. On a whisper she said, 'I am glad to see you.'

'Just glad?'

She swallowed before she could utter the words, *More than glad*.

When the tears welled in her eyes, his arms went about her once more, and with his mouth on hers he kissed her with heart-rending tenderness, all the love that had been accumulating over the months he had known her contained in that kiss.

Lisette swayed a little, for she felt the dizzying, heady aura of his masculinity, his vigour, the strong pull which she now knew quite positively was his love for her, wrap itself about her. While she had vainly set herself against the carnal forces Ross inspired in her, something deeper, something dangerously enduring, had been weaving its spell to bind them inexorably together.

Raising his head Ross looked down at her upturned face. 'I love you, Lisette. I think I loved you the first time I saw you—I remember you were wearing a pink, star-spangled sari.'

Catching her breath, Lisette raised her brows in amazement, silently questioning, hoping.

'When Araminta told me you had left Castonbury I went dead inside. You see, I had come to realise just how much you mean to me. I have never had any real feeling of love for anyone. I've had the experience of many women, but that wasn't love. Since I first set eyes on you, you had an effect on me and I wanted you and needed you more than I imagined I would ever want or need anyone in my life. You have caught me in the tenderest trap of all.' On a sigh with a whimsical smile tugging at the corners of his mouth, he admitted the truth of it. 'What we have transcends all else. You are a rare being, Lisette Napier. We'll never be separated again, my love. Do you hear me? Never.'

'Thank you for saying that,' Lisette whispered, an aching lump beginning to swell in her throat. Lowering her eyes she raised his hand and solemnly placed her lips against his fingers. 'I love you, Ross. I love you as much as it is possible for a woman to love a man. I have loved you for so long, ever since you jumped into the river and saved my life, and when you kissed me as I held on to you, it sealed what I felt for you in my heart.' Raising her eyes, she looked at him, and the gentle yielding and the love in their melting amber depths defeated him. 'Does that make you happy, Ross, to know I loved you from the start?'

'Happy? Bless you, my darling,' he murmured hoarsely. 'I don't deserve you.'

'Yes, you do. How did you know…?'

'Where to find you?' She nodded. 'I heard what happened and that you'd had to face the wrath of Aunt Wilhelmina, for which I am deeply sorry. Araminta told me you had left for London.'

'I didn't go to London. I went to Oxford to see my

father's lawyer. My father left me a legacy—more than I could ever have expected, which was why I decided to go back to India. I—I haven't decided what I will do when I get there….'

'That's not for you to worry about. Marry me, Lisette. Marry me today—now. Be my wife.' As she made to pull away from him, he held her tight. 'What is it?'

From within the circle of his arms, she stared up at him in wonder. 'Marry you?'

Ross probed for an answer. 'Do you understand, Lisette?'

'Of course,' she breathed. 'You want to marry me, you said.'

'Isn't that in the order of things when two people love each other?'

'And…you do love me?'

'More than anything. I'm sorry, Lisette. I should have made my intentions clear. If I had, perhaps you wouldn't have left Castonbury without seeing me.'

'Yes, you should. But it wouldn't have made any difference. Your family would never accept me and I wouldn't expect them to.'

'I have told you before, Lisette, that I make my own rules. Do you really think the difference in our backgrounds would make any difference to the way I feel about you? That sort of thing is not important to me.

Come, my love, why are we playing this game? The past is past for both of us. There is only the future.'

The thought of being his wife filled Lisette with many contradictory emotions—shock, fear and a burgeoning excitement she didn't dare consider at the present moment.

'I've had a lot of time to think on the journey down here and then waiting to see which ship you'd book your passage on. Araminta told me what you intended doing. I was disappointed that you didn't tell me about your legacy and that you meant to go back to India.'

'I'm sorry, I knew you could never commit... Your family, Ross? How do you think they'll respond if I become your wife?'

'I can't let them govern my life. My life is my own and I must live it how I wish. But if it makes you feel better, we have the blessing of Araminta, Giles, Phaedra and Kate. Aunt Wilhelmina will no doubt never speak to me again—but it can be borne, since she is not really a blood relation of mine. You know she is my cousins' aunt, not my own. My uncle, the duke, has his head filled with dastardly plans of receiving his grandson at Castonbury, of separating the mother from the child. There is no room in his life for anything else at this present time.'

Lisette stared at him in disbelief, unable to understand the duke's cruelty. 'He intends to remove the child from his mother?' Ross nodded. 'But…that is a wicked, cruel thing to do. He must be completely heartless. I hope your cousin's widow refuses to comply with his wishes.'

'My uncle is a powerful man, Lisette. He will have his way, although he has let the whole thing go to his head before it's even been settled.'

'Then I pray your family will make him see how wrong it would be. I have so much to learn about you, Ross. I'll never be able to live up to your position.'

He took her face tenderly between his hands and looked into her eyes, as if the only peace he could know would come from locking gazes with her. 'That's a trivial thing, of no importance to me. I'd like to gamble all I've got on the fact that I'll be the envy of every man who meets you. Now, ours is going to be the shortest courtship on record so I want your answer now. Lisette, will you marry me—now, here on the ship? The captain is prepared to officiate this very minute and Blackstock to bear witness if you accept. Yes or no?'

Looking at him now she no longer had any doubts. This man would always see her and know her, whatever she was doing, whatever she was wearing—his look had nothing to do with status or the concerns of the world. It was as simple as that.

'Yes,' she whispered, and the ship and the world seemed to tilt beneath her as he caught her up in his arms.

\* \* \*

Ross led Lisette to the captain's cabin where the captain, Will Blackstock, his face split from ear to ear by a wide grin, and a first mate were assembled. Lisette was astounded that Ross had already planned this. The time had come upon her in such a rush that she wasn't at all sure she was mentally prepared for the nuptials.

Ross smiled into her eyes and, reaching out to take her hand, pulled her against him. The unease that Lisette had felt a moment before dissipated as her husband-to-be slid an arm around her waist and pressed his lips against the hair above her temples. Her eyes were as brilliant as the champagne they would drink afterwards. They glowed with some emotion which seemed to be a mixture of satisfaction, hope, excitement and something else known only to them.

'Are we really going to be married?' she asked wistfully.

'Don't you doubt it.' Ross smiled gently.

The captain, a grey-haired, middle-aged man with kindly eyes, stepped near.

'You are Miss Lisette Napier?' he queried with a friendly smile.

'I am, sir.'

'And you are entering into this marriage of your own free will, without coercion of any sort?'

The question was unexpected, and she glanced up at Ross in some surprise. He squeezed her hand reassuringly. 'Did you agree of your own free will to marry me?'

Though Ross asked the question, it was to Captain Cookson that she looked and answered in soft tones. 'Yes, sir. Yes, I did.'

With a satisfied smile, Ross took her hand and held it tightly, and facing Captain Cookson, they spoke the words that bound them together, the words reverberating through Lisette's heart. Lisette could feel her eyes misting as she repeated her own vows, and she lowered her gaze to the strong, lean hands that held hers in a gentle grasp.

After celebratory toasts and much ribald banter, Ross took Lisette off to their cabin. Inside there was peace and semi-darkness. Only one candle was lit on this nuptial night.

Lisette came to her husband in pale beauty, her face pale and ethereal, her luminous eyes penetrating the very depths of his being. She paused to stand before him, wide-eyed, trembling. Her breath was fragrant from champagne and the freshness of her youth.

A great tenderness welled up in Ross and caught his throat. His hand moved out and gently touched her cheek. She reached up and grasped his hand. Moved by an impulse, he half turned her and lifted her in his arms. Her arms went around his neck. She shook visibly, laying her head on his shoulder.

'We are both going home,' Ross said. 'Whatever happens when I rejoin my regiment, I shall see that we are together always. Are you happy, my love?'

Looking up at him her trembling ceased. 'I have never been happier in my life.'

He undressed her and caressed her and laid her down. His gaze moved over her body, taking in its beauty. The soft breasts, the small waist and slender hips and thighs did not move him to lust as it had before, but to a kind of awed ecstasy. Instead of the urge to take her quickly, he felt the need to be gentle and tender, to caress with body, mind and spirit. Every part of them drew the other as if filling a vacuum, thrilling, vibrating. He loved her until they were both sated and she closed her eyes and snuggled into his arms and slept.

She was his wife, to have and to hold as long as they both would live.

When Lisette awoke during the night with her husband's arms about her, she knew a sense of protectiveness and belonging such as she had never dreamed possible. She seemed to be merging with him into the womb of timelessness, in which there seemed to be no bodies but a single entity.

\* \* \*

For Lisette the most surprising thing about sighting India at last was how familiar everything seemed. The gently waving palms against the lines of white sand and the splendid vivid blue sea—it was exactly as she remembered. On the shore she saw the native porters and coolies, naked except for a brief loincloth, baskets of spices and salt fish and wicker panniers full of oranges and limes, and the familiar smells of garlic, coriander and hot oil were wafted on the breeze. It was like finding herself back in a well-loved, well-remembered dream.

Standing by the ship's rails she looked at the beautiful clipper ships, the sturdy merchantmen anchored alongside. The water rippled deep gold in the sun, turning slowly with the sky to a lovely blue. She sighed and there was no sadness in that sigh, only sheer pleasure and satisfaction. When someone came to stand beside her she turned expectantly, her eyes gleaming in anticipation.

Ross smiled lovingly down at her. She wore a gown of apple green and silver grey. She looked lovely and elegant, her thick black hair neatly netted beneath her bonnet.

'Ready?' he asked.

Tucking her hand through the crook of his arm, she smiled up at him. 'I am now.'

They both took a deep breath and prepared to leave the ship.

Lisette knew she had come home.

* * * * *

Read on to find out more about
Helen Dickson
and the

CASTONBURY
PARK
*A Regency Upstairs Downstairs*

series…

**Helen Dickson** was born and lives in South Yorkshire, with her retired farm manager husband. Having moved out of the busy farmhouse where she raised their two sons, she has more time to indulge in her favourite pastimes. She enjoys being outdoors, travelling, reading and music. An incurable romantic, she writes for pleasure. It was a love of history that drove her to writing historical fiction.

Previous novels by the same author:

A SCOUNDREL OF CONSEQUENCE
FORBIDDEN LORD
SCANDALOUS SECRET, DEFIANT BRIDE
FROM GOVERNESS TO SOCIETY BRIDE
MISTRESS BELOW DECK
THE BRIDE WORE SCANDAL
DESTITUTE ON HIS DOORSTEP
SEDUCING MISS LOCKWOOD
MARRYING MISS MONKTON
BEAUTY IN BREECHES
MISS CAMERON'S FALL FROM GRACE

**And in Mills & Boon® Historical *Undone!* eBooks:**

ONE RECKLESS NIGHT

Did you know that some of these novels are
also available as eBooks?
**Visit www.millsandboon.co.uk**

# AUTHOR Q&A

**Apart from your own, which other heroine did you empathise with the most?**

I feel it is a little unfair to select one heroine in particular, since they are all appealing, feisty ladies. However, I do empathise with Kate. She comes across as being a mixture of rebel and conformist and I sense she would like to escape the confines of her upbringing. In possession of a sharp mind, she has the most pronounced views on most things. I like the fact that she devotes her life to worthy causes, that she has her own ideas on equality between the sexes, and is of the opinion that women should try and rise above their servitude.

**And which hero did you find the most intriguing?**

I have to say that the hero I find the most intriguing has to be Giles. Family circumstances and the loss of two of his brothers necessitate that he resign his commission. With a strong sense of duty—and little enthusiasm—he assumes his role as heir to the Dukedom, while, with tremendous fortitude, he romances his beloved Lily throughout all eight books, until he finally makes her his wife.

**What is your hero's favourite childhood memory of Castonbury Park?**

Ross's favourite memories of Castonbury Park are of the times he spent growing up there. As youths, Ross and his male cousins fought together and were wild, as young men are. As young as she was, his sister Araminta took after them. She was his only sibling and Ross treasured the times he spent with Araminta. She laughed often, for she was a madcap who revelled in all the mischievous things her big brother and cousins got up to.

**What are you researching for your forthcoming novel?**

At present I am researching my next book, which is set in medieval times. It is something quite different for me. I have set all my books after the Elizabethan period, so I am finding writing about knights and castles an enjoyable challenge.

**What would you most like to have been doing in Regency times?**

If I had lived in the Regency period I would like to have been born into a large and loving wealthy family—noble or gentry, either would do. I would enjoy all the physical pastimes the country had to offer and go to town for the Season's pleasures—and to relieve my mind from boredom. I would write romantic novels.

## AUTHOR NOTE

When I started writing *The Housemaid's Scandalous Secret*, I began by working out the structure, approach and theme for the story. But this book is not like my others, because threaded through is the continuity story and it includes characters featured in the other books in the Castonbury Park series.

I have always found the glory days of the British in India a time of enchantment—of vibrancy, oriental princes and potentates glittering with fabulous jewels living in medieval state in fantastic marble palaces. All this, combined with the heady images of sailing ships laden with spices and sumptuous goods from the east belonging to the East India Company, a uniquely British creation which took on the world, inspired me to use India as the setting for the prologue of my book. Books and television have vouchsafed me, as an outsider, a precious glimpse of India, but it is my dream that one day I shall visit and see for myself the *real* India.

Following the death of her parents, knowing she must earn her own living to survive, my heroine, Lisette, decides to return to England to find work. She has an unemotional approach to life. She is a reasoning person, yet passion burns nonetheless beneath the surface. It is an act of bravery for a young woman to embark on a journey that takes her from Delhi to Bombay, alone in a foreign land.

Masquerading as an Indian girl, she finds her life saved when Colonel Ross Montague pulls her from a raging river. Their lives become braided together by desire, but it is many months after this event before she is unmasked.

The story is set in the Regency period, which was one of the most turbulent, glittering and romantic times in our history, when rakes and dandies, outrageous gambling and scandals abounded. But Lisette, working as a lady's maid at Castonbury Park in Derbyshire, is as far removed from this glittering world as she had been in India.

The story is consistent with what I perceive to be the atmosphere of the times and the class divide. Lisette is aware of the gulf between her lowly status and that of Ross

Montague, a dashing soldier stationed in India who is home on leave. Men of his ilk are not for the likes of her. Lisette has to overcome many pitfalls and prejudice from below stairs before she attains her heart's desire—Ross—and is able to return to her beloved India.

Writing this book has been a challenge, but I found it an absolute delight to write.

**Don't miss the next instalment of Castonbury Park—**
*THE LADY WHO BROKE THE RULES*
**by Marguerite Kaye**

**'Your rebellion has not gone unnoticed…'**

Anticipating her wedding vows and then breaking off the
engagement has left Kate Montague's social status in tatters.
She hides her hurt at her family's disapproval behind a
resolutely optimistic façade, but one thing *really* grates…
For a fallen woman, she knows shockingly little about
passion!

Could Virgil Jackson be the man to teach her? A freed slave
turned successful businessman, his striking good looks and
lethally restrained power throw normally composed Kate
into a tailspin! She's already scandalised society, but
succumbing to her craving for Virgil would be the most
outrageous thing Kate's done by far…

# THE LADY WHO BROKE THE RULES

Marguerite Kaye

I'm so glad you decided to accept my invitation,' she said brusquely, for it was embarrassing enough, this girlish reaction, without letting him see it.

'I could not pass up the opportunity to visit this school of yours.'

It was most foolish of her to be disappointed, for what else was there between them save such business? Kate smiled brightly. 'I'm glad.'

Virgil frowned. 'Yes, but I'm not so sure that your family will be as enthusiastic. It is one thing to test barriers, as you said last night, but another to force an uninvited guest on people who, frankly, may not be very happy to receive me.'

'You *are* invited, for I invited you.'

'Did you tell them—the note you sent—how did you describe me?'

'As a man of great wealth and extraordinary influence, a business associate of Josiah with a fascinating history.'

She had not mentioned the one salient fact that he was sure would have been the first to occur to almost anyone else.

'You don't think,' Virgil asked tentatively, 'that it would have been safer to warn them about my heritage?'

'Why should I? I look at you and I see a man who has achieved what very few others have. You are rich and powerful and you have succeeded against overwhelming odds, which also makes you fascinating. Why should I tell them the colour of your skin any more than I should inform them the colour of your hair, or whether you are fat or scrawny?'

Or attractive. Really extraordinarily attractive. Which, she should remember, was quite irrelevant.

'Besides,' Kate said disparagingly, 'why encourage them to judge you before they have even met you?'

Virgil drew himself up. 'I don't give a damn—begging your pardon—about what your family think of me. I was more concerned about what they'd think of you.'

'My family can think no worse of me than they already do,' Kate said with a toss of her head.

'I don't doubt that. I suspect you take pride in being a rule-breaker.'

'Not at all,' Kate said. 'You misunderstand me. Breaking rules, even unjust rules, is far more painful than unquestioning obedience. I wish I did not have to be a "rule-breaker", as you call me.'

She looked quite wistful and Virgil found himself at a loss, for it seemed that they were speaking about two different things. He could, however, agree with the sentiment. 'I know exactly what you mean.'

Kate nodded, touching his sleeve in a gesture of sympathy he was already beginning to associate with her. 'Our cases are hardly comparable. There are a good deal of rules which ought to be broken, no matter how painful.'

She would not have said so if she knew the price he had paid for his disobedience. No matter how unconventional she was, she would likely condemn him for it—and quite rightly so.

Virgil rolled his shoulders, as if the familiar burden of guilt were a tangible weight he carried. 'I play by my own rules,' he said.

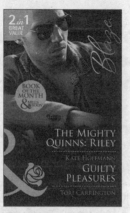

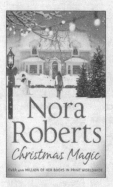

# Have Your Say

*You've just finished your book.*
*So what did you think?*

We'd love to hear your thoughts on our
'Have your say' online panel
**www.millsandboon.co.uk/haveyoursay**

- Easy to use
- Short questionnaire
- Chance to win Mills & Boon®
  goodies